A Mark like Cain's

By Jessica Marie Carlos

A Mark like Cain's
© 2018 Jessica Marie Carlos

All rights reserved. This book or parts thereof may not be reproduced in any form, stored in any retrieval system, or transmitted in any form by any means—electronic, mechanical, photocopy, recording, or otherwise—without prior written permission of the publisher, except as provided by United States of America copyright law. For permission requests and other questions/concerns, write to the publisher at the email address below:

carlos.littleJay@gmail.com

www.JessicaCarlos.com

Cover by Brandi Doane McCann

Dedicated to God,
my inspiration and my hope,
to Mom, Dad, Jake, and Josh,
and to my friends, new and old

Prologue

When danger lurks, charge it head on.

Uncle Riley was a weirdo like that. He gave questionable advice at best times, and at worst...

Yeah, let's just not go there. And do you want to know the problem with Uncle Riley's questionable advice?

Most people hear it and take it *way* too seriously.

See, for Harpers, it's a way of life. We charge danger because running never helps; it's like fleeing from our own shadows. No matter how far we go or how fast we get there, danger sticks to us like syrup. Have some of that dumped on your hair, why don't cha, and good luck getting it out.

And if danger's a shadow, imagine what happens when our black cloud's skulking form turns those harmless silhouettes into pools of darkness. We wind up swimming in trouble for it.

But if my mother's family, the Villenas, gave us the curse of the black cloud, then my father's family, the Harpers, gave us the ability to survive it like no one else can, courtesy, of course, of their unique way of dealing with—well, with everything.

But if *my* tale seems a little less Harper and a little more Villena, then I'd like to introduce you to my brothers, Jet and Charlie Harper, who were once the paragon of everything you shouldn't do. (In fact, sometimes, they still are, but you didn't hear that from me.)

And what separates what they were then from what they are now? What else but their inability to live in the moment. Sound familiar? It's a commonality among *Homo sapiens*—memory, a simultaneous blessing and curse.

Oh, by the way, I feel I should mention my brothers never had the "live" problem like I did. If anything, they lived a little *too* much, but it's *where* they lived and *when* they lived that really did them in. Charlie was stuck in the past, and Jet was stuck everywhere but the present. Their problems festered, like infected wounds, hideous and putrid, toxic in time. And together—oh, together!—they were two volatile chemicals. Add a catalyst and the resulting blast could level a mountain.

Even just feeling the shifting tides of the wind was enough to cue me in, and before long, I could actually see the massive storm brewing on the horizon. Worse, I knew I could do nothing to stop it. Did I really want to? Who knows? Somewhere in the back of my mind, I just couldn't wait for the escalating hostilities to explode into war and waste each other out.

Could my warning have spared them the worst of it?

Ah, who am I kidding? We're Harpers. We either do or die, and there's not a whole lot we can manage in the grey.

Besides, Charlie and Jet were renowned for tackling the impossible. It was ordinary for them, and for that reason alone, I may or may not have overestimated my brothers' abilities to cope.

Oh well, no use moaning about it now.

So, consider this instead: What do you get when you cross the lives of a pacifist priest and a trigger-happy contract killer?

Trouble.

And what happens when they both happen to be Harpers?

Well, possibly, the end of the world as we know it.

Chapter 1

Traffic laws are for sissies.

Really, that was the only thought on his mind at the time aside from, *Let's not crash.*

Of course, that second thought was more like an afterthought. High speed chases were his forte after all, and he almost wished he was back on his bike, feeling the wind split and wash over him, as much a nuisance as a thrill.

Almost.

But not really, because motorcycles were great for a lot things. Playing complicated games of cat and mouse was not one of them. No, in this case, his bike would just be a death trap on wheels, the subsequent crash an inevitably that would land him six feet under...*if* he was lucky.

Some things are worse than death.

He tried not to think about it too hard as he sped down the freeway, his dainty little fingers—that didn't seem right—

clasped around the black steering wheel of his blue Ford. His foot pressed down on the gas pedal, sinking it lower and lower 'til its rubber underbelly hit the floor of his '67 Mustang. It lurched forward with a jerk, the blaring horns orbiting around him urging him to go faster. In the narrow sight of his rearview mirror, a plateless Audi tailed him, engine revving so fast it left legal in the dust.

He weaved through traffic effortlessly, dodging unsuspecting motorists like he owned the road. Whoever they were, they were right on top of him. He veered onto the off-ramp around a swerving pick-up, forcing three cars into the shoulder that honked angrily at his reckless maneuvers. He ignored them all and drifted past the green light, through the shady underpass, and into the opposing intersection.

An SUV ran the red.

He slammed on his brakes, spiraling to miss the collision, the momentum forcing his car to tilt, tilt, *tilt*...

He swore, his car flipping once, then twice, then a third time before coming to a skidding halt on its hood. He hit the release mechanism on his seatbelt and crashed down, falling onto his side and struggling to right himself. Unable to see hide nor hair of his assailants, he could only hear the opening and shutting of a car door and the sound of his shattered window crunching under the weight of heavy feet.

He scrambled to get his uncoordinated limbs moving—why did he feel so sluggish?—but before he could even attempt leaning across to the other side of the car, a gun was aimed in at him, and a shot fired.

The sound slapped Jet awake with a hateful bang. Sweat glistened his brow, and his heart drummed like thunder. Cautiously, just as he was trained, Jet propped himself up in bed, took several deep, steadying breaths, and looked around.

Maps and pins decorated the walls, and spooled yarn sat on his desk atop a few forgotten files. A fine layer of dust coated everything. The entrance to his bathroom was open as always, and his bedroom door bolted shut. Everything was as it should be.

Jet sighed, falling back on his sweat-drenched sheets, hands scrubbing at his face. *Damn nightmares.* A lingering sense of foreboding sat heavy on his chest. He groaned and tried to shake it off.

And then he heard it, the faintest tick, a single decibel above impossible to hear. His muscles tensed, frozen in anticipation.

Jet didn't own a clock. They were way too loud for his liking. He'd upgraded the ventilation system, too, for the entire apartment block in fact, so that he could keep the fans off and the quiet, cool air coming. He'd also synched his television to the heart rate monitor of his watch, so if he passed out on the couch, like any ordinary guy might, the TV would shut off automatically. *He* was the only source of noise in the whole apartment.

So, when he heard that first, subtle sound, Jet knew immediately an unwanted guest was in his home. He just wasn't sure about the nature of its intrusion.

Rats had been a problem once, so had bats, but neither of those species of invaders had attempted to enter his domain in quite some time. They'd learned their lesson. Jet smirked to himself. His landlady, Mrs. Butterfly, as Jet was prone to call her, had hollered such impressively colorful words at him while he'd exterminated the vermin…

…with his revolver…

…while cackling maniacally.

Okay, so maybe he'd gone a bit overboard.

The soft, soundless whisper of rubber on tile pulled Jet from his reverie. He strained his ears and waited for the inevitable *creeeeeaaaaaaak* that followed, accompanied by a startled swear.

Jet sprung onto deaf feet, throwing on his nearest pair of pants and a clean v-neck. He'd known they'd fall for it. They always did. That small patch of wood flooring in his short hall might have looked like a style choice to anyone else, but Jet was always deliberate, and when all else failed, that trip wire could rouse his most stubborn sleep.

He yanked open the drawer to his metal desk, dumped everything sitting on top of it in, and lit a match. The figure behind his door rammed up against it. Jet had approximately three minutes.

No problem.

He dropped the match on his belongings, slammed the drawer shut, and locked it for good measure. By the time they wrenched that sucker open, all they'd find was a pile of smoke and ash.

Jet slipped a gun into the back of his waistband behind his blade, another in his left boot, and a three-inch throwing knife up the sleeve of the jacket he'd just tossed on. Then he was in the bathroom, swinging the door shut behind him and glancing around just to reassure himself someone hadn't managed the world's greatest Houdini.

Satisfied, Jet leapt onto the trashcan, a small cylindrical bin manufactured to support 192.5 pounds and not an ounce more. Then he removed a false panel from his decorative ceiling tiles, lifted himself up with ease, and slipped into the man-made crawlspace.

What Mrs. Butterfly doesn't know won't hurt her.

Jet slid the panel back in place and began to commando crawl towards the other end of the building. His sensitive ears detected the bathroom door giving way. He had approximately a minute and a half before that dodo found his escape route.

A minute and half could've been an hour and a half for all Jet was concerned.

After a few seconds of wriggling along, he dropped from the ceiling onto one of his neighbors' back patios. Alonzo Perez was hardly ever home. If he *had* been, the covered barbeque pit sitting just beyond his backdoor might have given him pause. After all, he didn't own a grill.

Jet threw off the deceitful cover to his favorite custom sports bike. Then he was zero to sixty in two seconds flat. The sound filters on his helmet, the only reason he could hear anything over the roar of the wind, picked up a hail of gunfire. Jet twisted around, his own firearm out and pointing at his would-be killer. With an exasperated eye roll, Jet shook his head, turned back to the road, and holstered his weapon. The moron was out of range.

Psh, what a waste of bullets.

Jet rode farther out of town, his apartment already on the outskirts of the city, and towards a small, private airstrip. Warehouses lined the streets left and right, but Jet sped past them all, turning down a dirt road before slipping through the slightly cracked door of a run-down hangar. He weaved around a few old-school Cessnas someone had abandoned mid restoration, sailed into the back office, shut off his bike, and switched it out for a cruiser.

Well, that had made for an eventful morning. Jet turned the ignition key, his baby's engine roaring to life beneath him. Then he tossed his helmet on the bench. *Now what?*

Jet scratched at the back of his neck idly and yawned. He considered heading into town for breakfast. He *was* kind of hungry.

But no, that ominous drum was still digging into his lungs like razor wire. Jet sighed again. Once more he was faced with reality and the trouble that came along with it. He scraped his tongue with his teeth and licked his lips, his face contorting in disgust. *Bleah!*

It tasted like responsibility.

Chapter 2

*B*zz.

Bzz.

Bzz.

Charlie didn't move, hands folded neatly on his desk, a pleasant smile plastered on his face.

Bzzzz.

His eyes didn't even flicker, just held the gaze of the man in front of him, devoid of all distraction.

Bz-zz-zzz.

Charlie Harper had spent four summers stuffed in a car with his younger brother, had shared a room with him for twelve years and ten more with various roommates. As a newly ordained priest, all he wanted was a little space, a place to call his own…like this office, even if it *was* just an overglorified closet they'd cleared out to make room for him. He had nestled in deep the moment they'd presented it and hummed contently to himself as he stacked his stuff wherever it'd fit. Yes, the claustrophobic spot between the restroom and the back door was all his.

But *his* spot had been invaded, by the evilest of sorts no less, an infestation of the worst kind. He'd tried so hard to maintain his dominion, but alas, his attempt at bloodless sovereignty was to no avail. After all the struggles of finally getting a place to work in solitude, he wouldn't surrender without taking up his sword and smiting the cretin who dared defy him.

This. Means. War.

"I've tried talking to her, Father, but she never wants to hear it."

Did it really think Charlie would just let it go? After this invasion of privacy, this betrayal of trust, this utter defilement?

"I know she loves me as much as I love her, but I just don't get it."

It could taunt him, demand his attention, mock him like cheese mocks mice, but he *would* have the last laugh.

"Well, what do you think I should do, Father?"

Wham!

The man jerked back in his chair, hands gripping the rests, eyes wider than the moon. Charlie's arm was up, raised to one side, the flat plastic of his swatter splayed against the wall behind him.

"Mr. Medina, what you and your wife need is honest, open communication. If she isn't listening to you, then maybe you're expressing yourself in a way that's hurting her, and you just haven't realized it. It may not even be intentional. Examine how you interact with each other, see what she needs, meet her needs, and reopen the lines of communication. It'll work itself out from there. Most importantly, pray together. Let God take control. He'll lead you exactly where you need to go."

Still stunned, the man merely nodded.

"Is there anything else?"

Mr. Medina shook his head.

"Alright then, have a wonderful day, sir," Charlie said, waving cheerily as the man exited. Then he moved the flyswatter down to his trashcan to cleanse it of his fiend.

"Father?" the secretary called, scooting in through the slightly ajar door. "A Miss Alma Hernandez called. Her mother-in-law has been moved into hospice and is requesting her last rites."

"Father Johann likes to do those, especially with faithful parishioners. He's known them a lot longer."

"Yes, Father, I know, but Father Johann's not here. Bishop called him to the cathedral, and he left in such a rush he must have forgotten to tell you."

"It's fine," Charlie said. "I'll take care of it."

Click. Click. Click.

You've got to be kidding me. Charlie slammed his hand down on the steering wheel and willed his car to come to life. "If You want me to get there," he said aloud, punctuating his statement with a poke at the sky, "You'll give me a way." He turned the key again. The car coughed and sputtered but refused to start. Charlie sighed. Yeah, he wasn't going anywhere.

Because, naturally, Miss Luna, their secretary, didn't own a car. Her son dropped her off at work every morning and picked her up every evening. And, of course, their bookkeeper was out of town, on vacation for the first time in *years*. And, just because God liked to tease him so, their custodian had only just changed his morning shift to afternoons. Charlie could've called a cab, but in this part of the States, he couldn't just stick his thumb out and hitch a ride, and by the time he phoned for one...

I could probably walk there faster.

Charlie sighed again, stared at the empty streets of their penniless people, gone to work or drunk in their sorrows, then began the long trek to Heaven's Gate Hospice. He was tempted to hitchhike once he hit the main road, but the thought of inconveniencing anyone kept his thumbs at his sides, well secured and unavailable.

Moments later, it began to rain.

Charlie tried not to visibly wilt in view of the passing traffic—*Why, God? Why?*—but he must've failed on some level because seconds later, a car pulled up to the curb and its window rolled down. "Need a ride?"

Charlie grimaced internally. He must've looked a real mess. But he swallowed down his reservations and smiled gratefully. "Thank you."

The man nodded, eyes on everything but Charlie.

Charlie felt a pang of guilt getting into the car, dripping with rainwater as he was, but the driver *had* stopped of his own volition, and he didn't seem very bothered by Charlie's state.

"Father Charles Harper," he introduced, "but you can call me Father Charlie. Most people do."

"Oh, right, sure." The man was jittery, nervous, and focused on the street far more than he should be with a stranger riding shotgun. "Where are you headed, Father?"

"Heaven's Gate."

"Isn't that a...a place people go to die?"

Charlie turned those words over in his head distastefully, choked them down, and rehashed a new set, "It's a home for the terminally ill, yes." He paused. "You don't have to take me all the way. The rain's letting up. Just let me out wherever's convenient."

"No, it's fine. I don't have anywhere else I need to be. I can get you there."

Silence was their language for the rest of the ride, and an uncomfortable knot formed in Charlie's gut that he tried to shrug off the moment they arrived. "Thank you again. God bless," he said, one hand arcing in a cross, the other resting on his travel kit.

The man's hands gripped the steering wheel tighter, his eyes staring hard at the window. When he made no move to answer, Charlie shrugged and opened the car door. "I was going to jump."

"Jump?"

"North Avenue Bridge—I was going to jump."

Charlie tensed, and for a moment, the synapses of his brain refused to fire. Then came the blinding panic, irrational and unnecessary, drowning out every lesson he'd ever learned and all conventionality.

With the last thread of his sanity, Charlie gave himself a mental shake, drew up all that rebellious emotion, all the anguish pulsing within him, and threw it out. A disturbing calmness settled over him.

"I'd finally worked up the nerve to do it. Then I saw you all dressed in black, walking there along the road, and I thought you were death."

Charlie blinked. "Sorry then."

The man's head jerked towards him. "For what?"

"For ruining your plans."

"But you're a priest. Aren't you supposed to be glad I'm not dead?"

"Oh, I'm not sorry you're alive. I'm just sorry I ruined your plans." The man tilted his head in confusion, questioning the difference, but Charlie didn't clarify. "Besides, at that height, the fall wouldn't have killed you. You'd have shattered both your legs, probably an arm, too."

Charlie's eyes roved over the man for a moment. "I take that back. You probably would've wound up fracturing your arm, you know, the kind where your bone juts out through your skin like a spear. And one heck of a concussion. Blood everywhere. Jumps are always messy, successful or not. And the paramedics would've had to set the bone in your arm on site, without giving you any pain meds since they wouldn't have known if anything else was in your system. Of course, if you had taken a dive, you definitely wouldn't have survived, but man, that would have been even messier, skin and skull fragments everywhere, the three B's in one go—blood, bone, and brain. So..." Charlie paused to let the image crystallize. "What now?"

The man's jaw had dropped, and his eyes were millimeters away from popping right out of his skull. He shook his head profusely. "I—I don't know."

"You got family, Owen?"

"Yeah, my dad."

"You get along with him alright?"

The man nodded.

Charlie locked eyes with him, filled himself with every ounce of fortitude he could muster, and let it leak from his brown orbs into Owen's. "Then you go straight to him, even if he's on the other side of the planet. You knock on his door, and you tell him everything you're feeling. Then you say a prayer and thank God for loving you enough to mess with me."

The man nodded, so Charlie stood from the car, moments away from closing the door. "Father?"

He stopped.

15

"How did you know my name? I never told you."

He bore a look of absolute wonder, and Charlie really considered letting the man think the information had been planted in his mind by the heavens above, but Charlie knew better than to play the divine, so instead, he stabbed his finger several times at a bill Owen had left on the dash. His name was printed on it in big, bold letters.

"Oh."

Charlie shut the door, turned, and walked away, carrying on with his original mission.

Death. How fitting. Was that how those accursed flies saw him, too?

Charlie let a rare, malicious grin slide onto his face. He rather liked the sound of that.

Chapter 3

At half past nine, Jet's Harley cruised onto a crumbling plot of asphalt someone had the gall to dub a parking lot. A ramshackle church sat off behind it, faded paint chipping off at every corner, bleached words that had once read *St. Augustine* only just visible against the sun. Jet swung his leg over the side of his bike and made for the small office nearby.

Silver bells hanging from the door closer jingled as he entered. No one was in the lobby, and any other person might've assumed it was a slow day, but Jet could hear a few members of the office staff humming along to the Christian radio station as they worked and, so, advanced with care. He hadn't really thought this trip through and could only hope he hadn't made the journey for nothing.

Despite the hollowness of the office, Jet knew better than to make assumptions. Doing just that had already cost him dearly, and Jet wasn't really the kind of guy to make the same mistake twice, so he watched the corners and shadows of the room with grand suspicion and marched towards the counter cautiously.

An elderly woman sat at the front desk, protected by a sliding glass pane and lots of wall. Her grey hair curled up in a bush by her ears, and she sported a pair of cat-eye glasses that magnified the blue and red blood vessels in the cue of her eyes.

His boots hit the tile in front of her heavy, and a pair of blues that fought judgment but found it anyways fell on his tousled hair, more brown than black with the summer sun, stubble shave, and dark orbs peering through his darker pair of Oakley's. She stood immediately, an unconscious response to his looming figure muscling over her frail limbs.

Jet paid her hardly any mind. "I'm here to see your priest."

It took her a moment to register his statement, and when she finally did, she jerked abruptly as if woken from a trance. "Oh, which one?"

"Charlie," he stated. She eyed him coolly, thoughts on disrespectful youth already swirling through her— "Could you tell him his brother's here to see him?"

In an instant, the woman froze, her startled features paling at the potential risk of her own judgment. "O—One moment please!" She scurried off to a door in the back, knocked briskly, then hurled herself through it.

Jet let his eyes drift over the large room and its remaining occupants, who were openly gaping at him like he'd made some sort of death threat. He held back a scowl. *Thou shall not curse thy neighbors no matter how annoying they might be*, he reminded himself.

Jet was spared further effort when the door in the back slammed open and the woman came scuttling back. "He'll see you now," she told him as she rushed over to unlock the door. Then she ushered him past her frightened coworkers, each one of them instinctively leaning away as he passed. He swallowed down his irritation. Charlie would not appreciate it.

He and his older brother were night and day, fire and ice, polar bears and penguins, if that makes any sense. Most of the time, Charlie was the calm, level-headed one, the clean-shaven model of impeccability. Jet was everything Charlie wasn't—disorder, chaos, a mess tied so well together he was considered by many to be a walking contradiction. There had once been a time when Charlie might have scowled at the incompetent right alongside Jet, but now they lived in two very different worlds, and the younger found himself down a kindred spirit.

Jet entered the tiny office first, followed by the reluctant senior. Charlie was flipping through a stack of papers on his desk and ignored them both. Loitering in the doorway for only a moment, the secretary excused herself without a word and tugged the door shut behind her like Jet might turn on her at any moment.

"You know, I really considered telling Miss Luna I was too busy to see you."

Jet gave Charlie's bowed head a shrug, pulling out the only empty chair and dropping himself into it. Already the crowding bookshelves and filing cabinets shoved into the leftover space from the desk and chairs were closing in around him. *How can Charlie work like this?*

"Next time, call. We can grab lunch or something."

Jet sighed. "I had a weird dream."

That caught Charlie's attention, if for no other reason than because Jet's tone suggested something sinister.

"Should I be worried?"

Jet sighed again and slouched. As always, a dull ache formed in his back almost instantly, and Jet used the pain to bolster his nerves. "I'll let you be the judge of that." His eyes scanned Charlie's desktop briefly, then jumped to the other visitor's chair, laden with boxes and files. Why was he here again? He glanced at Charlie, who still wasn't looking at him and, despite his misgivings, began to speak.

Charlie feigned disinterest, continuing his quest to find whatever sheet of paperwork he'd managed to misplace.

So, Jet gave him the short end of it, leaving out how the frightening conclusion had sprung him from sleep into consciousness like a shot from his favorite gun. Then Jet's blank demeanor twisted, and worry crowded his features. "Except...it's not me. It's Holly." Charlie's brow kneaded in confusion, but still, his eyes never left his task. "She was the one in the car chase, but I was seeing it through her eyes."

"Welp, that's sure not the weirdest dream you've ever had."

"Well, no."

"*But...*"

"I don't know. It just felt different. Real almost. Like a hallucination or something very similar."

"Like a vision, you mean?"

"Don't be ridiculous. Of course not." Jet tossed his head back to emphasize his mockery. Then, after a moment, his countenance shifted once more, and guiltily, he winced. "But Holly..."

Charlie sighed, dropping the paper he'd just signed and leaning back in his chair. For a moment, he merely studied Jet. "It was *your* car, right?"

Jet nodded.

"Well, what would Holly be doing driving your car anyways? You don't let anybody drive your car."

"That's true."

"Besides, Holly's off doing favors for the club. I don't think she gonna be involved in any high-speed chases any time soon. She's not the best driver."

"You're one to talk."

Charlie ignored him. "I'm more worried about you."

"Why? Even if, by some off chance, it happened to me, I'm a great driver. There's no way I'd ever flip my car."

"If you say so," Charlie answered, about ready to crack open a tome he'd pulled off the high shelf behind him.

"You got anything to eat?"

Charlie sighed. "You know, I wouldn't have a penny to my name if I had to feed you all the time. I pity your future wife." He reached into his drawer anyways and pulled out a granola bar, then set it down in front of Jet. "Now, if you don't mind, I have a lot of work to get done, and I'd rather not be here all night."

Jet rolled his shoulders and stood, unwrapping the bar and taking a bite. Charlie assessed him astutely and sniffed the air. "Did you ride here on your Harley?"

"Yup."

"*Jet,*" he wrung out, "there's a storm coming. Driving around on your bike in bad weather's insane. You're gonna get yourself killed."

"No worries, *Mom,*" Jet answered. "I'm gonna pick up my Mustang from Fuego's on my ride back anyways. Just got her detailed."

Charlie's eyes narrowed. Bringing his elbows onto the high armrests of his chair, he locked his knuckles in front of him and, with slow purpose, scanned Jet down and up again. "Be careful with that thing, too."

"Dude, I'm a fabulous driver. I'd never crash my car."

Charlie rolled his eyes, paused, then gave Jet another considering look. "I was having trouble with mine this morning. Any chance you can check it out before you go?"

"Sure, but it'll cost you another granola bar." Charlie huffed and opened his drawer.

"Thank—"

Wham!

Jet flinched, hands raised in a half-started defensive maneuver he only just stopped. "What the hell, Charlie!"

Charlie's swatter was on the wall beside him now, and as he pulled his instrument of death away, a dead fly dropped to one of his lower shelves. "They think they can win, but they don't know Charlie Harper."

Jet eyed him incredulously. "I always worry when you start referring to yourself in the third person."

Charlie merely shrugged, leaning his flyswatter against the bottom portion of his desk. "They're driving me nuts, okay? All I hear is *bzz*, *bzz*, *bzz* all day long. I can't take it anymore. It has to end."

The sound of a squealing rat echoed in Jet's memories. Maybe he was more like Charlie than he thought.

"In the name of Jesus Christ, I compel you to renounce your wicked ways, ignoble scum!" Charlie bellowed, suddenly on his feet. He slammed his flyswatter down once more, this time, on his desk.

Er…maybe not.

Chapter 4

"Why are people always trying to kill me?"

"Oh, I don't know. It might have something to do with your choice in career."

Charlie dumped his suitcase in the trunk of his car. Unlike Jet's smooth, blue stallion, Charlie's ride wasn't anything special. Jet's cars were pristine. Charlie's was economical. Half the time, he couldn't even name its make or model.

Charlie had just washed it, but some of the dirt clung to its shiny surface anyways and turned the black paint grey. The thinner metal of his jalopy was peppered with small dings. Regardless of anything Jet might say, most of them weren't actually Charlie's fault.

"Yeah, but I didn't even do anything this time." Jet paused a moment to think. "At least, I don't think I did."

"When has that ever mattered?"

Jet dipped his head in agreement, leaning up against the side of the vehicle as Charlie studied its contents.

Jet hadn't told Charlie how accurate his dream had been, but he hadn't needed to. Charlie knew. Before Jet's world had first been knocked off its axis, Jet, too, had accepted the truth of his prescience just as much as he accepted his need to breath.

Still, Charlie had to wonder. Had Jet's foresight always been this…erroneous? Charlie knew Jet didn't always understand what he felt and saw, and he'd never needed to, but Jet had driven an hour and half to tell Charlie about it this time—an hour and a half!—had acted like he'd just experienced something he'd never experienced before. Why the uncertainty?

Because there *had* been uncertainty as to who was who in Jet's second sight, and the discrepancies obviously hadn't ended there. After all, Jet was still alive.

But really, anyone with any sense could've expected that. Our capabilities stood on two opposite ends of a fissure, first fractured by our comparative distance to Uncle Riley and further widened by years of experience. So, in the actual event, Jet's quick jab at the glove compartment had dropped a gun in his hand, and no one was a faster draw than Jet.

But why had I appeared in his place to begin with? Why hadn't he just seen himself?

Charlie let his curiosity hang in the air above them like a guillotine. Jet had come to despise his gift of prescience, had even slipped into denial, so rather than start another pointless argument, Charlie left his inquiries atop their flouted cloud.

"Thanks for fixing my car."

Jet shrugged. "There wasn't anything wrong with it. You sure you were doing it right?"

"Nearly drive off a cliff *once...*" Charlie muttered under his breath, shaking his head. Louder, he added, "I'm pretty sure I know how to start my own car, Jet."

Jet snickered in response.

"Boys!" Mom called. They turned to her at once. "Food's on the table."

"We'll be right in," Jet answered. Charlie nodded beside him, and Mom disappeared back into the house. "If there's one thing I miss about living here, it has to be Mom's cooking."

"Is food all you ever think about?"

"You can't tell me you don't miss it."

"I wasn't disagreeing with you." Charlie dug through the contents of his trunk, double-checking his bags and ensuring he had everything he needed for his trip.

"Hey, Char?"

"Don't call me that."

Jet huffed. "Hey, *Charlie*?" The priest tensed, turning his head slowly to quirk an eyebrow at his brother. Jet had conceded *way* too quickly. "Your conference is in Chicago, right?"

Charlie's eyes narrowed, immediately suspicious. "Yes..."

"Well, I was thinking—"

"Oh no."

"—I've got some friends I haven't seen in a while—"

"I'm flying out tomorrow," Charlie interrupted. "Summer vacation just started. You aren't getting a ticket this late and definitely not on the same flight as mine."

"True, but I was thinking more along the lines of a road trip anyways."

"No."

"Charlie—"

"No!"

"Oh, *Father*," Jet sighed dramatically, the back of his hand pasted to his forehead, "I already told Mom we were riding together. You wouldn't want to make a liar out of me, would ya?"

"First of all, don't call me 'Father' either. It's weird. Second of all, you shouldn't have told her I'd agreed to something before I'd actually agreed to it."

"C'mon, Charlie, Mom was over the moon about it. She just wants us to stay connected."

"*Jet*," Charlie growled, arms crossed defensively.

"We can hang out, bond, contemplate life. It'll be fun."

Charlie sealed his lips, brown eyes scanning the trunk one last time before falling back on his brother. Jet had driven an hour and half to seek his counsel—an hour and a half. "I have to be at my conference in two days," Charlie finally bit out.

"Ah, that's plenty of time."

"Yeah, we'll get there with a whole hour to spare."

Jet ignored him. "You can fly back if you really want to. I can drive home alone."

"You can drive *there* alone."

Jet pouted, his big brown eyes like chocolate chips. His lip was jutting out just enough to be endearing, unlike other adults who tried it, and he'd somehow managed to make himself look ten years younger. How the pout still suited his face, no one would ever know.

"Fine," Charlie relented, "but you're on the pedal."

Jet's triumphant smirk wasn't reassuring. "No problem."

Charlie just rolled his eyes and grunted. This was a terrible idea. *Be positive*, he told himself. *Not everything involving Jet ends in destruction and death.* He turned to face his gleeful brother, fine eyes discerning the healing remnants

of a jagged gash hiding under the fringe of his little brother's brow.
Just, you know, most things.

Chapter 5

They took off early the next morning, leaving the sleepy town behind them and meeting little to no traffic even as they sped past cities and towns. The morning was too young for even the early risers to brave.

Despite all the teasing that usually passed between them, Jet and Charlie were fairly content that morning, the quiet, first rays of day unveiling the psalms and hymns of matins and lauds. Charlie's head drooped over his breviary, fighting sleep with skills earned from seven years in seminary, while Jet drove on, taking generous bites of the barbacoa taco Mom had made for him the night before. She'd been half asleep when they left. Dad…not so much.

Jet pulled through the checkpoint without issue, rolling his stiff neck and trying to relieve the tension in his spine. They'd been cruising for little more than an hour and a half, but already he could feel the beginning twinges of a muscle spasm in his mid-to-lower back.

"Pull over at the rest stop, would you?"

Vaguely startled by the sudden request, Jet chanced a glance at Charlie, who had slipped his prayers shut and readjusted his seat, but Charlie wasn't looking at him, and Jet could guess the reason they were really pulling in had less to do with Charlie and more to do with him. He grimaced out the window so his brother wouldn't see. "Okay."

Jet sailed into a parking spot parallel to the stop, locking the car in park with one jerky motion. Head titled slightly down, he slowly turned to face Charlie.

"I'm going to get a drink, and Mom wants me to call her. I'll be back in a minute." Charlie shoved the door open distractedly and took to the interior of the small building.

In some realm of disbelief, Jet watched him go, Charlie's black cassock twirling out with every turn and attracting the attention of baffled bystanders. Jet chuckled to himself. That never got old.

He waited several more seconds until Charlie was out of sight before twisting himself out of the driver's seat. He was no longer sure what the real reason was for this unexpected stop, but he would take advantage of it regardless. Raising his hands in the air, Jet stretched the aching muscles of his back and sighed in satisfaction with every pop of his stiff joints. Then he relaxed against the car in renewed comfort.

Jet had all but convinced himself this road trip was just a tribute to the past, a little stroll down memory lane if anything, but a small part of him, the part not in fervent denial, was flashing a neon sign in his mind with clear directions. He hated it. He hated it more than he thought he could ever hate anything.

Why he'd decided to heed the warnings now when he hadn't acknowledged them in years was really beyond him. Maybe it had been the car crash. I had never stood in for him in one of his visions before, and the thought chilled him. All the ways he could watch me die…

No!

It wasn't fair. He had no right to intrude on Jet's complacency. None. Jet jingled the keys in his hand. Oh, how tempted he was to turn the car around and defy his orders. But no, Charlie's flight had left hours ago. If they turned back now, his brother would never make it to his conference in time. Then they'd both be in trouble.

Jet eyed the windows of the small building for any signs of Charlie and found him standing by the vending machine with the phone to his ear.

Ever the impatient one, Jet gave up his passive wait by the car to take a short walk. Nowhere in his list of things to do had there been introspection. Jet shook his head as he trailed around the facility, weaving between picnic tables and crossing over to the side of the rest stop that welcomed southbound traffic.

Jet's fingers twitched by his sides. A scruffy man covered in tattoos was shouting profanities at a strawberry blond no older than Jet.

"Let go, you jerk," she snapped at him, trying to forcefully yank her arm from his grasp. With some fair effort, she managed to wriggle free, and Jet briefly considered turning back the way he'd come. The sharp pitch of a slap nixed that idea, and he strode without further pause straight up to the pair.

"Excuse me, but you're bothering people." They both looked around at the empty scene, one in rage, one in teary despair, both laced with confusion. Aside from the girl's—

and Jet could tell it was clearly the girl's—not a single car or pedestrian rested on their side of the highway.

The man shoved his companion back, and she glared at him through watery eyes. "Just leave him alone, Toro."

"Shut up—" The Spanish invectives that followed summoned a powerful glower from Jet.

"You, sir," he began dangerously, "are a disgrace to the human race. She has a name, and I'm certain it isn't any of the words you just spat at her."

"It's Penny, actually," she offered, still drilling a hole in Toro's head with her defiant gaze.

"It's whatever I say it is," the bull answered. He took a threatening step towards Jet and reached an arm around to the back of his jeans.

Jet tensed, anticipation running high, muscles ready for any necessary action, but the man merely whipped out a butterfly knife and flicked it open. Jet took his own step forward, blocked the incoming slice, and punched the man in the throat with a solid fist. Toro dropped the blade, hands latching onto his neck as he tried to draw in a full breath of air, failed, and found his way to the ground. On his knees, gasping past the harsh coughs scraping out of his cinching throat, the fool attempted to rise. Jet hardly spared him a glance, planted a well-aimed kick to the side of his head, and sent him spiraling into unconsciousness.

Penny only watched him, her mouth hanging open in shock. "He wasn't *with* you, was he?" That would pose a bit of a problem.

Her jaw snapped shut, and she shook her head. "He's my ex. This was the last place I expected to see him. I thought he was still in Mexico."

Jet nodded. *Crisis averted.* "So," he began, leaning back and raising his eyebrows, "where you headed?"

She blinked at him a few times before straightening up, shoving her shoulders back, and flipping her hair out behind her. "South," she said boldly.

"What a coincidence. I live down south. Maybe I'll see you around when I get back."

"Oh, yeah, okay," she mumbled, a blush mounting her cheeks. Her shoulders drooped forward as her finger caught a wayward strand of hair that she twirled innocuously. With a slight wave of her free hand, she strode off the sidewalk to her Camry, looking back at Jet only once.

Chapter 6

Charlie was just pulling a pack of peanuts out the vending machine, phone tucked between his cheek and shoulder, when he saw Jet round the corner. *Good, he's stretching.* Jet was notorious for suffering in silence, and Charlie often had to engage in a little discrete finagling just to get Jet to tend to his own needs.

Thinking nothing more of it, he finished up his phone call with Mom and slipped his cell in a pocket through the slit in his cassock. Then he tore open the peanut packing with his teeth and walked out the back door to seek his brother. He found Jet staring down at the crumpled form of a groaning man.

"Two minutes, I leave you alone for two minutes, and you just can't help yourself."

Jet smirked. "It was more like five, and he was going at it with some girl. Would you rather I'd just let him beat on her?"

"No, but you didn't have to be so drastic," Charlie grumbled.

"Ah, he'll be fine in a minute. I barely even tapped him."

Charlie shook his head. His brother was something else sometimes. Instead of commenting further, Charlie simply walked away, throwing over his shoulder a quick, "Ready to go?"

Jet smiled, then cocked an eyebrow of his own. "I thought you were getting a drink."

"Peanuts are better."

Then they were on the road again, sweeping along the dusty streets of Texas backcountry and boiling under the southern sun even in the early morning shades of light.

"Mom wants us to visit Aunt Hilda on our way to Chicago."

"And that's…?"

"Near St. Louis."

"Because…?"

"No one's gone to see her in a while, least of all us."

So, for the next three hundred miles, they enjoyed the homey comfort of their drive. Charlie dozed for a bit and dreamed of dead nights and never-ending grey ribbons of road. He knew he would. Uncle Riley had snuck his way into Charlie's subconscious long ago, and the results of their time together were stitched into his memory. Though Jet had jumped from the backseat to the driver's seat, Charlie's position hadn't changed.

When he wasn't sleeping, Charlie was thinking about whether or not they should stop for the night. A twenty-one-hour drive would be hard on anyone. But he knew if they did, then he'd definitely be late for his conference. He spared a glance at his brother. Jet had picked up a few useful skills from his former jobs. Working on very little sleep was one of them.

Jet caught Charlie's eyes for a moment and offered him a cheeky grin, then returned his gaze to the road ahead with a motionless shrug. They'd gone far enough for the tank to need refilling, so Jet cut off the highway and into a gas station. Charlie could only hope this stop would be a little less eventful than the last.

Feeling a little guilty over the night ahead, Charlie volunteered to feed the pump and fuel the car, so Jet lounged in the driver's seat, phone out and ready to dial. "Put that away," Charlie ordered.

Jet shot him a sardonic look. "You know that's partly a myth, right?"

"Jet."

"I'm not even close enough to—"

"Jet!"

"Okay, okay, I've gotta call a buddy. I'll be right back." Jet hauled himself out of the car, stretched again, and swept around to the shop.

Charlie almost stopped him, torn between the twin dangers of having Jet so near the car and having Jet so far out of sight. In his head, he counted the seconds 'til his brother's return. The pump clicked beside him, and begrudgingly, he sat himself back in the car, trying to catch sight of Jet's fit figure trudging back.

He jumped at a knock on the passenger's window. Jet stared in at him. "What are you looking at?" he asked through the glass.

Charlie just shook his head and waved dismissively. When had Jet even left the store?

Jet slipped into his seat with a thump. Immediately, the stale scent of nicotine burned at the inner skin of Charlie's nostrils, and the vague pangs of a second-hand addiction threatened his outer calm. "*Jet*!" he groaned, winding the crank of his manual window in an effort to air out the vehicle.

Jet rolled his eyes. "You are such a drama queen, you know that? It's not that bad."

"It's not that bad for *you*. You're surrounded by that horrible stench all the time. It's stirring up my sinuses. You know how sensitive my nose is."

Jet rolled his eyes a second time.

"Can't you quit already?"

"I could, but I don't want to."

"So you can't."

"I can, but I don't want to."

"The first step, Jet," Charlie began. Pausing with a pointed glare, he let the end of the adage hang between them.

"Sure, whatever."

Charlie growled and looked out the window. Mentally counting to three, he changed the subject, hopeful that his growing frustration would fizzle out into nothing. "Everything alright with your friend?"

"Huh? Oh yeah." Jet put the car in drive and prepared himself for the wiry roads of the city. "I was just letting him know I'd be stopping by."

"Who's this friend of yours anyways?" Charlie asked, watching the lower cityscape of Sugar Land merge into the towering structures of Houston.

"Oh…" His hesitancy should've set Charlie up to expect the worst, but with his senses tuned to everything going on outside the car, he completely missed the warning from inside. "Voight."

Charlie went cold, his whole body tensing like a tightened coil and the world outside ceasing to exist. "Please tell me you aren't actually going to Chicago to visit Voight the Void."

"I could, but then I'd be lying to your face, and I know how you are about honesty."

Charlie still hadn't relaxed, features pinched in phantom pain, hands clutching at the door and the three-inch, cast-iron crucifix dangling just below his chest. "Why would you want to visit Voight?"

"He's an old friend."

"He's a mass murderer."

"He's an assassin."

"Same difference."

"Big difference."

"No difference."

"I'm an assassin."

"A retired assassin."

"What in the hell does it matter to you!"

"It matters to me 'cuz I'm sitting two feet from you, and I'm *not* getting caught in the crossfire!"

So much for cooling the mood. Now they were both seething. Charlie tried to get a hold of himself, forcing his seized limbs to release their tension so he could grab a book he'd brought along with him. Jet, for his part, just gripped the steering wheel tighter, jaw set and unmoving.

It wasn't an hour later that he swerved into the parking lot of a diner on the north end of Houston. Standing on the curb, Jet pulled out a cigarette, thumbed his lighter, and lit the sucker, not bothering to so much as glance at Charlie as he walked past.

Charlie entered the diner and grabbed a booth near the window. He nodded at the waitress as she put a menu down in front of him. "Water, please," he told her.

Down the street, a group of kids kicked around a soccer ball, and Charlie was reminded of a summer he and Jet had spent on the road, well, partly on the road and partly in Florida at Uncle Riley's house. Charlie had met a kid named Simon that summer when they stopped briefly in Louisiana.

Charlie blinked hard. One of the boys was staring at him, watching him blankly. He must've been around fourteen, and freckles dusted his face. For a second, Charlie could've sworn it *was* Simon. Then Jet slid into the seat across from him and shattered their connection. Charlie blinked again and leaned sideways, attempting to get in another glimpse around his brother, but inexplicably, the boy had vanished.

"What are you looking at?" Jet asked, curious despite his irritation.

"Nothing, I was just thinking about the summer of '03."

Jet snickered. "You mean the first summer Mom and Dad dumped us with Uncle Riley." Jet perused the menu. "You know, that was your fault."

"It was not. You're the one who went snooping through their classified files."

"You used your sophomore class to recreate World War I."

"It was World War II, and they weren't getting the lesson the way Mrs. Dunbar was teaching it. I did them all a favor."

"Did them all a favor? 'Hitler' almost took out 'Roosevelt' in the cafeteria lunch line during finals."

"How would you know? You weren't even there."

"I have ears, Charlie. People talk."

Charlie sighed. "Whatever. If World War III ever breaks out, I bet none of *my* classmates will have been responsible for it."

The waitress set Charlie's water down with a thud, her wary demeanor making it clear she'd caught the tail end of his comments.

Charlie studied Jet while he ordered. His square face had loosened up, but his posture still spoke of tightly tied fury. *Voight the Void—why does it have to be Voight the Void?*

Sudden silence drew Charlie's attention. Both the waitress and Jet were watching him expectantly. "Sorry?"

Jet rolled his eyes. "She asked what you wanted, *Charles*."

Charlie glared at him, then swung his eyes to the woman and smiled sweetly. "Better company would be nice."

Jet and Charlie weren't strangers to flash fury. During the year and a half before Jet's departure to the navy, they'd become quite adept at riling each other up and striking each other down. Chairs would get knocked over, tables overturned. It never ended pretty. The neighbors had even called the cops once or twice.

Both knew the danger of palpable ire, especially *their* palpable ire. Poking the alpha wolves was a death wish for anyone with any sense. Sticking them in a confined space together was just asking for murder.

They drove on quietly, not saying much about anything. The buzz of strong characters clashing in too small a space didn't die, and it wasn't long before Charlie could bear it no longer. After so many hours of senseless stewing, someone had to do something.

Charlie took a breath and hoped the heat of their wills had dwindled enough to clear the air. Then he opened his mouth to apologize.

"Look, I'm sorry. I know you guys never liked my job, but Voight, he gave me a second chance. He's a good friend."

Charlie's mouth slammed shut at the sudden admission. For a moment, he didn't know what to say. Then he raised his eyes to heaven and slowly answered, "As long as he doesn't get you mixed up in anything, I guess it's alright." The car fell silent again, this time more comfortably. Peace reigned on for a little while longer. "What are the chances visiting hours won't be over by the time we reach Aunt Hilda?"

Jet smiled deviously. "I would worry about it. We'll manage."

Chapter 7

Charlie scowled at the receptionist's back as she searched for a pen, the contours of his face shifting only when she turned around with a Sharpie in hand. Internally, he was fuming.

She scribbled out Jet's name on a sticky label, which he took happily and applied to his shirt. Jet nodded at her in thanks, hooked an arm around Charlie's shoulders, and steered him away with a grin on his face.

To be sure, Charlie wasn't angry at the woman. She was just the victim. No, the source of his ire was currently manhandling him down the hall.

"See, that white collar of yours is useful for something after all."

"*This* is an abuse of power."

"Why? You didn't lie to her. You *are* here to visit a resident."

"Not in a pastoral capacity."

"But she never asked that."

"At times, omitting the truth can be just as bad as lying."

"Psh."

Mental institutions, like the one they were currently in, made both men uncomfortable. Charlie had been everywhere—hospitals, orphanages, prisons, war camps. Psychiatric hospitals were the only ones that made his knees weak and the hairs on back of his neck rise, an effect, Uncle Caleb once said, of knowing the fate of the family ended only in an early grave or the place where great minds unravel. Long, hardy lives are rare.

Jet wasn't faring much better. He acted like the moans and wails of the unstable didn't shake him, but crazed mutterings from a man in one of the rooms they passed made his skin crawl and brought to mind one of Uncle Caleb's more caustic warnings: Never assume a clinically insane person is actually insane. There are so many other reasons they might seem that way. Most of them aren't good.

They drifted down the halls, Jet's arm still slung across his brother's shoulders, now, to ground them both. The grin had fallen from Jet's face long ago, but he maintained his air of aloofness out of sheer pride.

Hilda Villena's room was at the end of a short corridor. Her name was tacked to the door, inscribed in lasting plastic, and a flickering light shuttered the hall in dingy florescence, casting odd shadows across the walls.

Charlie knocked out of courtesy but didn't wait for an answer before turning the knob and entering. Jet dropped his arm and watched, inching in slowly behind Charlie with less assurance.

The room was simple. A twin bed sat in the corner beside a glossy, glass window. The walls were white, the ceiling flat, and the floor laid with ceramic tile. Aunt Hilda sat on a recliner facing the window, where the boys could see the distorted figure of the full moon coating her face in a vintage hue. Lights were out for the night already, so they watched her in darkness.

Charlie took the bed beside her, searching her face for any acknowledgment that he was there, while Jet navigated around to her other side and leant against the wall to watch her watch the moon.

"Aunt Hilda?" Charlie called gently. "Tía?" he tried again.

She didn't respond, eyes glazed over and vacant.

"What's the point? She doesn't even know we're here." Jet crossed his arms, voice deceivingly bold.

Charlie only spared him a quick glance. "Aunt Hilda? I'm Charlie, and that," he said pointing, "is my brother, Jet." Still nothing. "We're Caty Harper's kids." There, a glint of recognition.

The icy chill of the ward was suddenly suffocating, and a nauseating pressure bore down on them. She turned her head to Charlie, greasy flat locks of black wire cascading over her shoulder. Then the whole room breathed, and the wrinkles of her face twisted, eyes suddenly animated and full of curiosity. "You're Catalina's sons?" came her scratchy voice.

"Yes, that's right," Charlie answered, a genuine smile lightening his features.

"Look at you. You're both still alive!" she said in awe.

Jet's eyes narrowed, and Charlie's face gave a solid twitch. He let out an uncomfortable chuckle in an effort to shrug off her comment.

She turned back to the window. "I like watching the moon, even if I can't see it so well from in here. It reminds me a Caleb. He always seems to find the worst sort of trouble under it. Is he still alive?"

Charlie nodded.

"And Caty?"

"Yes, she sends her love."

She nodded to herself, hesitated, then turned to Jet. She stared hard at him for a moment. "What happened to your legs?"

Startled, Jet fought the urge to look down. "My legs are fine."

"No," she told him.

"No?"

"No, they're missing."

Jet's hands fisted at his sides. Annoyed with himself, he gave into the urge and examined his legs. Nope, still there.

But Aunt Hilda stared at his legs as though she really couldn't see them. "Look at you hovering. It's really quite remarkable."

"I'm not hovering."

She was muttering to herself now, as if they weren't even there. "He's floating…like a ghost." Jet flinched at that. "A ghost…yes, he's a ghost. That must be it."

"Aunt Hilda?" Charlie called, trying to regain her attention. "*Tía?*"

"¿Qué pasó, niñito?"

"We just stopped by to see how you're doing."

"Did I tell you about the moon?"

Charlie threw his eyes to Jet, noting the unease in his posture and the moisture on his brow. "Yes, Aunt Hilda, it reminds you of Uncle Caleb."

"Uncle? Oh right, because your Caty's kids."

"Yes."

"But the moon, Carlitos," she began again, "it tells me so many things."

"It talks to you?" Jet asked derisively.

She ignored him. "He tells me that it will be okay. Todo bien."

"He?"

"*Him.*"

"Who's 'him'?" Jet asked.

She ignored him again. "It's pretty, ¿no?"

"Aunt Hilda!" Jet snapped, exasperated.

"No, no," she mumbled to herself, "can't be talking to no ghosts."

Jet stiffened, face growing paler by the second.

"Aunt Hilda, Jet's not a ghost."

She looked at Charlie, then back out the window. "Being a Villena's hard, but I think you'll be alright. You're Harpers, too, after all. You're different that way than the rest of us. The Villena name will die out soon, but the curse of our family will live on in you—that is, unless Caleb finds himself a resilient wife and makes a mother out of her."

"I don't think Uncle Caleb's going to be making a mother out of anyone, Tía. He's a priest, too."

"Oh, when did that happen?"

"Sometime before I was born."

The silence was unbearable, and Charlie knew he'd have to wrap it up soon. Jet looked about ready to bolt. "You're both very strong," she told them, drawing their attention as she gazed at the moon, "with will like lightning. It isn't there. It isn't there. And then it strikes, and nothing can stop it." Jet didn't relax at her acknowledgement. "Dangerous, difficult things always find you. You shouldn't always win, but the hand that wields you makes no mistakes. Trust will guide you, and faith will guard you." She paused, took a shaky breath, then commanded loudly, "Do. Not. Die!"

Thunder crashed without warning. Only Charlie jumped. "That storm came out of nowhere, didn't it?" he said, faking nonchalance. "We have get to Chicago, Tía. We'd better be going."

She didn't say anything, just stared out the window with the same dead eyes she'd had on when they first entered. Charlie gave her a gentle kiss on the cheek, laid a hand on one of hers, and prayed. Then standing, he waited for Jet to offer her a nod and followed him out the door.

"That was really creepy," Jet said as soon as they'd cleared the corridor.

The receptionist popped out from an adjoining corridor. This time, neither reacted. "I was just going to call you. The storm's getting pretty bad outside, and the streets around her flood like nobody's business. It's probably a good idea if you go now before it gets any worse."

"Thank you," Charlie responded, ever Mister Manners. "We just finished speaking with Miss Villena anyways." The receptionist froze, eyes locked on Charlie like he had signaled the Second Coming. "Is something wrong?"

"She spoke to you?" she asked.

"Well, yes," Charlie answered.

"With words?"

"Is there any other way?" Jet mumbled.

"That's...odd."

"How come?"

The receptionist gave them a weary frown. "Because she hasn't spoken a single word to anyone in over five years."

Chapter 8

Only the pitter-patter of rain on pane penetrated the queasy silence shared among them like an old friend, familiar though not entirely welcome. Jet saw another day of trudging through the trenches of the warzone he called life. Charlie saw another test of faith. He wanted to gripe about it, to be angry that no matter how far he went, no matter how much he gave, he'd never be free from the wind and hail of that damning black cloud.

But he didn't.

Uncle Caleb had warned him not to use the holy order of priesthood as an escape. It wouldn't work, he'd told Charlie. It hadn't for him. If anything, it had only made matters worse. And Charlie had promised that he wasn't trying to fool anyone by his ordination, least of all himself. It was true. It was honest. It was everything he'd ever wanted. He *had* been called.

But the black cloud hardly cared, and it took all Charlie had to suffer it gracefully like the good little servant he was.

Charlie grimaced from his seat in the car, one hand clutching the Benedictine crucifix that faithfully hung around his neck, the other pushing beads of the rosary he was praying. He almost dared mumble the mysteries aloud like Dad had done for years, but Jet had both hands on the steering wheel. Hunched over in his seat, he was treating the road like a minefield. Too much was going on there that Charlie wasn't quite ready to tackle, and breaking the hush would force him to do just that.

Jet had steadily been accelerating as the minutes passed, so much so that Charlie dared not drop his eyes to the speedometer. He really didn't want to know, but he caught a few glimpses of Jet, focused and burning out between rubber and road. The man was on a mission, and Charlie wasn't going to stand in his way. Besides, as long as Jet didn't shatter a window, they'd be fine, in the short term anyways.

He finished his prayers with a silently sung *Salve* and a request to safely get them to Chicago without Jet killing them on the wet streets first, and thankfully, at around two in the morning, Jet finally eased up on the gas pedal and relaxed back in his seat. He squirmed for a minute, trying to loosen the muscles of his back without actually taking a hand to them.

"Need a break?" Charlie asked. The shift in tension had woken him from his light doze.

"No!" Jet snapped, fighting the urge to tense again. Then, "No," much calmer. Then, "No!" as if he'd just realized his brother had volunteered to drive and was horrified by the notion. "Never."

Charlie rolled his eyes and turned his head, watching the streaks of rainwater fly off the window. "How's your back?"

"As good as it has been."

"And that means?"

"It's fine, Charlie, honestly. I just don't like sitting for so long."

"We could stop and walk around for a bit."

"We're only a few hours out. I can handle a little burn."

Charlie sighed. "If you insist."

Chapter 9

Grey—the skies were grey. Snow was coming. Charlie could just feel it. And boy did he miss home, where if it froze every once in a while, poor fortune had fallen.

Charlie watched as the first few flakes slowly drifted towards the ground. He really should've been paying attention to Doctor Halenbacker's Greek lesson, but something—he wasn't quite sure what—was pulling his thoughts into a downward spiral with those small, cotton-white puffs of frozen water.

"…to go through the tunnels. Wouldn't want any of our future priests dying of pneumonia, now would we?"

The tunnels beneath the school were creepy as hell. They'd been used long ago to smuggle alcohol during prohibition, attracting all sorts of trouble in turn, and the dim ambience only served as a reminder of their haunting history.

"Do let me know if any of you see Mr. Phillips while you're down there," the professor added.

Half the class groaned at the joke. There were rumors their old rector, Father Jerome, had sent Francis Phillips down there years ago as punishment for staying out past curfew. As the tale went, he'd never been seen again. Most of the students found it nonsensical. Others felt it wasn't worth their worry. A select few could be seen zooming down the corridors to avoid loitering too long in the ghastly vastness.

Normally, Charlie wouldn't have minded the trek, eager to be out of the biting, Chicago wind, but for some reason, at that very moment, a shudder rocketed through him, something that warned him away from those confined, cloaked quarters.

Noticing most of his class had already left, Charlie shook off the feeling, vacated his seat, and sauntered towards the door to the elevator that would take him down to the tunnels below. He waited several minutes for it to rise again. Most of his class had already ridden down, and now only the stragglers were left, most with other activities in the building to manage first.

Ding!

Charlie stepped aside to let an older group of men exit, then climbed in, swinging his backpack up over one shoulder and buttoning his coat. He was done with his classes for the day. Maybe he could get a little work finished in the library before leaving for his weekly jail visit.

The elevator doors parted with another ding, and Charlie stepped off the lift, the cold air washing over him in waves. He wrapped his black scarf around his neck tighter and marched on. Red brick ran the length of the tunnel, with lanterns jutting out of the walls intermittingly. The echoes of feet somewhere down the corridor drifted towards him. A group farther up the network was navigating near the dorms.

Charlie hit a fork in the tunnel and turned down the corridor that would lead him to the library. Several lights were out in the block, the shadows running most of the tunnel into a sea of darkness. Charlie stopped. It wasn't an uncommon sight, but…

The feeling was back again, cold and desperate. Charlie swiveled halfway. He could always study in his dorm room and hit up the library later.

A resounding click stopped him in his tracks.

He turned back slowly, one hand still on the strap of his backpack, the other resting at his side. A red-haired man edged out of the shadows, gun raised and ready for action. He had a permanent frown etched onto his face, eyes black in the lighting. He jerked his gun up twice, but Charlie didn't move.

Then the footsteps were louder, and voices accompanied them down the tunnel. Charlie raised his hands in mock surrender and took several steps back before the cock of the gun forced him to a stop.

The party of men had halted. They could see Charlie, his hands up defensively, and were sharp enough to know something was wrong.

"Whatever you're doing down here, it's none of my business."

The man's faced twisted into a sickening sneer. "You think you're so smart, don't you? Think you can talk your way out of this?"

"I just don't want anyone to get hurt." Someone was running…to get help, Charlie hoped.

"It's too late for that. It's been too late for that since you stormed your way into our lives."

Charlie squinted, suddenly very aware that the man in front of him was expecting recognition. "I..." Flaming red hair, baby blue eyes. "Simon?"

The man laughed. "Do we look that much alike?"

"Kenny, then," he answered more certainly.

Kenny nodded, a demented expression crossing his features. "Do you know where Simon is?"

Charlie shook his head.

"That makes two of us." He laughed again, a horrible, anguished laugh. "I haven't seen him since that summer you and your brother came to town." Charlie's eyes widened. "You damn Harpers screwed up everything."

"Ken—"

"Shup up! You must think I'm stupid. I know the only reason you were there was 'cuz the mayor hired your uncle to find his kid. Whoever took him only stuck around 'cuza you."

"Kenny, think about what you just said. If my uncle had been onto them, they'd have run, not stuck around. Besides, we were only in town for a few days."

"And yet they stayed anyways, 'cuz you all were *so* interesting. They hoped they could catch another glimpse of you, but when you never came back, they grabbed Simon instead." Kenny paused. "You know, Simon thought you were so cool. 'Charlie Harper can do this,' and 'Jet Harper can do that.' It's all I ever heard from him, and when your big brother thinks the world of someone, you start to think the same way, too."

"Ken—"

"I'm not finished! I spent years trying to find you so you could bring Simon back, like you were the answer to everything. But eventually, I figured it out. I figured out that you were to blame from the start. Still, I waited for you. I waited for you, Oh Great Charlie Harper! I waited for you, but you never came. Now I'm done waiting. Look at you, here, in your bubble. What a perfect little world you live in."

"Look, Kenny. I'm sorry about Simon. If I'd known he was missing, I would have tried to help, but I had no idea. We were just kids."

Kenny shook his head. "No more excuses, Charlie." He paused. "You think I came here to kill you, and I did, but I think I have a better idea now." Kenny shook furiously, aimed the gun at his own head—

"No!"

—and fired.

Charlie lunged for his crumbling corpse, but someone had wrapped their arms around torso and yanked him back. "Calm down, Charlie. It's alright now. You're alright now," Dr. Halenbacker whispered, wiping at the red droplets now blessing Charlie's brow. Chaos abounded, but Charlie only had eyes for his once-friend's little brother, sprawled across the ground, bleeding hot, crimson blood onto the cobblestone floor.

Chapter 10

Charlie had conked out at some point, his bobbing head bouncing the square frames off his face by the half inch. Jet frowned. He hadn't even seen Charlie put them on, and really, what did he need them for? His brother's eyesight had always been phenomenal, at least, when they were kids, and Jet wasn't convinced Charlie wore them for any other reason than to look sophisticated among his generally older peers.

"Charlie!"

Charlie jerked in his seat, eyes dancing everywhere even as his hand flew to his glasses. "What happened? What's wrong?" he asked, his panic evident.

The morning was still dark, the sky clear and bright with stars that sunlight had only just begun chasing away from its spot beneath the horizon.

"Nothing, I just wanna to know where I'm taking you."

Charlie glared at him, its effect dampened by his still slightly askew frames and the hand he had over his racing heart. "Thanks, Jet. I really needed that."

"Just doing my job."

"Uh huh." Charlie looked around at the city. *Where are we?* "A friend of mine asked me to check in at his old parish. I'm staying at St. Vitus's."

"Saint who?"

Charlie took a deep breath, a sure sign he was about to pay Jet back for the scare. After all, Charlie's favorite form of torture was prattling on about a topic no one cared about. He opened his mouth, then snapped it shut. Three vans had dashed out from an intersecting road, cutting off the flow of traffic both ways and drawing the attention of the entire block.

Jet hit the brakes, mindful of the cars behind him. It was early, but even in that quiet hour, the heart of Chicago pulsed with life, and the circus of cars around them were forced to a screeching halt. "Oh sh—"

"Jet!"

"What!?" *Charlie can't seriously be calling me out on cussing at a time like this.* He snuck a peek at Charlie, who'd braced himself for the sudden stop, but his brother's eyes were locked on the vans, so Jet turned to examine them himself.

They were white with no distinguishing features and windows that were tinted too dark to see inside. The back doors busted open on each, and over two dozen men spilled out, assault rifles ready for use.

Jet checked his rearview mirror. *Damn.* Cars were strewn across the width of the street. The confused civilian drivers had blocked their means of escape.

Jet yanked a handgun out from beneath his seat, slid the magazine in, and released its safety. "Charlie, get out the car."

"And go where?"

"Just get out the car, Char!" he shouted, shoving Charlie against the door. Charlie scrambled for the handle. "There's another gun in the glove compartment."

Charlie threw open the door and slid out, the first rounds of fire cracking his windshield and sparking off the pavement. He pushed his eyes up to the sky and spread across the lower side of his vehicle. "I'm just loving Your sense of humor," he said, wrapping an arm around his head when a stray bullet ricocheted off the open door. "We made it *to* Chicago safely, didn't we?" He let out a hysteric laugh.

"Charlie, the gun!" Jet yelled, still stuck inside. He lowered his window and ducked under it for cover, firing off a few rounds every couple of seconds and sending their assailants down one by one.

"Uh, no!" Charlie shouted back. "I'm a priest. We don't kill people."

Jet let out a frustrated groan, both because his brother was being stubborn *and* because he'd just emptied his mag. *Great.* He kicked Charlie out of the way as he reversed outside, grabbing his secondary gun and a few more magazines as he went. "Are you seriously doing this right now?"

"Hey, I try not to pester you about your career choice. Please don't disrespect mine."

"So don't kill anyone."

"I'm not going to hurt anybody either, Jet. Sorry."

"I hate you right now." Jet crouched behind the hood of the car, then dropped hard to the ground, shooting a few legs before delivering more fatal shots to falling bodies.

"Turn the other cheek."

"Don't you think you're taking that a little too far? There are people trying to *kill* us."

"Christ was tortured and crucified. I don't think this is far enough. Besides, I'm pretty sure they're only trying to kill *you*," he countered, watching Jet just barely dodge a shower of bullets. Charlie crawled to the back of his car and peered around at the injured innocents. He had work to do, it seemed. Wrenching his trunk open, he grabbed his kit.

Jet twisted back in time to see Charlie dart across the expanse of ruin. Injured bystanders were screaming out in pain and terror. Everyone else had cleared the street, and somewhere in the distance, sirens were approaching.

Jet cursed. He was down to his last few bullets and at least ten men were still standing. He took a breath of controlled adrenaline and shot out over the hood of the car. He emptied his last four rounds into the heads and chests of the most able gunmen and raced for the nearest target. Then he drew his favorite knife from the back of his jeans, swept under a slow hand, and slashed at the attached wrist. The man's subsequent hiss was cut short by the same knife meeting his throat.

Using his corpse as a full body shield, Jet reversed several steps to throw off their accuracy and strength. He crossed the street quickly and ducked behind another parked car, drawing fire away from his busy sibling.

But Jet didn't spare Charlie further thought, eyes set on the five men approaching. Three were out of ammo. Two were smug. All of them were careless idiots. They weren't pros. They were mercenaries pulled off the streets. *Too easy*.

The former assassin pinched the tip of his knife between his thumb and forefinger, wound his arm back, popped up, and hurled it at the first target his eyes fell on, dropping back behind the safety of the car before the dead man had hit the ground. He took several more seconds of gunfire before the last armed man appeared, but Jet, well, Jet *was* a pro. He grabbed the barrel of the gun in one hand, pushed it past him, and yanked hard. The man flew forward into Jet's waiting knee, and when the merc released his rifle, Jet kicked him in the chest and watched him topple backwards.

The remaining three men rushed him as one. Jet evaded their clumsy hits with boredom, elbowed one in the juncture between his shoulder and neck, then slammed the butt of his rifle into the skull of another, and kicked the third one back. Disengaging from all three, he drew the gun up and let out a round into two of them, and when the third charged him a little too close, Jet flipped him over, grabbing his head and twisting 'til it snapped. The man he'd robbed of his weapon twitched, so Jet let out one last shot into him before dropping the gun to the ground with a clatter.

The sirens were nearer now. They'd round the block any minute. He needed to not be there when they did.

Jet collected his knife and sought out Charlie, who was hunched over several moaning figures, rapidly spinning through Signs of the Cross, muttering a constant stream of words, and slathering every forehead he could find in oil. "Charlie," Jet shouted on the way back to the car, "we gotta go!"

Charlie ignored him and dropped to his knees by an injured woman. He spoke to her gently, and she mumbled something back at him, so Charlie merely took her hand and bowed his head in prayer.

Jet pulled up in the car, ramming two other vehicles to clear a path. "Charlie!" he called.

"I'm not finished yet."

"We gotta go now!"

"I'll meet you there," Charlie hollered back.

"Char—"

"I'm not leaving. Just go."

Jet huffed, then hit the gas, and tore down the street towards the lazy rising sun.

Chapter 11

Charlie was exhausted.

After he'd seen to the last victim, the police had briefly questioned him. Thankfully, they were busy trying to control the scene and had only asked him a few questions that he hadn't needed to lie to answer. Honestly, he didn't see why Jet couldn't have just hung around. He'd clearly been defending himself. Granted, Chicago was known for its strict firearm laws, but knowing Jet, laws were the furthest concern from his mind. He'd probably just wanted to foist the headache on Charlie instead of having to deal with it himself.

Charlie hailed a cab as soon as the police released him, sinking into the backseat with a weary sigh.

"You okay there, Pa-*dre*?" the cabbie asked.

"Wonderful."

The man eyed him through the rearview mirror but said nothing else.

Charlie and Jet had driven in at dawn. It was only seven-thirty now, but already Charlie was spent. So much pain, so much death, way too early in the morning. Was it too much to ask that he make it from point A to point B without nearly being killed?

"Pa-*dre*?" the driver called.

"Hm?"

"This is your stop."

Charlie looked out the window. Evidently, he'd dozed off at some point and hadn't even realized it. He reached for his wallet.

"Nah, it's on the house," the cabbie told him. "You look like you could use a break."

Charlie saved his grimace for the empty air. He must've looked awful. His hair was swaying in the wind, a sure sign it had lost its tidiness. He was hot, sweaty, and covered in an assortment of bodily fluids. One frightened man had even thrown up on him when his nervous stomach could take no more. Charlie pulled off his glasses, wiped them with a finger, and tucked them in a pocket he'd had sown into his sleeve when the action only served to make them worse.

Then, with tired eyes, he took a long, cautious look at the church in front of him. Internally, he swooned. He'd almost forgotten how beautiful some of the parishes in Chicago were—tall, dark, and Gothic. And St. Vitus was a beaut. Her tall center spire reached out for the heavens, framed by a pair of towers that stood as sentries beside it. A bell hung in the steeple, a real live bronze bell! The arches, the pillars, the architectural detail that dated its design to medieval times—Charlie forgot how to breathe.

A routine dog walker startled him out of his awe, her cocker spaniel releasing a torrent of barks at his obstructive placement on the sidewalk. The woman, clad in a pair of yoga pants and a jogging vest, only watched him with wide eyes, too surprised by his oddity to say anything at all.

Charlie watched her back for a second, then offered her a friendly smile, and turned towards the rectory. Touring the church would have to wait until he didn't smell so bad that a dog would complain. He sniffed the air and reeled in disgust. *Yup, I definitely stink.*

The rectory was across an alley, a two-story townhouse that stood adjoined to its office. Charlie marched up the steps to ring the doorbell. A middle-aged priest with salted brown hair answered, warm amber eyes narrowing in concern over Charlie's disheveled appearance.

"Father Charlie, I presume?"

Charlie inclined his head.

"Please come in." He stepped aside so Charlie could enter.

"Have you seen another—"

Jet was seated at the kitchen table, sipping a cup of water without a care in the world. He waved cheerily at Charlie, then downed the rest of his drink.

"Would this be who you're looking for?" the older man asked.

"Yes, thank you…"

"Father Martin Barnes." The priest held out his hand for a shake but snatched it back when Charlie raised his own. "Is that blood?"

It was blood. Years of first aid training had kicked in instinctively, and he'd grabbed several gushing limbs against the pained complaints of their owners and simply squeezed. The pressure had helped in most cases, staunching the flow of blood until clotting or the proper authorities had arrived in his stead.

"Yes." Two sets of worried eyes settled on him. "It's not mine."

Jet's gaze lightened immediately, but Father Martin studied him for several more seconds. "I wouldn't suppose this has something to do with the very…holy car currently occupying my garage, would it?"

"Turn on the news," Jet ordered. "You shouldn't have too many questions after that."

Father Martin nearly did but paused in the doorway separating the kitchen and the living room. "Would you like a shower?" he asked Charlie.

"Yes, that'd be great." Charlie made a quick stop at his ruined car through the back door of the rectory, then followed Father Martin up the stairs to one of the guestrooms.

"I didn't realize your brother would be joining us, but he's more than welcome to my other spare room. It's just me right now."

"Thank you, Father. I don't think he intended to stay, but after the morning we just had, I'm not really sure what his plans are now."

Father Martin nodded and left Charlie to his task.

The bedroom was small, with a twin bed in one corner, a dresser, a desk, and a door that housed its own shower—plain, simple, and just the way he liked it. Charlie dropped his bags by the bed, grabbed a change of clothes, and locked himself in the bathroom.

He stood in front of the sink mirror when he was done, dressed in a clean pair of black slacks and a white undershirt. Charlie's pale, narrow face looked back at him through tourmaline eyes. He combed his short hair neatly and frowned. A little pink scar on his lower shoulder was peeking out from under his sleeve. Charlie yanked the cloth down to cover it. He'd don his spare cassock in a moment so even *he* couldn't see it.

Eager to hide the blemish, Charlie exited the bathroom, groaning when he realized he'd left his garment bag in the car. He prayed it wasn't riddled with bullet holes, too.

Jet met him at the base of the stairs. "I guess I'd better be going," he said wearily.

"Father Martin's offered you a room."

Jet said nothing for a long moment, eyes searching Charlie's face. "Would that be okay?"

"He said it was fin—"

"With you?"

Charlie examined his brother carefully for any signs of mischief. He saw only anxiousness. "Yeah, it's fine, but heads up, the police'll probably be coming around soon to question me some more."

"And what are you gonna say?"

Charlie sighed in resignation. "I don't know."

And that would be his major stress of the day, not the death, not the violence, but his indecision over whether to offer full discloser or submit to his protective instincts, ingrained in him since the summer of '91 when that chubby-faced newborn had been laid in a cradle and dubbed *his*.

"Father Charlie, Jet, Mrs. McMullin from a couple doors down just brought breakfast. Care to join me?"

"Sure!"

Of course Jet would take the bait first. Charlie could practically hear his stomach growling, but Charlie didn't have much of an appetite himself, hadn't in a very long time.

"Come on, she always brings way too much for me."

Jet dragged Charlie along by the wrist, and Charlie could only look longingly at the back door as he was towed away from his comfort.

Father Martin seated himself at the table and grabbed a plate, pouring over the morning paper and distractedly cutting an egg. He was dressed in simple clericals but had lost his collar somewhere. Jet took a plate from the counter and shoveled food onto it. "There's orange juice and water in the fridge and coffee in the pot if you'd like some."

"We don't drink coffee," he said, already at the fridge. "Juice or water, Charlie?"

"What, neither of you?"

"Nope, unless Charlie's changed his habits?"

Charlie fought back a yawn. "No," he told them, "juice is fine."

Jet smiled at Father Martin. "Our uncle ruined coffee for us."

The older priest quirked a curious eyebrow at him, but Jet only smiled wider.

The kitchen fell into a cozy silence as Charlie and Jet ate. Father Martin sipped his steaming drink, eyes racing along the words printed across the page.

"I saw the news." Charlie startled but said nothing. He hadn't thought the man had attention for anything but the Tribune. "You two were in the middle of that?"

"Yup," Jet answered, model of nonchalance.

"They're calling it gang violence."

Jet snorted, and Charlie glared at him.

"They're wrong?" Father Martin asked, eyes leaving his paper and leveling on Jet.

Charlie answered, "It was an unfortunate attempt on my brother's life."

"For what?"

"I'll let you know when I figure that out, Father." Jet scooped up a large helping of sausage and egg and shoved it in his mouth to dissuade further questions, not that their unassuming priest friend would realize that, but Jet avoided eye contact with Charlie so he wouldn't have to see his disapproving frown.

"And you're alright?" the priest asked Charlie.

"Sure."

Jet swallowed. "It's fine. He's always getting shot at." Father Martin laughed good-naturedly, a sound that died in his throat when he realized Jet was serious. "You should ask him how he got that scar on his shoulder." Immediately, Charlie's hand shot out to self-consciously tug at his shirtsleeve. Father Martin merely watched in bewilderment. "His class got to study in Jerusalem their final semester, and they were caught in a firefight during an excursion into the city. Charlie took a hit to the shoulder rescuing one of his fellow deacons."

Charlie jumped out of his chair, the wooden seat scraping back across the tile. Somewhere in the back of his mind, he knew Jet was just displacing himself as the center of attention, but the breach of confidence had jarred Charlie's already frazzled nerves, and he channeled the thunder of their cloud onto his face for fury like no other.

A knock on the door spared them all, and Charlie's quickly vanished indignation swung his eyes to their host. Father Martin was leaning back in his seat. The tension choking the room had seized his body. He couldn't move. The knock came a second time, and Father Martin gave a rough jerk, snapped himself from his paralysis, and stood to get the door. He came back moments later with two detectives and a grey face.

"Father Charles Harper?"

Charlie bit back a groan. He wasn't in the right temperament to deal with the police. "Yes?"

The woman caught sight of Jet, who was leaning one arm on the table, pushed back defensively against his chair. "And who's this?"

"Jet Harper," Charlie answered, "my brother."

"Oh, good," the man said, glancing at Jet, "they're both here."

Jet's fingers twitched in Charlie's periphery, fighting the urge to reach for a weapon. The police could never have figured out that Jet was involved with the shooting, and definitely not that fast.

Charlie stepped forward quickly and snatched the hand of the woman, Detective Taylor, then the man, Detective Hall. As expected, Jet remained defensive but didn't otherwise react. Charlie was in his line of fire now. "Good morning, Detectives. What can we do for you?"

"Father Martin gave us a call." Two sets of eyes found the man now hiding behind their inquisitors. "For advice," Detective Hall clarified.

What?

"Who hasn't heard of the Harpers?"

"The club sent you," Jet stated.

"No," answered Detective Taylor, "our superiors in the department have assigned us to investigate the incident that occurred earlier this morning, but the club gave us a full briefing on the two of you when Father Martin rang."

Jet relaxed back in his chair, then, after a moment of indecision, began scarfing down his meal again.

Charlie's look of disgust went unnoticed, the attention of the entire room settling on his gorging brother. "What do you want to know?"

Three sets of eyes returned to him. Detective Taylor answered, "How about you just tell us what happened?"

Charlie glanced at Jet, who was steadily avoiding the conversation. Well, *he* wouldn't be of any use. "Someone's trying to kill Jet, but we don't know who. They blocked off the street and attacked. While Jet dealt with them, I aided the victims. That's all there really is to it."

"You took out forty-two armed men by yourself?" Detective Hall asked, whistling in appreciation.

Jet swallowed the food in his mouth. "Was it only forty-two?"

With a roll of his eyes, Charlie asked, "Anything else?"

"Witnesses say there were only three vehicles. Obviously, they couldn't have all come from the vans."

"Obviously."

Detective Taylor frowned in annoyance, but Detective Hall shook it off. "Did you happen to see where the rest came from?"

"Nah, I was a little busy, you know, trying not to get shot," Jet chirped.

Charlie smiled apologetically at the two.

"Are we going to find any evidence that either of you were at the scene?"

Jet turned to Charlie.

"Yes," Charlie stated plainly.

"Nah, hun, not of me," Jet said, smiling impishly. "I'm a ghost."

Chapter 12

The Rule is an assassin's survival guide. Personally tailored to an individual, mentors pass it on to their apprentices, who take that Rule and alter it to suit them. Voight had done the same for Jet, and like any good student, Jet had added a few of his own provisions and adapted a few of Voight's.

Cameras were tricky. Back when he'd first begun the game, he'd constantly been on guard for them. Those pesky things were everywhere, but his darling sister—yes, I'm aware that's me—had made friends with a genius named Twain, who enjoyed the use of human guinea pigs, voluntary or otherwise, and who had placed a microscopic chip in Jet's neck that forced his image out of focus on any and all recording devices. So far, it had not failed him.

Fingerprints were a huge problem. The easiest solution was to sear them off. Personally, Jet liked his fingerprints right where they were, so he never loaded barehanded, pain though it was, and rarely handled weapons without gloves at all. As an extra layer of precaution, for days like this where being that prepared was impossible, a good friend of Jet's had completely wiped him from the system. Had he ever been arrested? Nope. Military service? Never happened. Jet had been forced to forfeit his disability benefits for that one, but hey, contract killing paid more anyways.

So, in way of most forms of identification, he was covered. His DNA matched no one. His dental records matched no one. He did not exist unless he wanted to. He was, for all intents and purposes, a ghost.

He was *the* Ghost.

No one aside from his family knew his real identity, and that was just an act of trust, a gift he'd offered upon his return to life for the years he'd lived off-grid. He wasn't entirely sure he'd been forgiven for that yet, but it was a step in the right direction at least.

"So, you're a member of the Dragonfly Club?" It was Charlie who'd spoken. The detectives had gone, and Jet had momentarily fallen into review, a paranoid habit he'd picked up to ensure he hadn't missed anything.

"Yes," Father Martin answered, grabbing a bottle of water out of the fridge and joining them on the couches, "I only called them for advice on what I should do with you two since I wasn't sure what sort of trouble you were in. I guess they recognized your names and decided to address the situation themselves."

"Don't you ever feel like you're serving two masters?"

Father Martin frowned. "No, not really. It's a lot like being a military chaplain. I'd know. I was one. I counsel the members, provide for their needs. They don't ask me to do anything outside of my pastoral duties, and it's not like their practicing any weird sorts of rituals or pledging loyalty to some ostentatious icon."

Charlie nodded slowly, and Jet had to wonder what was going through his head—some argument, maybe, against the allying of the secular and the sacred?

They watched the news in silence for a moment, seeing but not really sparing the reporter much attention. "...*the third kidnapping in the county. State officials would like to assure concerned parents that the kidnappings are unrelated and that monitoring your children closely is enough to ensure their safety.*" The woman went on, but Jet tuned her out. Charlie sure seemed tired. "Weren't you supposed to be at your conference an hour ago?"

Charlie gave Jet a dead look.

"I don't think that's a good idea. You're about ready to pass out," Father Martin observed.

"I'll go to the second half tomorrow."

The news was still playing in the background, now a weather report for clear skies and mild temperatures. "Are the two of you club members then?"

"No," Jet answered, peering at Charlie who really did look like he could drop any second. "We're inheritors, but I joined the military straight out of high school, and the club doesn't hire assassins."

"You're retired," Charlie muttered.

"Maybe, but that's kind of my skill, and if the club can avoid death, it does. Where exactly does that leave me?"

Father Martin opened his mouth to question Charlie, but the younger man had already fallen asleep, head tilted back at an awkward angle. He'd have a crick in his neck when he woke. Father Martin smiled into his drink. "I'm heading to the office. Come over if you need anything," he told Jet.

Jet gave him a cursory nod before glancing at the form of his sleeping brother. Then he got up, shut the blinds, and locked the doors on his way out the back.

Jet shot one more look at Charlie, the hesitation in his movements so profound even he couldn't pretend like he wasn't taking a marginal risk leaving Charlie unguarded. Whoever was after him was likely after Jet Harper, not the Ghost, and that meant they knew about Charlie, too. Of course, there was the alternative, the one that meant his number was well and truly up. If someone had found the line where ghost and man merged, Jet Harper couldn't exist in peace anymore, and everyone around him was at risk.

The club would protect the others, but Jet had dragged Charlie into the middle of it. He had to know what he was up against, even if it meant leaving Charlie to his fate. He nodded to the wall and strolled out the door before he could convince himself otherwise.

Steven's Steakhouse was four blocks away. Jet had been there a number of times during his stint at boot camp, although he and his friends generally referred to it as the Pit, a pun even his less educated company understood. Known for its grill, the Pit was also a meeting grounds for the worst sorts of fellas. If you planned on starting a bar brawl, the Pit was the place to do it. If you were looking to watch a war council for the local gangs, the Pit offered you a front row seat. If you needed information on anything going down in Chicago, the Pit was a well of knowledge. All you had to do was know who to ask.

Jet slipped on his leather jacket as he walked the last block. The sun was sweltering for a guy like him, but he looked like he'd just swung off his Harley, and he needed the image to dissuade suspicion, so he ignored the heat, pulled out his aviators, and ducked into the building. Still early, the patrons of the Pit were mostly dining. Several heads turned to inspect him, but they accepted his presence as one of their own and returned to their business.

Jet hit the bar with ease, dropping onto a stool and leaning forward. He signaled the bartender, who was doubling as a waiter in the early hours of the restaurant.

"Bit early for a drink, no?"

"Just get me a screwdriver, would you?"

"Whatever you say, boss."

He waited a moment for the man to return, then spun in his seat to face the other occupants, elbows folded back on the bar top. At no part of the day were the Pit's patrons known for their decency, so it took Jet a minute to spot the dark figure huddled in a corner booth, eyes scanning the room every seven seconds. Jet downed the rest of his drink, savoring the mild zing, and subtly licked his lips clean of the acidic beverage. Then he stood, sauntered across the floor, and plopped himself on the bench opposite his target. The man jumped, eyes mapping every detail of Jet's face.

Jet did the same only far less conspicuously. He smiled, jerked a hand in the air, and ordered a beer from a flamboyant, fair-haired waitress that he didn't give the time of day. Even when she returned with his drink and leaned over promiscuously to flirt with him, his eyes stayed focused on the dark-skinned man in front of him. "Marsden Lamar," he acknowledged calmly, tipping his bottle forward in salute.

"How do you know me?" the man asked, tucking lower in his seat.

"Could you be a bit more obvious about your paranoia?"

"I'm not paranoid."

"Of course you are," Jet answered, taking a sip from his drink, "If you weren't paranoid, you'd already be six feet under…or dumped in a ditch somewhere and left to rot."

The man's eyes narrowed. "Who are you?"

"A concerned party."

"Concerned about what?"

Jet grinned as though genuinely pleased, took another sip, then, with a smile still stretching from ear to ear, said, "Now that really isn't necessary." Marsden's arm had barely twitched, but he stilled his gun hand anyways. "I'm not here for a hit. I just want to talk."

"I've heard that before."

"Habits are a dangerous thing for men like us. If I'd wanted to dispose of you, I'd have spiked your drink with ricin. It wouldn't be that difficult in a place like this."

The man jolted in his seat, leaning away from his glass like it might jump out and bite him.

"I didn't."

Marsden's eyes flickered up. "Concerned about what?" he asked again, forcing himself to calm down.

"Someone has it out for me. I want to know who."

"How should I know?"

"Because that same someone made you an offer."

"And how would you know that?"

Jet shifted in his seat, and Marsden tensed across from him. "Maybe it's a six sense," Jet said, "or maybe you just told me as much."

"You're him then," Marsden whispered, "The Ghost."

Jet narrowed his own eyes. "Maybe I don't like stupid people saying that tag out loud when I'm around." When Marsden cringed, he continued, "And maybe I'm starting to think I should put you on my blacklist, definitely not a place you want to be. Trust me." Jet held his glare several seconds before relaxing again thoughtfully. "Or maybe you could just tell me who issued the contract."

Marsden clutched his drink in clammy fingers, pushing the unsettling feeling of being threatened into his glass. "I didn't see." Jet growled. "I declined the second I realized you were on Claude's Nine."

Shock cracked his apathetic façade. "What?"

"I'd have to be crazy going after someone like that."

But Jet was still concerned with his previous statement. "What rank?"

"Sixth."

A mixture of pride and fear filled him. How had he managed that in such a short time? Were there really only five deadlier than the Ghost? ...And sixth? That spelled bad omen.

"Though the freakin' Grim Reaper's still first," Marsden muttered. "Damn assassin-killer."

Jet ignored him. Grim wasn't his problem right now. "I need to know who posted."

"Why should I help you?"

Jet gave him a look that said, "Get real, man," downed the rest of his beer, and slid out of the booth. "Hasta luego," he said simply, slinging an arm around the flirtatious waitress that was all too happy to follow him along. She stood perpetually between Jet and Marsden all the way out the door, where he merely tipped her, to her dismay, and trudged down the street.

Chapter 13

Charlie woke gradually, groaned, and sat up in the shadows of the room that mixed with the dancing, shining dust particles flurrying across the breaks of light. Swiftly, he rose to his feet. A bitter insomniac, Charlie needed only a few hours of sleep per day to function at his highest potential, and already he felt better than he had all morning.

Charlie made his way to the garage unhindered, glad to finally get back to his car and shuck on his cassock. The garage emptied into an alley, which Charlie took, looping around to the front of the building and striding into the home-turned-office. The bright light of the building stunned him for a moment, nothing like the realm of shadows that was the rectory and its lane.

An older man in jeans and a plaid shirt greeted Charlie the second he cleared the door, the parish deacon apparently, who was headed out to his second job. Charlie had never seen a homier office, with a fully furnished living area and a kitchenette available for public use.

Father Martin rushed from room to room, dodging his office staff as he bounced around, dropping papers on some stacks and picking up leaflets from others. Charlie jumped out of his way as the man dashed past him and nearly tumbled onto one of the room's many striped couches.

"Sorry," the priest offered. "I'm gonna be late for Mass."

Charlie waved it off. "Would it be alright if I joined you?" he asked instead, scooting farther out of the way as Father Martin rounded the coffee table to lay down a rim of flyers.

"Of course," he answered without stopping. "You can head over now. The sacristy's unlocked. I'll be there in a minute."

Charlie nodded and made for the door, more eager than ever to invade the church for a closer look. He wasn't entirely sure where Jet had wandered off to, but he was determined not to think about it. Jet could take care of himself. No point in Charlie getting an ulcer over it.

The neo-Gothic architecture was almost more brilliant inside than it was outside. Charlie grinned at the tabernacle. This place was everything he had dreamed it'd be the moment he laid eyes on it. Scratch that. It was better.

The church had been built in a Latin cross, and Charlie could see the lambent candles beyond the final row of wooden pews on each of the cross's short ends. A confessional stood on the left side of the nave, the old-fashioned kind that was laid up against a wall with two doors that kept the priest and penitent from mingling in more than words. The sanctuary rose up a step, railed off from the public, aside from a gap left for solemn processions. A second step acted as a dais for the altar and the presider's chair. Behind Charlie was a set of stairs that led up to the choir loft and the chain that brought the bell to life.

Ah, life is good.

Charlie marched up the center aisle with little worry, even as the weekday regulars refocused their eyes from their rosary beads and prayer books to the unknown collar strolling casually through their church. An elderly sacristan stalked him into the sacristy. "Is something wrong with Father Martin?"

Charlie was already rifling through the closet for a spare alb. "No, sir, he's fine. He'll be over in a minute. I'm just visiting for a few days."

For a brief moment, the man was a beacon of relief. Then wary suspicion tightened the corners of his eyes. Before he could say anything else, Father Martin flew through the back door, the bells of noontide spurring him into an uneven skip. He barely spared his parishioner a glance. "Victor, is everything alright?" he asked, dropping his own alb on over his head. He sighed tiredly when he realized it was backwards.

"No, no, I'll just be going now," he said, vanishing out the door.

Charlie was now fully draped in white, the thin chord of a cincture tied in loops at his waist and a green stole hanging from his neck like a permanent fixture. "Your parish is gorgeous. I'd love to be assigned to a place like this."

Father Martin gave him a sidelong glance, then shucked on his green chasuble. "You think so?" He smiled smartly. "Just wait 'til you hear Mrs. Abernathy sing."

Chapter 14

Devon Davis was a six-foot-six, lean, mean, running machine, and as he dashed through the winding paths of Jackson Park, freedom sung in his blood like a prelude for eternity. He loved running, and he hadn't felt this alive since, well, since yesterday, when he'd last been on a run. With the breeze in his hair—his crew cut, to be exact—and the pavement beneath his feet—or foot, if we're being honest—his euphoria exploded into endless energy that could've powered Wall Street for a week. The tap of his steps set the tempo, percussed by the rhythmic puffs of air expelled from his lungs.

At the next grove, a second pair of feet fell into step behind him. Devon jerked to a stop, ears on high alert. He spun around to find…

…absolutely nothing. Devon shook his head in exasperation. Paranoia was a bi—

The click of a gun at the base of his skull brought all his orchestrations to a grounding halt. Then his face twisted in fury. One arm flinging back, he turned abruptly, words of rage pistoning his tongue, "Why you—" The stoic figure of Jet greeted him, and all anger fled. "Jet Harper?"

Jet broke a grin.

"Son of a gun! What the hell you doing here, boy?!"

"Ah, just visiting."

"Well, why the hell didn't you tell me you were coming? I could've planned a big shindig for yah."

"I was just in town. Thought I'd say hi."

"Hella'va way to say hi. But then again, you always were one for bringing the boom."

Jet smirked sheepishly, running a hand along the nape of his neck. They began walking again, this time, with camaraderie. "How's the leg?" Jet asked.

"What, this one?" Devon joked, shaking his good leg at Jet. "Or did you mean this one?" Devon patted the outer thigh of his left leg, chuckling hard. He stared down at it for a moment, fingering the place where his skin met the curb of the silicone cup. "It's fine." They roamed in companionable silence for a few more seconds. "How're yours?"

"Great, thanks," Jet answered. "It's my back that's always reminding me of my limitations."

"Trouble?"

"My legs give out occasionally, but other than that, I'm good."

"Oh, is that all?"

They crossed a short, wooden bridge. The water lay stagnant beneath them even as the wind fluttered the leafy green trees above. A power-walking couple came into view up ahead, earphones blaring music a little too loudly. Devon and Jet sidestepped them and the odd looks they garnered, a one-legged runner and his biker friend.

"Wanna race?" Devon asked.

Jet snorted. "Why? So I can eat your dust? Thanks, but no thanks."

"Then beat it. I still got another six miles."

Jet smiled, nodding gently. "Yeah, alright."

"Hey, the Shoe Crew's around. We heading to Mackey's tonight. Wanna come?"

"Ah, I've actually got some stuff."

"Dude, c'mon, it'll be fun." Devon tapped a fist on Jet's shoulder a few times, traces of his emphatic cajoling still lingering in his knuckles.

"What time?" Jet relented.

"Eight."

Nodding slowly, Jet assented, "Yeah, I can make that, but I gotta be somewhere after, so don't expect too much."

Devon issued him a cheeky grin. "Wouldn't dream of it." Then he bound away like a deer with only Jet's sigh to bid him farewell. For a moment, Devon felt kind of bad for pressuring him. Jet hadn't seen most of their old crew since the incident. Davis had only reconnected recently himself.

Ah, the kid would be fine. Jet needed a little action in his life. Seeing the Shoe Crew would be good for him. What did that baby-faced Mexican have to worry about anyways?

Chapter 15

"...And I absolve you of your sins, in the name of the Father, and of the Son, and of the Holy Spirit. Amen."

Confession was one of Charlie's favorite priestly duties, and despite what Uncle Riley thought, it had nothing to do with all the juicy *chisme* involved. The Seal of Confession prevented Charlie from speaking about anything he'd heard, and the grace of God prevented him from thinking about it later. He could sit there for hours, and all he'd come away with was an overwhelming sense of pain and hope, all heartbreak one second and healing the next.

So, Charlie exited the confessional high as a kite, just as refreshed at the woman who'd gone out before him.

The rectory was quiet when he entered. Charlie guessed Jet was still out and Father Martin was at the office. *Ah, what peace.* He'd grab a bite to eat and read for a bit, maybe start prepping for his next homily, and figure out a way to win his own pastor's forgiveness for missing the whole first day of his pre-paid conference.

Charlie turned to the staircase, only to be met with the business end of a .45. He backtracked into the living room where a grunt from behind him drew the corner of his eye. Father Martin was tied to a chair, gagged and sweating. His fear was radioactive, so Charlie fought to control his own. Fire feeds fire, Uncle Riley had taught them. Best not add any fuel to the flame.

A second chair was tied behind Father Martin's. Charlie reversed into it. "You're Charles Harper, correct?"

For the first time, Charlie turned his brown eyes to the gunman. He was big, burly, and covered in hair, with a thick mustache and a full beard. He wore a pair of jeans, boots, and a tactical vest that was at least one size too small. But Charlie's real focus was on the man's eyes. They were coffee-colored and a little too dark, like someone had overbrewed the pot. The swollen black of his pupils pressed the brown into a slender ring.

Outwardly, the man was calm, a repeat amateur that had never gone pro. Jet's eyes only got like that when he was in the heat of battle, guns firing and reflex covering his every move. Jet was a professional. This guy was not, but his cool head told Charlie he'd done this enough times to be dangerous, so Charlie bolstered himself for the coming inquisition.

The man threatened to whip him with the gun.

Oh, right, he'd already been asked a question. "Yes, I'm Charlie Harper."

"Where's your brother?"

"My brother?"

"The Ghost, the Specter," the man said in response. "You were seen riding with him. You're either brothers or cousins.

You look too much alike not to be. So," he continued, tapping Charlie with the barrel of his gun, "where's your brother?"

Another man, a little thinner than his partner and wearing a black bandana across his lower face, appeared from the hallway. "All clear."

The larger one signaled him to tie Charlie to the chair and waited as he did so. "Where. Is. Your. Brother?"

Charlie said nothing. He'd done this once before, and the two buffoons in front of him had nothing on his previous captors.

The speaker left Charlie to stand before Father Martin. "You Christians have this thing about defending each other, right?"

Charlie refused to speak.

"Okay, suit yourself."

Charlie heard movement, then the sound of the gun colliding with some part of the man behind him. The priest's head jerked back into Charlie's, and the older man let out a moan of pain. Charlie felt his heart rate soar and gritted his teeth to ground himself. He didn't know how far he could let this go. Not that it mattered. He really *didn't* know where Jet was.

"Where *is* he?"

"I wouldn't know. He goes where he wants."

"Wrong answer."

Charlie saw the leg rise and winced in sympathy when the large man brought it down on Father Martin's shin. The older man let out a yelp and groaned, then allowed his head to drop against Charlie's.

"One last time before I start putting bullets in all the most painful places: Where is your brother?"

"Am I my brother's keeper?"

"Aren't you supposed to be?"

Charlie's skin prickled. Someone was watching him, some shadow in the hall leading out to the garage. Charlie sighed. "Sometimes, I think he's more mine."

"Wha—" The smaller man was on the floor unconscious before he could finish asking the question.

Jet had appeared in a flicker, and ducking under a jab meant for his face, he swung an uppercut into the bigger man's gut. Before his assailant could recover, Jet had reversed the man's grip on his gun, pushed the barrel up into the soft flesh beneath his chin, and with the man's own finger, pulled the trigger.

Blood splattered everywhere, and Charlie's nose wrinkled in disgust. Jet was completely clean, of course. Father Martin had only taken a few drops himself. Charlie, on the other hand, could feel the blood trailing down his skin, sullying the inside of his collar and cassock as much as it had the outside.

Jet cut Charlie free first, and Charlie rose, wiping blood and brain matter from his vestments in annoyance. "You couldn't have snapped his neck or something?" Father Martin looked up in astonishment, so Charlie quickly added, "Not that I think you should have killed him at all, but a broken neck would have certainly been cleaner."

"The less I tussled with him, the less evidence I might've accidentally left behind."

Charlie gave him a sardonic sneer and turned his attention to their host. "Are you alright, Father?"

The older man rubbed his head and groaned, but Jet was already checking him over. "Minor concussion at the worst. He'll be fine."

"What about your leg?"

Father Martin raised it and winced. "It hurts, but I don't think it's broken."

Jet gave it a quick look anyways and nodded in agreement. "It'll hurt like a bi—a lot, but you should be fine."

Father Martin nodded.

Then Charlie caught sight of himself in a decorative mirror. He looked like a psycho from a horror film, a maniac who'd just hacked someone up with an ax or a chainsaw or something. You could've lined him up beside other notorious sociopaths of the twentieth century, and he'd have fit right in—deranged lunatic!

Charlie's perpetual frown deepened, and he narrowed his eyes at his sullied reflection. *Well, damn,* he thought to himself. *There goes another cassock.*

Chapter 16

The club detectives swooped in not ten minutes later. They had the scene processed and cleaned while Jet and Charlie waited upstairs, stewing in discomfort.

Charlie was not at all pleased. Still, after he got out of the shower, *again*, he grabbed the nearest book off the shelf, a dictionary he was too proud to put back, kicked his feet up on the edge of the bed where Jet was sprawled, and pretended to read.

Jet would throw him a glance every few minutes, open his mouth, and shut it without a word. He stared up at the ceiling for a while before his eyes drooped and he finally conked out. It was a testament to his trust in Charlie that his nearest weapon was more than three feet away.

After a few hours, Father Martin limped up the stairs to retrieve them. Charlie grimaced at the man's obvious pain all the way down. "We can't leave you Harpers alone for more than a few hours without all hell breaking loose, can we?"

"The world's not ending just yet, but give us a couple more days."

Detective Taylor was less than impressed.

"Who's going to tell us the full story here?" Detective Hall cut in before his partner could trade any jabs with Jet.

Jet smirked. "I would, but I only arrived in time to catch the end of it."

Charlie sighed in exasperation. "Those men tied up Father Martin and me. They were looking for Jet, sort of."

"Sort of?"

"They didn't know him by name, and they were only assuming I was his brother because we were seen together earlier and we happen to look alike."

Jet frowned at that. "Someone must have been watching from the crowd earlier." His eyes narrowed. "And someone's got a picture of me."

"So? I'm sure lots of people have pictures of you," Detective Taylor muttered.

"Not lately. I've taken measures to ensure it. Whoever issued the contract must have known me awhile. It's not like I was lazy before."

Now Detective Hall frowned. "Do you know who's after you? Because it sounds a lot like you might."

"I've got my suspicions, but I want to check them out before I say anything. You can't make accusations like that without causing a real stir. I've got information coming tonight. I'll know then for sure."

The detectives nodded. "We'll keep you all posted on our end, and we've put a few uniforms out front for the remainder of your stay. You'll be safe here." Detective Hall turned to Jet. "We'll keep you in the small print of the pages back at the department for whatever they find on you from the scene."

Jet smirked. "Don't expect them to find much."

"Fine," the man said, nodding at Jet and waving at the others. Detective Taylor was already half way out the door. Father Martin chased after them.

"I don't think she likes me very much," Jet whispered to Charlie.

"Gee, I wonder why?"

Jet shot him mischievous grin. "I promised an old buddy of mine I'd meet up with him and some friends tonight, so I'm going out around eight."

"You're socializing at a time like this?"

"Yeah, why not? If I die tomorrow, I don't want to have spent my last day lying around with my brother and his priest friend. No offense," he told Father Martin as he reentered the room.

"None taken?"

"In the meantime," Jet yawned. "I could do with some food and another nap."

Chapter 17

Jet was annoying, Charlie decided. Being anywhere near the miscreant was the dream of a masochist, which Charlie definitely was not. Away from Jet, the rectory was an eerie kind of quiet, and Charlie just wanted a little easy peace, so disregarding his better judgement and the ache in his belly warning him to turn back, Charlie went for a walk around the block.

After only a few minutes, his phone beeped, and he slipped it from his pocket to see half a dozen pictures in his inbox.

Thought you might need these. ~ Uncle Caleb

Charlie rolled his eyes. *I hate it when he does that.* Still, he cast a glance at the first image.

Jet must've been one or two at the time. Charlie was standing behind the couch, eyes peering around it in deep thought, watching Jet rearrange his toy blocks. "Wow, I was a creepy kid." It took Charlie more than a few seconds to figure out why his five-year-old self was studying Jet with such a look of intensity.

Initially, Charlie had been curious about the little, wiggly bundle of blue blanket his mother had brought home from the hospital. Jet was his specimen, something to be studied, so like any good scientist, he'd experimented, first with cause and effect. He started by taking Jetty's teddy, Fluffy. Baby Jet had cried and cried and cried until their temporary nanny had tracked Charlie to the treehouse out back and forced him, under threat of rice kneeling, to give up Fluffy. Charlie's knobby little knees had protested madly.

Then Jet had started walking...maybe running is a more accurate term. Charlie spent most of his spare time playing hide-and-seek with the little terror and figuring out how to bottle chaos. He'd become an expert at psychological manipulation...at least, until Jet began circumventing his tactics. Maybe he should have been more careful with what he was teaching the tyke.

A few years later, Charlie had outgrown his play thing, and a new one came along that he also wanted little to do with. He let them have each other, watching from a distance but never getting too close. Jet and I had our own fun, and Charlie's machinations were largely set in a corner where they slowly shriveled up and died. Still, Charlie was vigilant. He'd watch his siblings, if for no other reason than to be sure nothing went awry.

Then the summer of '03 had happened, and '04 and '05 and '06. Stuffed in a hot car together, crossing the country with Uncle Riley, not that Mom and Dad had known that, things had changed yet again, forced to bond or die of boredom.

Then Jet had turned sixteen, and everything had gone to hell. Charlie found himself desperately wishing he hadn't been born a whole three years before Jet. Out of the house for college, he didn't have the slightest clue what was going through Jet's mind anymore. It was like one second, Charlie had mastered the game, the delicate dance of the Harpers, and in the next, Jet had rewritten the rules completely, obscuring them from sight so Charlie couldn't even see what they were anymore.

"Ey, you!" The shout drew Charlie from his thoughts.

Charlie looked around. He'd wandered a few miles without even realizing it and into an unfamiliar part of town. A short, muscular Latino wearing a wife-beater headed towards him, tattoos covering both arms. "Yes?"

"Charlie, jefe, it's me, Lazaro!" A few others joined him from the shadows of a nearby alley. Charlie's eyes fell to the various bits of exposed flesh, recognizing the overlapping lightning-shaped S's of their Sur Seis tats almost immediately.

"Lazaro," Charlie acknowledged, genuinely surprised, "last time I saw you, you were in prison." Yeah, him and six other guys, all arrested on a drug raid. Charlie had met them on pastoral assignment, ordered to minister to the men behind bars. "I thought you were serving five to ten?"

"Ah, you know how it is, good behavior and all. And you? How long 'til you get promoted?"

"Ordained," Charlie corrected kindly, "and a few months ago actually."

"Really?" The man looked surprisingly proud. "Padre, then. That's great news, jefe." They started walking, Lazaro's four lieutenants flanking the man.

Sur Seis was one of the most organized street gangs Charlie had ever seen. Its influence stretched from border to border, and Lazaro was one of six generals. With scars lining his face and grey in his hair, he was no stranger to the hard life.

Charlie had met Lazaro in county when the law had first cuffed him. They'd talked, a lot, about things Charlie dared not repeat, and after months of visitation, Lazaro had turned over a new leaf. "Anyone who messes with la familia—I'll put the fear of Sur Seis in them," he'd told Charlie.

Well, it was a step up from outright killing them.

"And how are you doing, Lazaro?"

The tough man grinned. "Great. I've been thinking a lot about what we talked about in the joint, too, and I spoke to El Jefe. We might be trying something new soon with los muchachitos. You'd like it." He nodded to himself happily. "You know, Sur Seis started thirty years ago with a group of six barrio boys just looking for someplace to call home."

They marched in peace, the fading sunlight setting them aflame in orange rays. "It sounds like you've got a lot going on."

"No more than usual. What about you, Padre? What are you doing in Chicago? I thought you lived in Tejas."

"I do. I'm actually only here for a conference. It's just a couple days. Then I'll be headed home."

"Ah, well, the offer stands as always, Padre. If you need anything, anything at all," Lazaro said, pausing to allow conjurings of what *all* might mean, "just give me a call. I'll take care of it. I owe you."

"You don't owe me anything, Lazaro. Really. I didn't help you to help myself."

"Still, I've got your bac—"

The screech of tires drew their attention as a shower of bullets lit up the evening air. Someone jumped in front of Charlie, grabbed his arm, and dragged him behind a dumpster, where hot metal scraped past them in sparks. Lazaro's lieutenants returned fire, while Charlie ducked for cover. This was not how he hoped his afternoon walk would go.

His eyes fell back to Lazaro, who was staring at the green metal of the dumpster, one hand pasted to his belly. In the background, the bangs continued. "It's not Sucre. I've never seen them before, Lazaro," one of the men said, tossing a look over his shoulder when his boss didn't answer. "Jefe?"

But Charlie was already there, peeling back the pale hand shielding a crimson pit. "Lazaro?" The man dropped. "Lazaro!" He was semiconscious, shock staving off the pain and yet drawing him nearer to death. Charlie didn't have his oils. He didn't have his books. The prayers were escaping him. *Oh, God!* He was panicking.

Charlie pressed down on the wound as hard as he dared, draping his fascia over it to help stem the bleeding. It wasn't doing a whole lot of good. Lazaro grimaced. Weakly, he raised his hand to Charlie's. "I—I'm s—sor—ry. Lo siento!"

"This isn't your fault," Charlie muttered, trying to ground himself.

Lazaro grunted in return. "Am I—going to die?"

Charlie wasn't a doctor, but he wasn't stupid either. Lazaro's blood was pooled all around them, his face whiter than a sheet, his skin cool and clammy. Nowhere did Charlie sense help coming. He bit his lip. "I don't know."

"Lo siento," Lazaro wheezed.

"It's not your fault."

"—siento."

He seemed stuck on it, so Charlie indulged him. "For what?" he asked, attention settling completely on Lazaro. Forget the damn paramedics. They weren't coming, and once they came, they'd be too late. They were always too late.

Lazaro's hand settled in Charlie's. "I've do—done so many bad things, hurt so many people. Padre, tengo miedo. What if He doesn't want me? How can He love someone like me?"

Charlie had seen people die before, sat beside them in hospital rooms as the life drained out of them, watched as their heads were blown off by violence born of hatred and malice, but this, this was different. This was slow and agonizing. This was heartrending. *Please, help me.*

"Of course He wants you." Charlie hardly felt the tears rising in his eyes. Pain—there was so much pain. He didn't know what to do, what to say. His heart ached for this man. It burned in a fervent blaze that swelled until it consumed him, and Charlie was flooded with warmth. "He loves you," he barely heard himself say.

"*I love you.*"

"*¿Padre, me amas?*"

"*Sí, mijo, te amo mucho.*"

Lazaro was crying now, silent tears that spilled forth from the corners of his eyes onto the bloody pavement, but Charlie couldn't see, couldn't know, couldn't witness.

"*Te amo.*"

"*Te amo.*"

Because Charlie knew only love, an impossible love that brought tears of consolation to his eyes, a love he inadvertently pushed into Lazaro until his corporeal body could receive it no more. The warmth left Lazaro's light orbs as life left him, and the divine bliss in Charlie's own heart dissipated until nothing was left but the cold.

Charlie walked away with a dark face.

The police had told him it was gang-related, like they thought the morning shootout had been, but they were wrong. Lazaro's lieutenant had said it wasn't Sucre. It wasn't their enemy. They hadn't known *this* enemy. Charlie did. This was Jet's enemy, and Jet would have to answer for it.

Chapter 18

"You broke it." Charlie wrapped his small fingers around a cherry red microscope. One of the lenses was cracked, and there were angry tears in his young eyes. "You broke it, and now it doesn't work anymore."

"I'm sorry, Charlie. It was an accident."

Seven-year-old Charlie pouted. "Dad told you not to kick the soccer ball in the house. He said you'd break something, and you did. You're a bad boy, Jetty, a very bad boy."

"But Charlie, I said I was sorry."

"You broke it, Jet."

"It's broken," a different voice called out.

"Broken," said another.

A plethora of different voices assaulted him, ones of every age and gender.

"It's broken, and no one can fix it." That was little Charlie again.

"Broken."

"Broken!"

"You broke it, Jet. I'm telling Momma," I cried. I was even younger than Charlie, maybe four or five, wavy hair all frizzy and wild.

"I'll get you a new doll, Holly."

"It won't be the same!"

"Hol—"

"I'm gonna tell Momma, and you're gonna get it."

Jet was running. He wasn't sure where. In the darkness, there was no place to go. Light drew him out to a familiar cliff. *Bam!*—Jet was falling—*Crack!*

Broken.

Broken.

"Jet." I was there again, all grown up as Queen of the Dragonflies, dressed in black and pink and ready to kick some. "Don't break."

Broken.

"Don't break!"

Broken.

"Really done it this time, haven't you, Harper?"

Jet came awake with a jerk, hand reflexively reaching for his knife. He scanned his unfamiliar surroundings. Oh, right, he was at St. Vitus's, in its rectory, passed out on his borrowed bed.

He sat up fully with a groan, his free hand rubbing at his lower back.

Broken.

Damn it! he cursed, slamming a palm onto the spongy mattress. He hated those stupid dreams. He'd take his PTSD-drawn nightmares any day over the horrors of his unreliable second sight and all the odd monsters that came along with it.

So, Jet stewed through a shower, letting the hot water soak the knots in his back and slowly draw out the tension. He could almost taste the residual stain of the black cloud on him. Jet cringed. Grabbing a washcloth, he tried to scrub off the uncomfortable sensation, but it lingered still, and he came out of the shower not feeling any cleaner.

Jet heard footsteps on the first floor as soon as he stepped out of the bathroom. He stilled and listened, then relaxed when he recognized Charlie's smooth gait. It was quicker than usual. Actually, he sounded agitated.

Offering himself a shrug, Jet continued dressing. He had to leave for Mackey's or he'd be late…or later than he already planned on being anyways. After all, predictability was dangerous for people like him. Jet laced up his boots and snagged his leather jacket off the back of a vacant chair.

Father Martin didn't appear to be in, but Charlie was fidgeting down in the living room. If his older brother was upset about something, now was as good a time as any to address it. It would be a long night for Jet, and though he'd never jinx himself, the possibility existed that he wouldn't be coming back.

Charlie was pacing around the furniture when Jet descended. Whatever was going on, it wasn't good. "Where are you going?" Charlie asked.

Jet raised a brow at him, noting the crusted blood on his hands that couldn't be his own.

"Where are you going, Jet?" he repeated, grinding his teeth together.

"Like I said earlier, I'm going out with some friends."

"You're going out with friends." There was rage there, a rage Jet didn't entirely understand, a rage he hadn't seen since he'd signed up for the navy without a word to anyone, a rage only Charlie could call up and deliver. "You're going out to party with your friends while people are out there getting killed 'cuza of you."

"Killed?" Jet eyed Charlie's soiled hands again. "Father Martin?" he asked wearily.

"Don't know. Don't care."

Oh, this is so *not good.* This was worse than anything Jet had ever gotten. Charlie's true fury was notorious in their youth, but never before had it been aimed so assuredly at Jet. "I'm working on it, Charlie. I've got a meeting set for tonight."

"And then it's over?" The black cloud hovered like a mist.

"No, my contact will tell me who issued the contract on me. I'll track 'em down after. *Then* it'll be over."

Charlie shook his head angrily. "It's so easy for you, isn't it? You'll slaughter anyone who gets in your way."

Jet's shoulders dropped back, and he drew himself up to full height. He'd always cowered beside that insatiable rage, no matter who the target was, but Charlie was edging over the line. "Don't go there," he warned, voice taut with fury.

"Is owning up to it such a problem?"

"Shut up!" Jet shouted. "What do you know? You think you've got me all figured out—"

"What's there to figure out, Jet? You've got the bloodlust of a parasitic tick." Charlie stomped his foot loudly and drew up a question that would prove his point: "Tell me, Jet, what are you gonna to do when you find the guy who's responsible for all this?"

"I'm going to put one right between his eyes."

"Why is killing always your answer for everything?"

"Killing's what I know."

"But it's not the *only* thing you know. You spent eighteen years in a house with Mom and Dad, all peace, love, and play nice."

"You don't get it, do you? After I got hurt, I had nothing, Charlie. Nothing. Voight saved my life, gave me back control of it. Before Voight, I had nothing!"

"You had nothing because you wouldn't accept anything. You had nothing because you left everything behind. You're so full of stupid, selfish pride, and worse, you can't even see it."

"Oh, and what about you?!"

"What about me?!" They were both shouting now, and it was a lucky deal the next-door office was closed for the night.

"You're a thespian. 'Oh, look at me,'" Jet mocked. "'I'm Charlie Harper. I preach peace and prosperity, but I've been in more fights than a gangbanger. I just won't fight now 'cuz I'm a sniveling coward.' You know, I bet you became a priest just to hide like the spineless snake you are."

"Don't you dare question the intent of my ordination."

But Jet was already shaking his head, stinging words eager to go further, to hurt, to maim, to kill. "What would you have done if I hadn't come back when I did? Would you have let Father Martin die? No, wait," he added suddenly, faux enlightenment filling his face. "You already had, hadn't you? The moment you let yourself get tied to that chair is the moment you gave up your life and his. I used to kill people who deserved to die, Charlie, but you wouldn't raise your fists if it meant world peace."

"You don't know what I would or wouldn't do."

"I know enough. You'd betray us, let us burn, just so you could keep pretending like peace is all *you* know."

"I'm not the one who turned my back on everything that mattered, Jet."

"Then what do you call this? You pretend like your life's so perfect without me, like everything bad that happens is *my* fault. You're a Harper in freakin' denial, pretending like the black cloud doesn't exist. Well, news flash, it does, and it hangs over all of us, even the Holy Harper, Charles. You know what you are, Charlie? You're a sanctimonious, bellicose basta—"

Charlie swung a right hook that struck Jet on the side of the head and sent him careening into the wall. Jet caught himself, swept down to pick up his fallen jacket, and stormed out of the building.

Charlie paced heatedly, then turned and stomped up the stairs to his room where he paced some more. *Jet. Jet. Jet. Jet. Jet. Jet. Jet.* It was all Jet's fault.

He grabbed a vase off the nightstand by its slender neck, irately stared at it for a second, then flung it at the wall with all his might. It shattered spectacularly, pieces flying every which way. With rage that swallowed his whole being, Charlie let his world turn red.

The landline phone went first, slid off the dresser with both hands and thrust at a hanging mirror that cracked on impact. The end table went next. He swung it like a bat at the desk and wall until only a single leg remained. Then he tossed even that behind him precariously and reached for a drawer. It was empty, so he slammed it to the ground, followed by the next and the next after that, with all its stored trinkets still inside.

His sheets were gone, pillows scattered all across the room. Charlie didn't remember disturbing the bed, but even the mattress was off its frame. Nothing in the room was where it had been, and Charlie was sure he would've broken a window if his room had had one. He panted, fury slowly thawing with the lack of breakable objects nearby.

"Did a real number up here, huh?"

Charlie turned towards the door where Father Martin had appeared. "I'll pay you back for the damage." Slipping from the high but not quite back to Earth yet, Charlie couldn't muster the energy to look remorseful.

Father Martin waved him off. "I'm sure you will." The older man flicked his head in the direction of the door, and Charlie followed him down the stairs, out of the garage, and in through the back door of the church. "Your brother had a pretty shiner when I saw him earlier."

"He drives me nuts sometimes." They took a seat in the front pew. Father Martin had left all but the sanctuary lights off, so they sat shrouded in darkness.

After the long walk from the rectory to the church, Charlie had managed to grasp some semblance of control. He flexed his still bloody knuckle, scratching a bit of Lazaro off his finger. "I'm sorry about the room. I haven't lost control like that in a long time."

Father Martin nodded. "Feel better?"

"A little."

"Breaking things is a popular form of stress relief."

"But it's not the best way to cope."

"No, but you don't need a lecture on that." They stared at the altar for several minutes. The tabernacle gleamed in the light of the Lamp of Christ, red and radiant.

"It's my fault." Charlie took a breath. He'd spent seven years in seminary, and he'd never really dealt with the issues of his past. He couldn't. Every time they came up, he'd argue his way out of doing anything about them.

"What is?"

"All of it," Charlie began. "Jet, Lazaro, all of it." He felt the confusion in Father Martin without having to turn and look. "I met Lazaro while on pastoral assignment. He runs…ran with Sur Seis."

Father Martin nodded, and Charlie could sense his interest. "He's dead. I left the rectory. The police didn't follow. I should have turned back the moment I realized that, but I was glad they hadn't and just went on my merry way." Charlie paused to collect himself. "Lazaro was trying to do better, has been since I met him. You should have seen him, Father, lying on the ground, scared that God wouldn't accept him for all the wrongs he'd done in life. And you know the worst part? He took that bullet for me. Sometimes I don't understand why God does that."

"Why does God do anything?"

Father Martin hadn't really understood Charlie's statement. Only a Harper could. The real curse of our family isn't facing the black cloud. It's watching those around us suffer for it. They languish, and we thrive.

"Lazaro died in a shootout this evening. Some friends of Jet thought they'd put a couple in me." Charlie shook his head. "Jet was right. People die around me because I purposefully blind myself. Leaving the rectory put everyone I crossed paths with in danger. I *know* better, but I did nothing because I thought I could escape the will of God."

"You're a priest," Father Martin stated incredulously.

"And I thought that was enough. I could handle the weird flare of our family mixed into my priestly life, but that's not what I got. That's not what I keep on getting. I get death and violence and everything *they* get on top of the batty-catty crazy priest stuff *we* get. I mean, when was the last time someone held *you* hostage in a confessional?"

"Yeah, Mrs. Gabon does that every other Saturday."

Charlie gave him an unamused glare. "You know that's not what I mean."

"Well, I don't know what you want me to tell you, Charlie. You're pretty much screwed."

"Father!"

"Why do you think God puts that kind of stuff in your path?"

"He's poking me with a stick."

"Charlie," Father Martin scolded. Charlie sighed and slumped farther in his seat like a chastened schoolboy. "It must be genetic."

"What?"

"Why were you so angry at Jet earlier?" the older man asked in lieu of an answer.

"It was easier to blame him. Seeing him like this, blowing people's brains out like it's no big deal—he's got his own set of problems."

Father Martin sighed. "Yup, it's definitely genetic."

"What is?"

"Charlie, you were covered in carnage earlier. I was in emotional shock for an hour just for being involved, and you just shook it right off. How many people do you think can do that?" Father Martin sat back in the pew, letting his eyes roam the high rafters of the church. "Why do you think killing people doesn't bother your brother as much as it should?"

Charlie gave a sloppy shrug. He really didn't know how Jet's brain worked, not anymore at least.

"Well, what's the reason that *you* don't react normally?"

"By the time I get to the blood and the gore and the death, it's already too late to stop it. And then after…it seems so pointless to be concerned. Other than praying, what else is there to do? I mean, if there's other people involved, there may be need for consolation, but that's really it." Charlie paused to consider his own words. "It's wrong that I won't have nightmares about being drenched in blood, isn't it?"

"Odd, maybe. Wrong, I don't know. Somehow you still know killing is immoral." Father Martin paused to collect his thoughts. "Do you like watching people die?"

"No!" Charlie sat up straighter. "Hence, your guestroom."

"But you weren't angry because he died. You were angry that he died because of you."

"Everyone dies, Father. I'm not supposed to help them get there faster."

"I see." He said it so resolutely, like it all finally made sense. Charlie was overtaken by unease.

"You see what?"

Father Martin took a deep breath. "You and your brother...maybe your whole family, you're wired a little differently. That's not exactly your call," he said, giving Charlie a pointed look before continuing on, "and maybe that's what this is all about."

"Huh?"

"Why are you so resistant to God's plan for you? Are you afraid?"

"No," Charlie mumbled uncertainly, "it's just very confusing. Why can't I just be an ordinary priest?"

"Why can't you just be an ordinary Charlie Harper? Is it so hard to be yourself?"

They lapsed into silence as Charlie pondered those words. When *had* he decided the cavalier lifestyle of the Harpers no longer suited him?

Oh yeah, when Jet had lost his freakin' mind. "So, this *is* all Jet's fault."

Father Martin squinted. "I thought it was your fault."

"It's my fault that it's Jet's fault." The older man said nothing, so Charlie took it upon himself to explain, "Jet went a little wild on us. I guess it was normal teen stuff mixed with whatever trauma we garnered from our time with Uncle Riley and typical, everyday black cloudiness."

"Black cloudiness," Father Martin whispered to himself.

Charlie ignored him. "I went to college in the area, so I'd go with him, sometimes, when he was being particularly wicked, just to make sure he didn't get into too much trouble." Charlie hesitated. "One night we went downtown. Jet wanted to hit up a bar, but we were both still underage, so there was no way I was agreeing to that. Went to a party instead, which wasn't much better, really. These tough guys said something to us, and Jet got smart with them. What else is new? Needless to say, they were not happy. We wound up out back, ready to throw down, or Jet was. Five against two. We could've taken them, but I was just so tired of it, of baling him out of his messes." For a long time, Charlie said nothing. "I left."

Father Martin waited.

"I saw the betrayal in his eyes, and I left anyways. When he showed up at home later, he had a black eye, a split lip, and a couple of broken ribs. Signed up for the navy the next day, and once he left, he didn't come back, at least, not for a very long time."

"If you're on better terms now, why not just apologize and move on?"

"An apology doesn't really cover it, Father. See, I have these…abilities. One of them allows me to make my presence as big or as small as I want. I can make everyone notice me, or I can make sure no one notices me. Jet has his gifts, too, to see the future, the past, the ghosts that haunt us. We *never* used them against each other. Ever. It'd been an unwritten rule between us since we were little." Charlie drew a shuddering breath. "I did that day. He wasn't the target, but it did affect him. I let myself disappear just enough that those little punks let me walk right past them. Jet and I, we've been through so much together, and we always looked out for each other, not matter what we were arguing about or whose fault it was that time, and I betrayed everything."

"When was the last time you saw betrayal on his face?"

"About a half hour ago, when I landed that right hook." Charlie stared at his hands hard. "No one else could've done it. He'd have seen it coming."

"Charlie, I think you should apologize."

"That's not enough!"

"I know, but I think it would help. You and your brother, you're both here-and-now kind of guys, and staying fixated on that point in the past isn't helping either of you. Maybe you nudged him in the wrong direction, but he's his own man now. He makes his own decisions, and he's got to figure it out for himself."

Charlie nodded. He could appreciate the truth in that.

"Whatever reason you feel God's plan isn't for you, maybe it's time you reevaluate it." Charlie only stared ahead blankly. "So," Father Martin asked, "what are you going to do now?"

Charlie just sighed in response. Did it matter? He wouldn't be getting much sleep tonight anyways.

Chapter 19

Jet strolled into Mackey's a full hour late. Oh well. He'd needed a little time to cool down from his fight with Charlie anyways. Honestly, he was still kind of miffed with the man, but he didn't have time to deal with that now.

Davis and the rest of the Shoe Crew had claimed the round table at the center of the establishment, and Jet dropped himself into the only vacant seat.

Mackey's was the exact opposite of the Pit, a family friendly bar and grill that still served the good stuff to anyone with a card and steady hands. Jet ordered a beer from across the room the second he got there.

"Well, well, well, if it isn't the lucky devil himself," said Marcus Ren, a pale man with messy black hair.

"Where you been? I was starting to think you weren't coming," Davis hollered.

"Ran into a little trouble."

His old friend examined him. "More like trouble ran into you. Nice eye."

"Thanks."

"How'd you get it?"

"My brother."

The whole table gaped at him. "Isn't your brother a pastor or something?"

"A priest," Jet corrected solemnly.

"Wow," Davis said in awe, "you must've done something real bad to piss a priest off enough to take a swing at you."

"Ah, you know," Jet said, not eager to elaborate. "What's this?" He stole a rib off Ren's plate and gnawed on it happily.

"Hey!"

They chatted good-naturedly for several minutes. Jet was somewhat in awe himself. When Davis had told him the Shoe Crew was in town, he'd expected a few of the guys, not the whole ding-dang squad, or what was left of it anyways, five of the leanest, meanest hell-raisers out there. "Y'all on leave?"

"There's that Texan lilt," Coffer teased. He'd always been the most talkative of the group. Never could quite get him to shut up.

"Sort of," answered Brian Song, a.k.a. Bird. "They put us on rotation with some new hotshot boy band. Technically, we're just off-base for a couple hours, but those featherweights are first up on the call board for the next op. We won't be going anywhere for another week at least." The Asian man ran a hand through his hair in frustration.

Jet shook his head in sympathy. Their kind of missions were few and far between as it was. Having to share them with another squad really sucked. "You still in command, Wick?"

The blond man across from him grimaced. "Yeah."

"Ah, stop pretending like you don't love going all Sergeant Ban on us," Coffer snipped.

"Sergeant Ban? More like mini Hitler or Smarty's mother," Davis quipped. The whole table laughed, although the other Latino at it, Sergio Martinez, glared half-heartedly.

"Oh yeah, I love keeping everyone in line," Wick admitted, "but calling the shots on the field's a pain. I was doing just well and dandy being second." That shut up the table quick and easy, each of the men stuck in some moment of the past.

"Did you need anything else?" The waitress was pretty, slender, and wearing a tight shirt that was probably a dress code requirement. She hovered over Jet's left shoulder.

"I'll order, thanks. Give me a basket of baby backs, one of those eight-ounce steaks, a fully-loaded baked potato, green beans, and a slice of apple pie."

"Somebody's hungry."

Jet shrugged. "I missed lunch."

"And to drink? Another beer?"

"Water."

She left to put in the order. "She's so into you," Coffer pouted, mussing his red hair in hope of attracting more attention from the ladies of a nearby table. He winked at one who giggled, then waggled his eyebrows at her.

"How you doing?" Ren asked with a flick of his head.

"Just dandy."

"Please," Davis countered, "he told me earlier that his legs give out on him sometimes."

Ren jerked in his seat, clearly startled by the revelation. "What? Is it serious? What have the doctors said?"

"Dude," Jet stated, raising his hands in a placating gesture, "chill." Ever the mother hen of the group, Ren huffed at him, eyes imploring Jet to answer. "It's fine, really. It's just pressure. It doesn't happen very often, only when I've *really* over done it. I'm good, honest."

Before the man could respond in any way, the waitress, named Sheila, returned with Jet's food.

"What're you boys celebrating?"

"Old friends," Davis offered.

"Yeah, the Shoe Crew is back, baby!" added Coffer.

"What are you, a fraternity?"

"Do we look like a bunch of frat boys, missy?"

She smirked mischievously. "Maybe."

"We were all in the navy together."

"Oh, sailors." Her smirk grew. "Why do they call you the Shoe Crew?"

The whole table smiled victoriously at her. "Because ain't nobody get to us before we give 'em the boot!" they shouted.

Sheila laughed alongside them. "Very nice." She turned to Jet. "You sticking around?"

"Nah, sorry, not interested. I've got work to do. Then I'm headed home."

"That's too bad." She twirled her hair and laughed.

"Why do you always get the girls?" Smarty complained. "You didn't even flirt with that one."

"Yeah, what's the matter with you?"

"I told you, I've got stuff going on."

"Yeah, but you *never* take 'em home."

That would be pretty stupid considering his profession. "Maybe I'm just waiting for the right one."

"Dude, you are such a hopeless romantic."

Jet smirked into his cup. "That's why the ladies love me."

The Shoe Crew broke up around ten-thirty. Only Davis hung back for a minute when they made for the street. Jet kept his vigilant eyes wide and roaming. "You know if you ever need anything, I'm here for you. Well," he paused smiling, "most of me is."

"Funny." Jet wasn't laughing. "But hey, I might take you up on that someday."

"You're in deep, aren't you?"

"Yeah, but I'll be fine. I'm a world-class swimmer after all. I'm always in deep."

Davis walked away then, and Jet headed down the street. He had to scamper a bit to make it to the Pit on time, and when he did, he stuck to the shadows. Catching sight of Marsden Lamar in the window, Jet signaled him out. They strode a few blocks down the road to a secluded vacant lot. Public places were great for amateurs on the run, but even Jet couldn't keep track of all the movement to ensure he wouldn't get shot in the head by a passing stranger.

"What do ya got?" Jet asked, lighting up a cigarette.

"I tell you, and I get to live, right?" Lamar was sweating bullets, clearly concerned about playing both sides.

"Believe it or not, I don't actually enjoy killing people." He halted the motion of his cigarette half way to his mouth, as if it was as much a revelation to him as it had been to Lamar. "I don't actually enjoy killing people," he repeated back to himself. It was something he hadn't thought about in a very long time, the only aspect of his commitment that hadn't quite been complete, as an assassin, his greatest weakness. He'd always been torn between despising the fact and loving it. *Focus!* "I don't have all night, Lamar."

"I don't know who put out the contract on you. Looks like only the one who picked it up is privy to that information. But I did find out who the assassin is, the one who put the bounty on your head for anyone with a gun. She goes by the name of Belladonna, number four on Claude's list."

"Aw, she thinks she's good."

Lamar oozed incredulity. "Are you crazy? Aren't you worried?"

"If you don't think you can survive the game, then you really shouldn't be playing it." Jet paused to take a drag. "How long am I going to have to wait for you to tell me whatever it is that you don't want to tell me?"

Lamar started. "I—I'm sorry. She's still pretty new from what I understand, a real rookie. Someone's been teaching her the trade. Marks are still fresh. You might be dealing with a vet behind the velvet curtain."

"Or she could just be showing off. Rookies make those kinds of mistakes all the time."

Lamar nodded. "True." Then he waited. "So…can I go?"

"Not until we're through."

"But—"

"Do you honestly expect me to believe that you went snooping around the Market and didn't catch any heat for it? She knows I'm looking, so what was her move?"

Lamar sighed. "You know, I've been doing this nearly twenty years. I thought I could help—" He pulled a slip of paper the size of a business card from his shirt pocket and handed it to Jet. "—and spare you the moral dilemma."

Jet took the paper and read it. "There's no dilemma. Here." He handed Lamar a pill, then popped one in his own mouth. Lamar cast uneasy eyes on his. "Something of my own creation. It counteracts most poisons by strengthening the body's natural defenses, but it only lasts a couple of hours. With a name like Belladonna, I'd take it. Just in case. Consider it payment for your services."

Lamar nodded uncertainly and fled.

Jet took another puff of his cigarette, then dropped it to the ground and stomped on it with the heel of his boot.

Hostages...Jet hated hostages. They always made the situation more complicated than it needed to be.

He didn't have a lot of time. Belladonna had made sure of it, giving him just enough to reach the rendezvous. Clever. And bad news. Belladonna knew what she was doing.

She'd been taught well.

Chapter 20

The rendezvous was in a derelict neighborhood. Most of the homes and businesses were abandoned or breathing their final breaths, and the empty streets made the four square blocks look like the modern Lost Colony. All they needed was the word Croatoan carved into one of the power line poles.

Jet stood on the road in front of an alley, a commandeered warehouse on one side and vacant apartment complex on the other. It was dark. A city streetlight popped out of the curb like a weed, but it wasn't working, flickering on and off every ten to twenty minutes. The only steady source of light came from one of the high warehouse windows, but it was vague and veiled at best.

They were waiting for him, a group of six mercenaries, armed with various rifles and handguns. Jet maneuvered around a broken down car at the edge of the alley and entered.

One of the mercs had his arm wrapped around the collar of their hostage. Penny stared back at him fretfully.

She was just as pretty as she'd been the last time he'd seen her, even with bloodshot, terrified eyes and knotted hair. Jet's sharp eyes roved over her. She seemed unharmed, save for some defensive bruising.

The click of a heel alerted Jet to the arrival of the only other woman on scene, Belladonna, who crept out from a dark crevice, a personal aide at her side. Jet expected a skintight bodysuit that accentuated a name like Belladonna. He got practical combat gear instead, right down to her formfitting bulletproof vest. His spine tingled.

"What a great pleasure to meet you, Specter."

Italian accent, Tuscan to be exact.

"I wish I could say the same, Belladonna, but I'm never pleased to see other assassins. It generally means someone's screwed up."

Penny tensed, and the arm around her neck tightened.

"Fair enough. You do know why you're here then?"

"You want me dead, or well, your client does."

Belladonna smiled wickedly.

"Now, are you going to give me Penny, or is this going to be a problem?"

"She's very beautiful. You have good taste."

"I don't even know her. I've been in her company all of five minutes."

Belladonna fingered her gun cheerily. "How unfortunate for her." She nodded at the mercenary nearest to her and said, "Kill them both."

Penny's struggles increased, and Belladonna spun back to the warehouse like the amateur she was. Jet's fingers twitched for a gun, but the men had gotten in close. He wouldn't have time to pull a weapon. Penny let out a war cry, then stomped down on her captor's foot and elbowed him in the gut with all her might.

The man harrumphed, and the momentary distraction was all the time Jet needed to draw his gun and a throwing knife simultaneously, and his knife met one man's neck just seconds after two of his bullets reached two others. Penny's captor recovered quickly, and almost had his arms back around her when Jet's fist collided with his face. "Penny, run."

She darted around the remaining two, saved by Jet's last minute grasp at the back of one's shirt, and vaulted over the car out of sight.

Saving Penny had cost him. The man he'd punched issued a kick to Jet's back while he was distracted. Fire lanced up his spine, and for a second, Jet blacked out. When his vision finally swam back into focus, he was lying on the dirty pavement. Jet tried to push himself up, but the pain returned or had never really left, and Jet flopped back to the ground with a thud.

The three remaining mercenaries towered over him, their frustration giving way to satisfaction. In white, hot agony, Jet was undone.

Chapter 21

Jet was undone.

The Shoe Crew had been assigned a blind jump. In other words, they'd been kicked out of a helicopter, literally. Whoever happened to be closest to the doors was shoved out first. They always drew lots for spots.

Their CO had given them a coded map that did little more than lead them to their target, which could have been a weapon or a person or a fancy cigar for all they'd known at the start. As always, they weren't really on the mission they were on, partly because they didn't really exist and partly because whatever it was they were retrieving didn't really exist either. If they were caught, the higher-ups would tuck their blinders behind them and call plausible deniability. There were many names for this kind of mission. Jet personally preferred "ghost op" because they were there and not, there and gone, without the slightest trace of their existence left behind to tie them to the tide.

Back then, Jet was the rookie, the little brother of the group that was annoyingly good at everything. He was the best all-around marksmen, the most versatile in close quarter combat, and smarter than a newbie ever should have been. But all the medals he'd picked up, all the honors and awards, all the recognition in boot camp and beyond had turned Jet into a cheeky little brat, or at least, a cheekier little brat than he already had been.

And well, rookies always make mistakes.

Their little outfit didn't have an official name because, like I said, they didn't really exist. The eight of them were decked in night gear, assault rifles in hand. They had a buddy system working for them that made Jet feel more like a boy scout and less like a highly-trained soldier, but this particular squad insisted on pairing up. Reminiscent of his youth as it was, Jet didn't bother complaining. The familiarity was a comfort he hadn't expected to find.

The mission went pretty smoothly. They'd cleared the enemy post, whoever the enemy might have been, gotten in, found the target, and gotten out. All that was left to do was make the eight-mile hike to the extraction point.

By the tall and wet vegetation and the Spain-*ish* Spanish shouts, Jet surmised they were likely somewhere in South America. The hot, icky climate screamed Venezuela. He wisely kept that information to himself.

The sun was racing them back to their destination. As always, they'd be removed in the cover of darkness or not at all. Jet looked over the cliff they were navigating into the expanse of trees. He was up for a couple of weeks leave and was considering going stateside. All he really wanted was an authentic fajita taco. The chefs back at base couldn't tell a cow from a rubber duck as far as he was concerned.

Geoffrey Stonefield tapped Jet's helmet to wrestle his attention. The white, dirty blonde with dirt perpetually clinging to his skin was their squad leader. He'd insisted on partnering up with Jet to keep an eye on their youngest squadmate. The man always seemed to know when Jet's thoughts were wandering. On base, he was a real hoot about it, often egging Jet on or getting real deep, real fast. On the field, he was all business. With fifteen years under his belt, Stonefield's experience squashed Jet's prodigious talent and the measly handful of years he'd acquired himself.

Jet felt the corners of his mouth twitch up in an innocent smile. Then the nauseating sound of steel *clink*, *clink*, *clink*ing along rock met his ears. "Grenade!" someone shouted.

Jet wasn't sure where it had come from. All he could think was ambush. He dove between a gap in the rocks, and adrenaline made the resounding boom that followed that much louder. Two others stood beside him. Neither was Stonefield. Jet cursed colorfully, then hoisted himself up against the protests of Bird and Smarty, who were attempting to wrangle him back in and keep track of the mess that had sent them awry. Another blast, stronger this time sent Jet staggering madly. He caught sight of Wick hauling a limp Davis to cover.

Jet scanned the grounds. Stonefield was twenty feet away, struggling to stand, shrapnel sprayed across his flesh. For a split second, Jet had to wonder how Stonefield had gotten so far away. Then he gulped, and the guilt set in. With the cover of trees farther than it really should've been, Jet took off towards the man. Bullets sprayed at Jet from somewhere far below, but Jet ducked closer to the ground for cover, geometry assuring him he wouldn't be shot.

Open pain filled the field, the moans of the long dead rising up to assault him. Jet shoved aside his second sight and threw himself beneath Stonefield. The man passed out almost immediately, blood loss and shock the least of his problems. Jet took his full weight with a grunt.

Even back then, Jet prided himself in his strength. He could pump iron alongside the best of them, but Stonefield was no small thing. The man was easily a foot taller than him and built like a bear. Jet ran for all he was worth anyways, the gunfire continuing to whiz past him from below. Thankfully, their squad had more or less regrouped, and while Ren tended to Davis, the others returned fire. Jet gave it all he had, pumping his legs harder and willing them to move faster.

He saw it with his second sight too late, and Jet could do nothing but cringe when the atmosphere exploded once more. By some miracle, he'd evaded the shrapnel, but a dangerous set of tremors slammed into him, and with no limbs to spare, still feet from the rest of the squad, Jet was thrown over the cliff, Stonefield leaping from his shoulders to tumble down before him.

The drop wasn't vertical. Jet only discovered that when the first impact came too soon and was quickly followed by a second and third that spun his body like a barrel. He scrambled for purchase, anything to slow him down.

He found nothing.

But seconds later, a tree found him. Jet slammed into it hard, his back bending around it unnaturally. At least one of his bones let out a sickening crack, and Jet screamed in agony at the worst pain he'd ever felt. Stonefield continued his descent for several more meters, and as Jet tossed his vibrating skull around to the side, the image of Stonefield splayed across the ground unmoving was all that greeted him.

A stomp of boots drew nearer, as did the sharp sound of gunshots. Then there was only darkness.

He woke up in the hospital tent back at base. Davis was laid up next to him, not looking so hot himself. Marcus Ren, who was the closest thing they had to a doctor in their actual squad, was seated between them reading a book. "Ren," Jet croaked.

The man startled. "Oh, heya Harper, you're up earlier than I thought you'd be."

"Davis?" Jet asked, welcoming himself to the water Ren was holding to his lips.

"Lost a leg."

Jet swore. "Stonefield?"

"Don't remember much, do you?" Ren sighed. "You two rolled right into them. They killed Stonefield, clipped you pretty good, too, but we gave 'em hell for it and chased 'em off."

"I don't feel anything." Jet tried to push himself up in his cot, but the molten lava that sprang from his back dropped him down and forced a whimper out of him. In any other circumstance, he would have died of mortification right then and there. "My…I can't feel my feet or my legs or…" Jet issued his worst curse.

"No, you wouldn't. You busted your back pretty bad."

"I'm paralyzed." Breathing was suddenly very hard. "I'll never walk again."

"That's what they always say," Ren answered, sympathy mixing with determination, "but if anyone can tell 'em what kind of senseless morons they are, it's you."

"Ren?"

"Yeah, bud?"

"Is it okay if I go back to being an arrogant world-conqueror *tomorrow*?"

Ren frowned. "Yeah, bud."

Jet nodded and looked over at Davis. "Any other casualties?"

"Not on our end."

"Why am I laying on my back?"

"To alleviate the pressure on your gunshot wound."

"That's stupid," Jet muttered as he stared at his sheet. "My back's definitely worse off than my lousy leg." Of all the things that could've happened... How could he have seen it coming and yet not been able to do a damn thing about it?

And just like that, Jet was undone.

Chapter 22

Charlie had just turned the street corner when a figure slammed into him, toppling them both to the ground. He bounced up quickly to help the other, a woman, it seemed, who was shaking off the fall.

She was strawberry blonde, or at least, she'd died her hair that way. Thin but fit, she moved like an athlete. But her hard hazel eyes were dark and bloodshot. For a moment, Charlie suspected she was on something. Then the fear on her face registered, and her mouth was moving. "Oh my gosh, Father? You *are* a priest, right? These guys kidnapped me because of this man I met on my trip home. They said something about being assassins. Then they started fighting, and I felt bad just leaving him there, but he told me to run."

Oh, Jet, Charlie groaned to himself. "You must be Penny." Her quizzical look pushed him back into action. "Come on. I'll take you to the police station." They jogged several blocks to get there, and Charlie's profile of her held up. She kept pace with him without issue, save for a little bob of her head as she ran, and he could guess that that and the discoloration of her eyes were a result of sleep deprivation and stress.

The officer working the front desk looked up with a jerk as they hurried through the glass doors. "Can I help you?" she asked, taking in Penny's odd appearance. Her clothes were rumpled, and her hair had come undone, pinkish strands sticking out every which way like an overused broom.

"These guys—"

"We'd like to speak with Detective Taylor or Detective Hall," Charlie cut in. "It's urgent."

"Detective Taylor's gone home for the day. Let me see if Hall wants to see you. What did you say your name was?"

"Just tell him it's a priest."

Detective Hall met them in the foyer several minutes later, and once they were in the safety of the station's small conference room, Charlie told him Penny's tale, ignoring her surprise when the incident at the rest stop came up. Detective Hall eyed him warningly, so Charlie schooled the impatience on his face the way he'd once been taught.

"Stay here. I'll get the cavalry on it."

But for once, Charlie didn't feel like sitting idle and leaving the trouble up to professionals. His gut was telling him Jet couldn't wait for the cavalry, and Charlie couldn't ignore his own intuition, not where Jet was concerned, so when Detective Hall turned away from them to summon backup from their slumber, Charlie put a finger to his lips to silence Penny and slid out the door. Detective Hall could curse him all he wanted. Jet needed him, and no way in the nine circles of hell was he was going to fail his baby brother a second time.

Charlie hated calling in favors, but Penny hadn't remembered exactly where she'd run from, so he sucked up his reluctances and prowled around for an outfit of Sur Seis. He found one huddled around a fire pit, smoking pot on the seedier side of town in tribute to their fallen friend. Gangs with as big a reach as Sur Seis have eyes everywhere, so it came as no surprise when, after some mild persuasion, they told him exactly where Jet's meet had been arranged.

Charlie hailed a cab that dropped him a block from the alley. He approached with extreme caution, his urgency tempered by the deadly silence of the night. He edged around the broken down car and found Jet lying face down on the ground. Other than the six clearly dead bodies surrounding him, no one else was present. Charlie's heart skipped a beat, all sorts of horrors coming to mind for an end he couldn't fathom.

He darted towards his younger sibling, the gravel of the rocky asphalt digging into his knees as he plunked himself on the ground beside him. Charlie let out a quiet sigh of relief the second he caught sight of Jet's ribcage expanding and compressing in a steady rhythm. "Jet?"

Jet groaned in response but didn't otherwise react, so Charlie shoved both hands beneath him and began attempting to flip him over. The younger gave a startled shout, white, razing pain blowing across his features. Charlie halted at once and called a little more urgently, "Jet!"

"Ch—Charlie?" The agony was so pronounced that Charlie worried his breathing might displace the air around Jet enough to make the pain worse, but the fear—the fear was so much more devastating. It seeped from his brother like lifeblood, and with it, his spirit. "I can't move my legs." The colored drained from Charlie's face, and his first instinct was to place a hand on his brother's shoulder in comfort. The next was to call an ambulance, but before he could whip out his cell phone, the warehouse door slammed open and a dark shadow emerged. "Run, Charlie. Run!"

The figure held a handgun towards them, squinting through the darkness at their figures. Charlie stood calmly, flicked open his glasses for a moment, then tucked them back in his sleeve.

An odd kind of fury filled him, one he hadn't felt in a very long time, something primal and protective. Who dared do this to Jet, *his* little brother, his *only* little brother? Charlie ground his teeth and locked his cold, steel eyes on the figure, clearly back to finish the job. The streetlight flickered on, and their would-be killer was suddenly very aware of just *who* he was squaring off with.

"Look, Father, I don't want to hurt you. This doesn't concern you. Just go now, and we'll both pretend like you were never here."

Charlie said nothing. Instead, he began to walk. Step by step, he closed the distance between them, a dark shadow with black eyes gliding across the abyss. The man raised his old Barretta incredulously and fired off a round, then another and another. Charlie marched on, not the smallest flinch, not a skip in his step, the embodiment of calm, certain confidence.

The man continued his litter of bullets, but with every missed shot, the shaking of his limbs increased, and his incredulity turned to desperation. Charlie came to a halt two and a half feet from the shooter, the barrel of the gun not an inch from his forehead. Charlie challenged him with the sharp, brown windows of his soul.

The trembling man blinked, then pulled the trigger. *Click.* Horror. *Click. Click.*

Charlie watched him with hard, unblinking eyes and swiped at the gun with both hands, disassembling it in one swift motion. Then he jerked his whole body forward harshly, and in extreme fright, the man fainted.

Charlie spun on his heel and returned to Jet, who had latched onto a crate and the low hanging end of a fire escape to drag himself back to his feet. Charlie threw one of Jet's arms across his shoulders and took the majority of his weight. "Should you be standing?"

"If I can, I will." Jet winced, gnashing his teeth together to conceal his pain. "It feels like someone stabbed me in the spine with a hot poker." He took a step and swore violently, but Charlie didn't chide him. Not this time. The anguish Jet wore was laid bare for all the world, and Charlie could offer little more comfort aside from that mild reprieve. "We have to get out of here before—" Jet hissed. "—before they figure out I'm still alive."

Charlie tried to not make it obvious that he was half-dragging Jet down the street, his younger brother clinging to his side like child, but it was hard to hide. He steadied his breathing so Jet wouldn't know how much of a struggle it was just to keep them both upright. Jet had other things to worry about. His brow was drenched in sweat. Just how much fear must Jet be feeling that he'd use pain, of all things, to mask it?

Charlie tightened his grip on Jet's back, careful to keep his arm high enough to prevent pressuring his injury. There weren't any cabs around in this part of town, so they continued their slow trek towards civilization. He'd drag Jet all the way to the hospital if he had to, throw him over a shoulder and carry him there. It didn't matter.

Jet's foot caught on the ground, simply because he didn't have the strength to raise it any higher, and they both pitched forward. Charlie caught them both with considerable effort. Jet moaned at the jerky movement, a pitiful sound that only strengthened Charlie's resolve. "I got you, Jet. I got you."

"Charlie?"

"Yeah?"

"I don't think I can…"

"Yes, you can, Jet. I got you, and I won't let you fall. I promise."

Chapter 23

Charlie lingered in the doorway for a moment, watching Jet flop down on his bed face first like he simply couldn't be bothered to stand anymore. They'd decided to recover in Jet's room since it was closer to the stairwell and not still in shambles from *someone*'s angry tirade.

Father Martin shuffled in with a heating pack for Jet, then dodged around Charlie to his own room with a quiet, "Good night."

Jet turned his head from the pillow, raised the cord of the heating pack and stared at it despondently, so Charlie took it, plugged it in, and draped the pack across Jet's back. "Hand me my bag, would you?"

Jet always packed light, so Charlie dropped his brother's only bag, a black duffel, on the bed beside him. Jet raised his head to search it but gave up quickly with a muffled groan. "The Vicodin, please."

Charlie rustled through Jet's stuff to find the pill bottle and, grabbing a glass of water off the nightstand, handed him both. Jet pushed himself up long enough to down the meds, then collapsed back on his bed, stifling another groan with his pillow. "I still think you should see a doctor."

"Namywoatedanousbusounnesry."

"What?"

Jet turned his head to the side. "Not only would that be dangerous, but also completely unnecessary."

"Jet—"

"Really, Charlie, I'll be fine. I just need a little sleep. The Vicodin will take care of the rest."

"It's just a painkiller, a highly addictive one at that."

"Yeah, but I don't think that idiot did any real damage, and this'll be the first and last pill for a while."

Charlie huffed in exasperation. Stubborn was a word applied to most members of our family. Jet was no exception. "You couldn't move your legs, Jet. You might have aggravated your old injury. If you don't get treatment, you could permanently damage your spine."

Jet slid onto the ground, heating pack falling onto the bed as he maneuvered to his feet. He bit back another groan so he could rise in practiced stoicism. "I didn't aggravate my injury. I *can't* have aggravated my injury. And even if I had, what does *permanent* mean anyways? They told me I'd never walk again, and look at me. I'd say I'm more than capable."

"I wasn't suggesting that you aren't. I'm just saying maybe you shouldn't risk it by pushing yourself so hard."

"Charlie, people are trying to kill us, so I *have* to bring my A-game, no matter how hard I have to push or how much I have to risk."

For a moment, Charlie said nothing. Then, "Do you miss it? Do you miss getting paid to kill people?"

Jet sigh miserably. "I miss the high. I miss feeling like I'm completely in control all the time, like I'm unstoppable, untouchable—" No one but Marcus Ren had heard that hitch in Jet's breath since he had turned sixteen. "—unbroken." More silence. "I miss being on top of the world, making things happen, playing…playing God," Jet announced, voice laced with hysteria.

The self-deification chilled Charlie. "Then why'd you stop?"

Jet raised his eyes skyward and growled. "Because I missed you guys more. I missed you and Holly and Mom and Dad. I missed dating and hanging out with old friends. I missed—I missed—I missed walking into a church and not feeling like everyone there was judging me, like they could see everything I'd done wrong and I was dirt beneath them for it. I hated feeling like a monster, a murderer, freakin' Cain the Cursed."

"Jet—" Charlie started.

"I know, alright? I know. Don't preach at me. I know. It's just…" He took a breath. "…it's easier said than done. I couldn't exactly walk into confessional and promise to try and do better when I had every intention of doing exactly the same thing over and over again." He shook his head. "I don't like killing people, Charlie, but the rush of coming face to face with your own mortality and escaping with your life is so damn addictive, and holding someone's life in your hands—that's power."

Charlie opened his mouth to argue, but Jet shook his head, acknowledging the flaw in his own statement. That kind of power was a lie, a self-fed deception. So what if you could choose whether someone lives or dies? You can't cure cancer. You can't bring the dead back to life. You can't own the world no matter how hard you try. Killing is just a choice, like paper or plastic, except with considerably larger consequences. Jet already knew that. But it was having the choice at all that gave him some sense of security.

"You don't know what it's like, Charlie, to see everyone else doing what you know you never can. We use our legs for everything, Charlie. Do you get that? Everything! You wake up in the morning and get out of bed, and I couldn't. For the longest time, I couldn't even *leave* my freakin' bed, Charlie! And when I could, I couldn't just pop on up and go for a walk. Do you know how hard it is to navigate your way into a wheelchair? It feels like the freakin' Olympics, maybe not after you've figured it out, but when you first start, it's the end of the freakin' world, Charlie."

The hitch was back again, accompanied by a pair of glassy eyes that took Charlie back to the days when Jet would wake up screaming from dreams of horrifying futures and forgotten pasts. He thought maybe he should say something, provide some sort of comfort, but Jet wasn't finished yet, and Charlie realized Jet needed this, an emotional breakdown he wouldn't have permitted anyone else to see.

"I needed other people just to do what you do without thinking every day. Do you know how much it sucks to need help just to take a bath? Do you know how humiliating it is? And then, you go out there—" He pointed. "—and you see everyone else merrily strolling on their way without a care in the freakin' world. And you just—you can't." The water in his eyes welled. "You can't run. You can't dance. Do you remember what I was like as a kid, Charlie? You couldn't pay me to sit still. Remember, Charlie? You tried, but I wouldn't. Do you think anything's changed?"

And once the tears rolled, Charlie could restrain himself no more. He took a hasty step forward Jet was too tired to evade and pulled his brother flush against him. Jet tensed for

135

a moment—being held was just so unfamiliar—then wrapped his arms around his big brother and buried his face in the soft, black fabric of his robe.

"I never wanted to feel that helpless again, Charlie," he mumbled into his shoulder. "And I—I thought it would help. It felt like it was, like I could do anything if I got to choose who lived and who died. If I could make that choice, then I could choose to walk again."

"Jet, you're not helpless. You've never been helpless, and even without your legs, without your arms, without whatever, you wouldn't *be* helpless. It's no in your nature. I know it'd be hard at first—it always is—but you don't have to figure it all out by yourself. That's what you've got us for, Jet. That's what you've got me for. I'm your brother. I'm not going anywhere. When you need me, I'm right here, even when I'm not actually here. You know what I mean?"

Jet nodded. Yeah, he knew. When the two of them were in sync, they could be on opposite sides of the globe, and it wouldn't matter. He pushed away from Charlie slowly. Tempted as he was to wipe at his wet cheeks, Jet didn't. Dad had always told them that real, unselfish tears weren't meant to be hidden.

"There are other ways to cope with fear, Jet."

"I know, and I promise I'll try harder, but…I have to do this first."

"Jet, listen—"

"No, Charlie, you listen," Jet interrupted. "These guys, they'll come after you, all of you. Mom, Dad, Holly—no one's safe. You've been with me all of one day, and how many times have you almost died? They'll get to me through all of you, and they won't stop 'til *I'm* dead or *they're* dead. Do you really want me to just hand myself over? I will if you really think I should." Jet stared at Charlie intently, his eyes contorting between treachery and hope.

Charlie stepped back. "No," he stated resolutely. "You might die a martyr someday, but today is not that day."

"Why? Because you don't want me to?"

"No, because there is still work to be done."

Jet quirked an eyebrow at him inquisitively, so Charlie tried backpedaling to reason. "Besides, they kill you, and then what? They won't stop murdering people. Heck, they'll probably come after us later just because we're Harpers and we've got that kind of mark."

"So let me finish this."

Charlie shook his head again. Where was the peaceful solution, the bloodless answer? There had to be one. There always was.

"I've got an idea…if you'll trust me." Jet's displeasure was enough to tell Charlie exactly what his plans were.

"That bridge was burnt and rebuilt." On one side anyways. If they were going to truly fix this mess, Charlie still had his end of the bridge to rebuild. He took a breath, braced himself, and blurted, "I was diagnosed with anorexia in seminary." Okay, not the route he'd planned on taking, but it'd get him there nonetheless.

"What?!"

"I didn't really have anorexia, but I had this really bad habit of skipping meals when I was busy, and well, I was always busy, so I lost a little too much weight. A few of my professors were convinced I had a problem." Charlie rubbed the back of his neck. "It all got a little out of hand."

"Why didn't you tell us?"

"Us?" Charlie questioned. "You and I hardly spoke at all back then." He moved on without further remark, "It wasn't really a problem. I hadn't lost *that* much weight, and I started paying more attention to my eating habits afterwards so my professors would stop looking at me like I'd keel over any second. When I lived at home, we always ate together, and now, people shovel food at me by the ton. If I don't eat it, it goes to waste. Sure, when I'm alone, I have to remind myself not to get so wrapped up in whatever I'm working on that I forget to eat, but it's not a *huge* problem."

"Wait, but they diagnosed you? Who was the idiot that did that?"

"It's kind of a long story. I wanted to analyze their reactions to…" Insert sheepish head scratching. "Never mind. It's not important."

Jet eyed him wearily. "Then why are you telling me this?"

Charlie readied himself— "You shared something. I thought I should, too." —and chickened out.

Jet just watched him disbelievingly. "I thought you had some great connection, a point to be made, awe-inspiring wisdom from above."

Charlie shrugged.

"Dude, you are the worst priest ever." And then Jet laughed and laughed and laughed. Charlie helped him back into bed and dragged a chair over to sit beside him.

Honesty—yes, Charlie treasured honesty. He could do this. He shut his eyes for a minute to work up the nerve. "Actually, the staff had a good reason to suspect I was starving myself. They were pretty sure I was depressed. I don't know. Maybe I was." He paused. "Kenny Jude is dead."

For a moment, Jet said nothing, eyes fluttering, mind searching. Comprehension settled like an old house, loud and unnervingly. "Yeah?"

"I ran into him at school. Blew his brains out right in front of me."

"Damn," Jet muttered. "What a jerk." His eyes roved over Charlie, and for the first time in forever, he saw a crack in Charlie's perfect mask, a chink in his impenetrable armor. It was different than their earlier fight. Anger had been such a common occurrence between them before Jet had left that the few good moments shared between them in recent months hadn't healed their wounded bond.

Vulnerability was foreign, frightening, and fraught with complications. "Charlie?"

"Simon's missing. Kenny figured it was the same guy that nabbed Mayor Donaldson's kid. They'd have gotten the hell out of Dodge sooner if we hadn't been there, and they never would have taken Simon. Kenny blamed us, and he wanted me to bleed for it."

"Charlie," Jet began, noting the drops of guilt forming on his brother's brow.

"I know, okay? I know it's not my fault, any of it. I knew that then like I know it now, but..." He paused, breathing deeply. "...it hurts, Jet, like nothing I've ever experienced. It hurts, and I don't know how to fix it, how to make it stop. What's the point?" Suddenly, Charlie looked very tired and old. The look didn't suit him. "What are we?"

"Broken."

"Isn't everybody?"

"Maybe *that's* the point." Jet's eyes glazed over, and Charlie knew Jet's second sight had eclipsed the first. Oddly, Jet's face didn't sour. "Broken isn't damaged."

Charlie's frown deepened. They definitely weren't talking about him anymore. "You're not damaged, Jet."

"To rule the world is but an illusion. To find yourself beneath it, the place of Man."

"*And with un-blinded eyes, see, accept, and become the ruler of your own self,*" Charlie finished coolly, arms crossed over his chest.

Jet eyed him, the second half of the adage still hanging off his elder brother's lips. Most everyone excluded it in favor of the first, and Jet often forgot how much Charlie read in their youth.

"Not beneath the world, Jet. Beneath the illusion. To give up control of everything out there and embrace it for everything in here." Charlie placed a hand on his chest, fingers spread wide. "*What are we? What are we that remain on the sand, who long for the rocks, though we cannot stand? / What are we? What are we that have leapt from the sand? 'Can the rock be our home?' speaks the folly of Man.*"

Jet nodded mildly in agreement. "You've been reading a lot again."

"Are you kidding me? It's Holly. Every time I see her she starts spouting off poetry."

"I know, right? Carlioni, Cezán, and whoever the hell Fontane is—I thought she was just doing it so I'd leave her alone after the whole Devenay fiasco."

"Sisters," they muttered in unison.

Jet smiled in reverie, relaxing sleepily, so Charlie took a calming breath. *Now's as good a time as any.* "I'm sorry, Jet."

"For what?" he mumbled, already half asleep.

"For leaving you."

Jet's eyes came open with a start, and he searched Charlie's faced intently. "To which occasion are you specifically referring?"

"The Westwood Party, '09."

For a moment, Jet didn't move, eyes boring into Charlie's with serious consideration. "I bet you are," he finally said, tilting his head so he wouldn't have to look at him. Charlie's heart clenched tighter, not even aware of the strain in his chest until just then. "It seemed like such a big thing at the time," Jet added, still turned away from Charlie, "like you'd given up on me." He paused. "I was so pissed at you."

"You still are," Charlie noted.

"Just a little."

"I didn't give up on you. I just gave up on trying to reach you. I don't know. Maybe that's the same thing."

"And now? Am I savable?"

"That wasn't ever in question, Jet. I just couldn't be the one to do it. I regretted leaving almost the second I did, but we were both just stupid kids trying to own the world, to be in control of everything. We couldn't do that then, and we can't do that now."

Jet sighed loudly. "Charlie," he said simply, turning his eyes back on him. Charlie read them—honest, sincere, and forgiving.

Charlie nodded to himself. "Do you really want to do this? I know what you're planning, and I see a profound lack of control in your near future."

"Yeah, yeah," Jet grumbled. "Man, I really want a cigarette."

"Okay." Jet shot him a quick glance in surprise, but Charlie wasn't reaching for the pack on Jet's dresser or his dime-store lighter. Instead, he was stretching out his hand to lay on Jet's injured spine.

"What're you doing?" Clearly, Charlie had learned some sort of weird church healing magic or something in seminary. What else could it be?

"Shut up. I'm praying."

"*What?*" The exasperation was clear.

"Do you want to feel better? Then shut up and pray."

Silence reigned once more.

"…Then can I have a cigarette?"

Chapter 24

They went their separate ways the next day. Splitting up was dangerous, but Charlie had determination written all over his face, and Jet was certain only God Himself could stop the priest from making it to day two of his conference. So, Jet said nothing, just watched him go and did something he hadn't done in a while.

"*Pater noster, qui es in caelis...*"

It wasn't like he'd ever really fallen out of his faith. His belief had never faltered. Only his trust had. And while the notions themselves may have seem rather intrinsically linked, they only partially were. His belief could exist without his trust, but his trust could not exist without his belief.

Jet sighed. "*...sed libera nos a malo. Amen.*"

Maybe it was time he stopped blaming God for the odd happenings of his life because, really, he'd never actually believed the fault lay with Him to begin with, but shame and fear had tapered his wisdom and drug him into despair. It was easier to lie to himself than to admit that most of his aches and pains had come from his own pathetic decisions, decisions he'd made for the sole purpose of keeping up his impervious front.

Jet sighed again.

He hadn't had a heart-to-heart with Charlie in quite some time. They'd been used to solving problems together, the result of sharing a room for twelve years and Uncle Riley's unorthodox teaching methods, but it had been such a ridiculously long time since they'd helped each other out with anything serious that it felt surreal to return to that.

So much had changed in so little time, and it seemed like the stone had been rolled away, the air cleared, the stuff that haunted their nightmares vanquished…well, most of them anyways. A young, girly voice still whispered in Jet's ear to be careful. Last night's adventure had been the closest to leaving him legless since the original event itself, something he was definitely not too keen on revisiting.

Alright, understatement of the century much? Honestly, he'd never been more scared in his life.

Jet sighed for the umpteenth time.

Okay, that wasn't quite true either. The time he'd almost gotten Charlie possessed—yeah, that was pretty dang horrifying. Jet's face twitched. He had a whole list of memories just like that that still haunted his dreams.

But being stuck in that damn wheelchair was the latest of them. He'd sat there watching what others could do and only ever dreaming he could do it with them, told constantly that it would never happen. He'd have died of humiliation if Charlie or I had ever seen him like that. Mom and Dad didn't count. They were his parents. They'd already seen him at his weakest.

The strangest thought occurred to him then, something he hadn't bothered considering when he'd first been confined to his prison on wheels. What if he *had* gone home? Could they have made him feel any better? He'd always reeled at the thought of their pity, but would they really have been so cruel? It was hard to picture on Charlie's face, despite Jet's constant suspicion of his motives. Sadness was all he could picture on mine.

"People mistake pity for condescension, this patronizing act of false sympathy that breeds nothing but inaction," he'd once heard Charlie preach. "But people are wrong. Pity is love, compassion, and mercy. Pity is our humanity bringing us to our knees beside our brothers and sisters, calling our hearts to break from their stone castings to bleed for another as the heart of Christ bleeds for us. The only question is, can you accept that? Can you accept mercy? Can you accept love? Can you accept solidarity and let the Christ in them tend to the hurt in you?"

It was true, Jet decided, after a quick Google search. He couldn't find a single definition of the word *pity* that connoted anything but good will, and could accepting mercy mean anything but relief?

Jet hadn't wanted to rely on anybody the first time. After being told of all he couldn't do, he was determined to shake off their condemnation and rise above it. He *could* do it. He'd show them...

But we had never suggested that he couldn't. We had just wanted him home. Could everything have been so much easier if he'd done just that? He'd been determined to go it alone, like he always ha—

With a bitter shock, Jet realized that he *hadn't* always gone it alone. At the very least, he'd had Charlie, and at the very most, he'd had the family. The only time he'd ever felt like he'd *had* to be alone was…

Voight.

Charlie had been right all along. No matter what happened, Jet would still have everything he needed, with or without the use of his legs, like he always had and like he always would have.

Detective Taylor stood on the curb of the street beside the unmarked suburban Hall was seated in. Stirring her morning coffee, Taylor jumped at Jet's sudden appearance beside her. "Oh, you're alive."

"Don't sound so disappointed."

"After the story Hall told me, I wasn't sure *either* of you were still kicking."

"Yeah, well, for the time being, you're stuck with us." Jet sighed, then leant up against their car so Detective Hall could hear him through the open window. "I have a standing invitation to join the club, and I've decided to accept it."

Detective Taylor dropped her coffee cup.

"Look, stuff's going down. I need to talk to your Admin, like, yesterday. Now, I could march up right up the front steps of HQ and ring the doorbell, but I don't want to step on any toes. Are you gonna to help me or not?"

"You know where HQ is?" Detective Hall asked curiously.

"I'm an inheritor, remember? The information is available. I examined it. Besides, for anyone who really cares to look, it's pretty obvious."

Northern headquarters wasn't in Chicago, so Detective Hall asked to take the rest of the day on account of the late night he'd had. Then he pulled Penny out of the conference room she was snoozing in and brought her out to the car. She almost ran when she saw Jet. "You!" she hissed once she was safely in the car. "You're the reason I got kidnapped, dragged across the country, and nearly killed."

"You know, my sister got kidnapped seven months ago, dragged *out* of the country, across Canada to Alaska, almost killed, dragged across Canada back *into* the country, almost burned at the stake, married to a madman, and almost killed again. And none of it had anything to do with me."

"*What?* Your family must have the worst luck ever."

"Nah, life is just too easy for us, so the Big Guy upstairs makes it a little more challenging." She frowned. "Nice moves by the way. If you hadn't distracted them like that last night, we'd be facing St. Peter hand in hand."

She blushed pretty like she had the first time they'd met. "I've taken self-defense."

"You're a professional dancer, or if it's a side job, it shouldn't be."

She looked away coyly. "How'd you know that?"

"It's all in your moves…and physique."

Her blush darkened, only made worse when Jet smiled at her candidly. "Where are we going?" she asked Detective Hall, twirling her hair and pointedly keeping her eyes off Jet.

"Somewhere safer."

"Than the police station?"

Hall hesitated. "Yes."

Jet leaned back in his seat still smiling. Though the day was young, it was treating him well. First, he'd woken up with only mild soreness in his back. *Unbelievable.* And Jet was certain it would fade completely once he loosened up some more. Now he was getting to spend two hours in a car with an intelligent, gorgeous girl—er, woman. He could see the feminist in her already.

Oh, yes, what a wonderful morning it was turning out to be.

They pulled up to NHQ without any issues, and Jet stared at the building in bemusement. It wasn't anything like southern headquarters. SHQ stretched up five stories, plain and square. Northern headquarters was sleek and modern. Jet wasn't sure he could've described the shape if his life depended on it. Buildings, he decided, should not have that many curves.

They were led inside, past the receptionist that Jet knew was packing heat, and up through an oddly winding set of stairs. This place was great for losing people, and only because Jet was trained to keep track paths and orient himself did he know exactly where they were in the building and how to make a tactful retreat if necessary.

The three of them entered a spacious office. The occupier of the desk's chair, who Jet surmised was the Northern Admin, sat facing the window. His guests were ignored. Already Jet didn't like him. *What a boorish attempt to look cool.*

But Jet had to admire his office. Like the Southern Admin, he had bookshelves everywhere, scattered all over the wall for an unobstructed view out of the floor-to-ceiling windows. From his office, the Admin could see everything.

"Detective Hall," the Admin said, finally turning to face them, "what brings you here?"

The redhead scrutinized Jet intensely, and Jet mentally shook his head. Clearly, *she* already knew why they were there. Just what kind of game was she playing? He really didn't have time for this. "Penelope Belmonte is here for protective custody." She nodded. "And Jet Harper's here to join."

Jet wasn't anticipating the startled look on her face. Quite frankly, he was a bit surprised Detective Taylor hadn't called ahead in warning as soon as they'd driven away. "Take Miss

Belmonte to the lounge. It appears Mr. Harper and I need to chat in private."

She barely waited for the door to close behind them. "I deny your request."

Jet frowned. "You can't do that. I'm an inheritor."

"You must be in good standing with the Dragonfly Club to be admitted into its ranks."

"I am in good standing."

"You're an assassin."

"A retired and reformed assassin."

"Then why have the streets of Chicago turned into a warzone?"

"We humans have these things called pasts, and try as we might, we just can't seem to get rid of them." Jet crossed his arms and forced aside the scowl he wanted to let loose. It wouldn't help right now. "Look, you can do this now, or the Southern Admin can do it when I get back, but I *will* be admitted. The severity of the situation's about to go from warzone to hell. Now you can either put a leash on me to minimize the casualties, or I can go about this the way I really want to and lay this land to ruin." Okay, so maybe he'd exaggerated just a tad, but the rigid redhead didn't need to know that.

She glowered at him. "Sit down."

The Admin was young, maybe forty, too young really. She must've just taken the title. Her inexperience was making her quick to judge, but he trusted the system to work. If she was the Admin, she deserved to be. He just had to survive her hulkishness long enough to get her on his side.

"You're right. I could admit you if you're really in as good a standing as you seem to think you are, but if I did that, I could also bench you and keep you off your warpath entirely. Why would I send an assassin out there to kill other assassins? That's not how we operate. I'd rather send some of my own agents out to capture them, not kill them."

"Oh yeah? And how many of your agents are you willing to murder to make your point?"

"Excuse me?"

Jet continued, "The guys you've seen so far are a dime a dozen, Admin. The top guns on this are professional contract killers, two of Claude's Nine."

"*What*?"

"Claude's top nine assassins." When the confusion didn't clear, he elaborated, "Claude Moreau was once considered the top assassin on the planet. He got old, retired, and disappeared. About six years ago, a list pops up on the dark web labeled Claude's Nine, his top nine favorite, living assassins, and I guess you get what I mean by favorite."

"You pick up contracts via the dark web?"

"Don't be stupid. Of course not."

He didn't elaborate, so she moved on, "Do you know the people on Claude's list?"

"A couple."

"Are you on it?"

"I'm ranked sixth." He could taste her hate. Jet wasn't sure how that was possible. "You don't have to be active to get ranked. It's not like you just stop being good when you leave the Market."

The Admin sat back in her chair. "The people trying to kill you?"

"Belladonna's ranked four, and I'm guessing her mentor's in the top three."

"And do you know the top three?"

Jet sighed. "No, not really. I haven't seen the latest list. I don't have the right tech at the moment to reach it either, but I know the Grim Reaper's on top—Grim's always on top, has been longer than the list has been around—and I know Belladonna's four because an informant told me as much."

"So, is this a revenge thing?" Her green eyes were now intrigued, like she was trying to solve a complicated puzzle.

Why does everyone always think it's revenge? "Psh, revenge? Nah, revenge is for kids with too much time on their hands, sweetheart. When you've seen war and it's taken your friends, you know there isn't any one person to kill, just the enemy, and you can't kill everybody, don't even really want to, no matter how good you are at it. No, this is a protect-my-family thing, a protect-my-friends thing, a protect-everyone-I-care-about thing. If you send your field agents out there, they might get past the hired hands, but by then they'll have tipped off Belladonna and her sponsor, and then they'll just die."

"We don't hire assassins."

"You want me to capture them? Fine, I'll try, but I won't make you any promises. Capturing assassins alive is no cake walk, and I'm not about to get my head blown off to prove my loyalties, especially since my loyalties are exactly where they need to be."

She picked up a pen and fiddled with it, contemplation on her features. "And how will I know you're really trying?"

Jet sighed. He hated big brother, the metaphorical one anyways. "When my sister had her op, they had her wear these video camera contact lenses. I had a subcutaneous jammer injected into my neck a while ago, but I'll talk to the guy who put it there and make sure it doesn't affect your signal so you can watch." He took a breath and rushed forward, "But I won't have you yammering in my ear the whole time like they were with her. You'll get me killed like that."

The Admin's eyes had squinted. "Your sister?"

"What, have you been out of the country for the past six months?"

"As a matter a fact, I have been."

Jet frowned. "My sister, Holly Harper, Queen of the Dragonflies."

Her pen dropped. "Your sister's the Dragonfly Queen? Really?"

Jet had never thought he'd see the day where his little sister had gained fame on him. "Yeah."

A slightly different intensity filled her gaze now, like the puzzle had doubled in size and she suddenly had more pieces than she knew what to do with. But the phone rang, and she jumped, snatching it quickly off its cradle in aggravation. "What?" Almost immediately, her demeanor shifted to concern. "No, I'll handle it." She hung up and stared at Jet some more, this time, with consideration.

"Charlie Harper is your brother, correct?"

"Yes," Jet answered warily.

"He's a priest?"

"Yeees."

"And he's at a conference in Chicago at the moment?"

Jet only nodded slowly. He didn't like this hesitant line of questioning one bit.

She grimaced. "I'm afraid I have some bad news."

Jet's stomach dropped. *No, no, no, no, no!* "Is he dead?"

"No."

Somehow, Jet found little comfort in that. "Then how is he?"

"At the moment, fine."

Boy was he ready to wring her neck. "Then what's the bad news?"

"Have you heard of the Aureate Society?"

Jet wracked his brain. "It's an extremist cult, isn't it?" That wasn't really his area of expertise, but he'd come across the name during a job or two.

"Yes." She paused dramatically, and Jet nearly pounced. "We've just uncovered a plot that involves an attack on the Chicago clerical conference." Jet stiffened. "I'll make you a deal, Jet Harper. Prove to me you are more than just an assassin. Stop the attack with as few casualties as possible, catch as many of the cultists as you can, and don't let anyone discover the club's part in it. Do that, and I'll admit you to the club and sanction your op."

"Why not just send in the guys you have in the area? It seems like an awfully big risk to wait two hours."

"One of our fulltime coders picked this up. We have no way of explaining our involvement."

"You could 'tip' someone off."

She grimaced. "They'll want to trace something like that back to its source, and we don't have time to cover our tracks. Besides, seeing how your brother's life is in jeopardy, I'm sure you're the most equipped to handle this situation and have the strongest motivation to ensure its success."

"But two hours is a long ti—"

"I know I've been peevish, Mr. Harper, but please don't underestimate me. Do you really think I don't have slightly faster means of transportation on hand than a car?"

Chapter 25

Their penchant for trouble seemed worse than usual, like their constant black cloud had turned category 5 hurricane without any notice. Well, maybe there had been some signs. Regardless, when Charlie woke up in bed early the next morning and the sky wasn't falling, his room wasn't on fire, and no else had died, he was feeling pretty good about his day.

Then he and Jet had sat through a quiet yet comfortable breakfast with Father Martin. No problems there. Jet had left almost immediately after, eager to "get this day over with already," and Charlie had lagged behind long enough to wash his vestments, *again*, and pull himself into something resembling a respectable rookie priest. Still, all was well.

Charlie had even made it to his conference while it was still bright and early, thanks, in part, to Father Martin, who'd given him a ride. Yes, everything was fine.

So then why did it feel like everything was very much not fine?

Charlie moped under the Newberry Hotel's entrance awning, trying to vivisect the warning he felt rumbling through his gut. After an unenlightening five minutes, Charlie simply sighed. *It's never that easy. Might as well just deal with it.*

Just before he could enter the building, a fluttering of wings drew his attention to a nearby tree. He'd expected mourning doves, like the kind he'd seen on his walks while at school. Charlie paused in cold consideration.

Ravens.

A conspiracy of ravens haunted the bountiful branches. Most of them, Charlie noted, were eyeing him suspiciously. They were silent on their perches, peering down at him with their obsidian eyes. Their feathers were ruffled, like they'd been through a great deal of trouble to land there for him to see.

Ravens.

Something was coming.

Charlie signed in with only an odd look from the receptionist and joined his brother priests in the large reception hall of the hotel. Most were mulling about and mingling, discussing the latest hot topics and reconnecting with old friends.

For the first time in a several weeks, Charlie felt the weight of his inexperience. As far as he could tell, he didn't personally know a single priest in the hall. Oh, he'd heard of some of them. He was sure the French-American priest chatting amiably a few feet from him had his own segment on the Catholic channel, and at least one of the speakers off to his left was a well-known representative of the Vatican. Charlie tapped his foot in growing anxiety. He couldn't even remember what this darn conference was supposed to be about.

A wave of nerves flooded Charlie. Too many strangers were gathered together in a single space. He didn't like that, so he gripped his notebook tighter until the metal spiral dug into his skin and reminded him it was there. Then he took a breath, molded his unflappable Harper mien, and searched the room diligently. Smack dab in its center was a table that appeared half empty. If he accidentally stole someone's seat, they'd just have to deal with it.

Charlie marched through the room calmly, dodging busybodies everywhere he went, found his chair, and reclined into it leisurely. He didn't recognize any of the four priests at his table, but he hadn't really expected to.

"I didn't see you here yesterday," said a young Italian, whose name tag read Lorenzo, because he'd have noticed a young diocesan priest in a cassock. Not too many Americans still did that.

Charlie smiled. "I got a little held up and couldn't make it. Family trouble. Besides, I'm not staying at the hotel. I promised a friend I'd meet up with his old mentor as St. Vitus's."

"Interesting," an older priest said, "that you'd choose your family over your duties as a priest."

Charlie smiled, unabashed. "No, Father Baxter, my family is a part of my priestly duties."

Father Baxter's face soured, but Lorenzo just looked curiously amused. "Your first duty is to the people of God."

"When did our families stop being part of the people of God?"

Lorenzo's snicker was silenced by Father Baxter's glare, and the two other priests, an Indian currently going by the name of Matthew and a redneck named Buck, stifled their own amusement.

"Forgive me, Father," Charlie offered sheepishly. "I've been verbally sparring with my brother since we left home two days ago. It's not quite out of my system."

"Where are you from?" Lorenzo asked.

"South Texas—Diocese of Brownsville."

"That explains a lot," Father Baxter jibed.

Charlie ignored him. "My brother decided we should come together so he could visit some friends. I should've known better.

"Oh yeah?"

"He's a bit of a trouble magnet. Then again, I guess I am, too. Oh well, everything'll turn out the way it should."

"Do you really believe that?" Father Buck asked.

Charlie smirked. "Oh yeah, Father, when you have a big, red target painted on your back by the Creator Himself, you learn trust one way or another."

A tapping on the mic drew the hall's attention as a cardinal took center stage. Charlie estimated somewhere near three hundred priests were present, all seated around circular tables in well-cushioned chairs. It was expensive décor for an expensive reception hall in an even more expensive hotel.

The cardinal droned on about some theological issue, but Charlie was finding it difficult to focus. He'd gone through such an array of emotions in the past two days that he wasn't quite sure what to do with himself. Anger, frustration, sorrow, fear—they were generally so foreign to him these days that experiencing them in quick succession had left him a little restless. And the cold fury he'd felt when Jet had begged him to leave, to surrender him to death… *As if!* Had Jet really thought Charlie would do that? He had abandoned his brother once, but it definitely hadn't been to certain death.

He scribbled something down in his notebook to feign attention. Charlie hoped the men at his table didn't want to discuss the topic at any point because he really didn't have a clue what the cardinal was babbling on about.

Charlie's jobless pen froze. His skin tingled in the same way it always did when something bad was about to happen. He flashed his eyes around. No one else had noticed, but the open doors of the hall were suddenly closed, and a shady looking man was standing by the dais at the other end of the room.

Charlie reached a hand into his sleeve and plucked out his glasses.

He'd thought glasses were an odd ordination gift, especially coming from his sister, but he'd smiled at me nicely and accepted them anyways. He heard me say something about my friend making them, but Charlie had shrugged it off, of course. He didn't really need glasses.

Then, in mock delight, he'd plastered them on his face as he was unpacking in his new office, only to realize he had in his clutches one of the neatest gadgets he'd ever seen. He'd smirked to himself excitedly. Glasses made him look smarter anyways.

Charlie peered through the lenses, and years of being a Harper meant the outline of a gun was visible even under the suspicious man's coat. He adjusted his glasses to disguise his change in sight, which revealed a Glock and a large knife hidden on the back of the man's figure.

Charlie visibly grimaced. Was this one of Jet's friends? The man didn't seem too concerned with Charlie, or he simply hadn't acted on it yet. "Something wrong, Father Charlie?" Father Baxter asked from beside him, his irritation quite clear.

"Brace yourself," Charlie warned.

One. Two. Three. Four. Fi—

Then the Glock was suddenly pointed at the cardinal, and the assembly erupted into frenzy. "No!" the gunman shouted. "Everyone sit down and shut up." He shook his gun at the cardinal to make his point, and most of the priests had the presence of mind to calm themselves. Others were forced back into their seats by their companions. "I feel I should warn you," the man announced, "you're all going to die, so say your prayers. I'll give you a moment for that. No need to thank me."

Charlie read the fear on many faces. They were priests, but they were also human. Fear in the face of death is almost instinctual, and death by murder is certainly not an appealing thought to anyone.

"Cardinal Weatherford, you and your compatriot—what's his name?—Cardinal Neumann, will get the VIP treatment. God won't even recognize you when we're through."

"Blasphemy," the cardinal spoke, a paragon of courage. "Martyrdom doesn't scare me. If you have no fear of God, do your worst? It is not *I* who will truly suffer."

"Such wisdom, such strength," the man mumbled in a craze. "It's a good thing I don't need your fear to inspire it in everyone else."

Charlie bit his lip. Under normal circumstances, he'd just let this business run its course like any other priest would. But for once, the idea gave him pause. Inaction could be just as bad as wrongful action, and the difference between him and everyone else was that he was actually in a position to do something about it. Charlie sighed to himself. What was he actually supposed to do? The wrong course of action could still be worse than failure to act.

Charlie growled lowly, and the priests at his table shot him strange looks. Well, one thing was for sure: he *always* tried doing nothing, and it *always* ended badly for him. Maybe it was time to change it up a bit.

"Everyone in this hotel will die," the man said, waving around a gas mask, "and you damn Christians'll be to blame for it. You'll see. Well, actually you won't see because you'll all be dead, but not to worry, I'm sure heaven will grant you a front row seat." His laugh was maniacal, and something inside Charlie snapped. *Just who does this guy think he is?*

Charlie stood abruptly. At first no one seemed to notice aside from those nearest to him. Then Charlie took a breath, drew himself up to full height, and demanded the room's attention by his presence alone. He gripped his rosary tighter, wrapped around his fist like a binding.

"Can I help you?" the man asked, curious but no less sure of himself.

Charlie spoke calmly. "It seems we have a problem," he ground out. Slowly, he ambled towards the dais, eyes trained entirely on the threatening figure before him. Charlie wondered what the cardinal must be thinking of his grandiosity, but he wasn't about to lose his focus trying to find out.

"Oh yeah?"

"Yes." That guy had a god-complex, a really bad one, and his overt pride coupled with Charlie's own gift gave Charlie the chance to get in close. After all, the man had no reason to think a young priest was any threat to his grand scheme. Charlie climbed the steps and stopped several feet from gunman, his back to the other priests, the cardinal in his periphery. "You see, God and I have an agreement."

"Oh, really?"

"Yeah, really," Charlie said, twisting the rosary tighter in his fist. "He puts me in situation like this so that I can deal with them accordingly."

The man's brow furrowed in ire.

Charlie sighed. *Bring it down a notch, Charles.* "Look, you can do whatever you want with me. People don't need to see the red of the cardinal's cassock to react the way you want them to. Just, let everyone else go, okay? There are innocent people here."

"How selfless of you, Father, but I'm afraid a cardinal would be far more effective, and we have no intention of letting anyone out of this hotel alive."

Charlie raised his eyes to heaven, hands out in front of him as if to say, "See what I have to deal with?" Then he pulled his left arm across his stomach, and with his right, made the Sign of the Cross. *God forgive me.*

Charlie's stainless-steel rosary came loose around the man's free hand. Instinctively, his gun hand swung around to aid his captured limb. Charlie took the opportunity to shove the weapon skyward. He twisted the man's wrist 'til he dropped it, then spun around his assailant, the man's seized hand pulled over his own shoulder by Charlie's metal lasso. His free hand reached behind him to swipe at Charlie with the blade from his belt, but another nerve pinch forced him to drop the weapon, and Charlie bound both hands together with the slack of his rosary. He gave the man a two-fingered shove and watched him stumble back and fall.

"Who—Who are you?" the man stammered.

"Who am I? I'm Charlie Harper."

The man slapped his back to the ground to retrieve his fallen gun, but the click of another weapon stopped him. "Move another inch, and I splatter your brains all over the floor." When the man made no move to test him, Jet whipped him with the butt of his gun.

Charlie's face twitched. "Was that really necessary?"

"What, the threat or the knockout out?"

Charlie didn't honor his question with an answer.

A light gaseous mixture plumed from the air vents, and the concerned mumble of the priests grew in volume. "Don't worry," Jet announced over the speaker system. "I've replaced the deadly nerve toxin with a sleep agent. It's probably better the rest of this guy's buddies think you're dead for the time being." The cardinal was affected first. He dropped like a rock into Charlie's arms. "Don't worry," Jet repeated. "You'll all wake up in a couple of hours, just about the same way you passed out."

"Allergies?"

"I did a check. Honestly, Charlie, have you no faith in me?" Jet turned his head when Charlie didn't answer. He was swaying beside the cardinal. "You know, I was going to let you pass out in peace, but," Jet said, fishing out a small pill from his pocket, "you're welcome to join me, for old time's sake."

Charlie snatched it from his hand and swallowed it dry. "I'll manage Cardinal Neumann. You just deal with everything else." They waited a moment for the concoction to take effect. Then Jet nodded and led the way as Charlie gazed over the slumbering assembly. Somehow, he didn't think Bishop was going to be very pleased with him.

They slunk out of the hall into the corridor. Everywhere they went, employees and patrons were strewn out on the floor unconscious. "You checked the files on all these people?"

"Charlie, relax. The dosage was safe for just about everyone."

"Just about?"

Jet sighed. "I checked everything twice. The margin of error's less than 1%. If I hadn't knocked everyone out, they'd be in a panic, and the Aureates would've opened fire on any and everyone. I know you're worried, but this is the best I got, and worrying that my best isn't good enough isn't going to save anyone else, alright?"

Charlie nodded. Jet was right. They both had to focus on what they *did* know.

Jet caught him at a cross-section. They could hear the muffled voices of the Aureates just beyond. "I didn't know there were two high-profile cardinals making an appearance here."

"We do have our secrets." They paused to listen, but the gas masks of the cultists were muddying their speech. "Now, you want to fill me in on what's going on?"

"The Aureates have taken over the entire hotel. That's about all I know."

"And you found out how?"

"A club coder picked it up. I'm handling it for them."

Charlie cocked an eyebrow at his brother. "Proving yourself?"

"Yeah, and you know, right place, right time."

"As always," Charlie responded.

Jet nodded in agreement. They did always seem to find themselves in the most opportune position to be of assistance. Jet twitched at a memory of the last time he and Charlie had dealt with occultists. They'd just been kids then. "So, is this Cardinal Neumann important?"

"I'd assume so."

"You don't know?"

"I'm a newly ordained priest. You think they actually tell me these things?"

The voices grew louder, and Jet stormed the hallway while Charlie took cover. Jet worked methodically. Jab to the throat. Remove gas mask. Knee to the gut. Remove gas mask. Kick to the head. Remove gas mask.

Well, that was easy. Three Aureates lay unconscious in the corridor thanks Jet's fast-acting sleep agent. Jet signaled Charlie to join him. "Who are these Aureates anyways?"

"You don't know?" Jet asked in mock awe.

"Jet!"

"Alright, alright. They're a cult of some sort. Honestly, I don't know much else. All they told me is that they particularly dislike Catholics. Sucks for you."

"You're Catholic, too."

"Yeah, but I'm not a priest, and for once, that actually seems to be a good thing." Charlie rolled his eyes as they turned another corner, then chucked Jet back behind it and threw himself against him. "What's up?"

A hail of bullets answered for him. "Where are we going, Jet?"

"The cardinals were sharing a suite at the other end of the hotel. Cardinal Neumann should be hanging out there," he paused and took a breath, "maybe."

"Maybe? *Jet—*"

"I haven't been given access to all-things-club yet, and I didn't have time to do my own recon. Cut me some slack here, Charlie. I'm not a miracle worker."

"Fine. Do you know where we're going?"

"Um, further into the hotel seems like the logical choice."

Charlie released a frustrated groan, then scanned the walls for a map of the emergency routes. "Look," he gestured to Jet.

Jet strained his eyes at the wall across from them and fired off a few warning shots of his own. "I can't see that. It's way too small."

Charlie pulled out his glasses again and planted them on his face, adjusting their view as he did. The bleary insect-like letters grew and focused. The exchange of bullets continued, but Charlie took a moment to map the hotel. After a couple of seconds, he blinked. He was *so* out of practice. No way would he remember all the possible routes. He adjusted the view on his glasses, and this time, they captured the image and ran lines across each lens. Charlie sighed and reviewed their route again just in case. "Alright then, let's get a move-on already."

Jet eyed his glasses but said nothing.

"Jet!"

"Sorry, okay? I'm not used to having to worry about not killing people. It's so much easier to not have any rules."

"It always *seems* easier to do the wrong thing." Charlie scanned the hall separating them and the cultists.

"Except when you're trying to do the wrong thing. Then it's pretty hard."

Charlie rolled his eyes. "Hand me a gun."

His younger brother froze, finger hovering over the trigger and head turned to stare at Charlie with startled confusion. "What?"

"Just give me one."

Jet pulled a semi-automatic from the back of his belt and handed it to Charlie. "You still remember how to use that?"

Charlie released the magazine to examine the contents, jammed it back in, and pulled back the slide to load the first round. "You remember when we used to play cops and robbers with Mom and Dad?"

"Yeah," Jet said wistfully, "those were the days."

"Remember how we used to beat them?"

Jet smirked. "What do you have in mind?"

"Harper vs Harper: Scenario 3."

"Are you sure you're up for that, your priestliness?"

"Don't worry about me. I'll be fine."

"Want me to go first?"

"Still trust me not to blow your head off?"

Jet's eyes twinkled. "On my mark." He waited. *Three, two, one.* Jet released one more round of shots and darted around the corner, Charlie swinging out behind him and maintaining his position.

The Aureates leapt from their spot, only for Charlie's gun to fire at their longest strands of hair. The bullets shot passed Jet's running figure and warned their enemies from the open. Charlie could see Jet fighting the urge to raise his own gun and just halt them, permanently, in their places. Instead, he rolled low across the next corner and moved into hand-to-hand combat, adding an occasional shot to stray limbs that were a little too troublesome, and by the time Charlie arrived at the next corner, Jet had dropped every single one of them. Jet joined him back behind their next blind, now his turn to recover. "You're up."

"Don't talk. I'm concentrating." This time Charlie ran full force towards the next intersecting hallway. Jet's metal brushed past him much closer than Charlie's had, the result of being a more efficient marksman. Charlie ignored it. *Focus!*

He suddenly wished he didn't have a gun occupying one of his hands, so he slid it across the floor to their next cover and moved into fighting position, setting up for strikes with minimal damage.

Charlie rushed his first target. Grab wrist, strike elbow, strike neck, remove gas mask. Lock wrist, twist arm back, strike back of knee, remove gas mask. Turn. Palm strike chest, double arm sweep, double knife hand strike neck, remove gas mask. A gun appeared feet from him, too far for him to counter. The crack of a shot firing squirted blood onto the beige tiling. Remove gas mask. The wound was bleeding out, but Charlie couldn't find the seconds to bind it, and he sincerely hoped the lost soul wouldn't die.

Jet yanked him back behind cover. An elevator descended at their backs. "Route," he demanded.

"Stairs."

They climbed.

No one was on the stairs. Regardless, they sprinted up in their alternating pattern, never a pair more cautious, but before they could exit the stairwell, Aureates spilled onto the landing below.

Jet pulled a metal cylinder that was clipped to his belt. *Flashbang*, Charlie thought, plugging his ears, pinching his eyes shut, and turning away. Jet snipped the pin and flung it to the floor below, shielding his own senses just as the resounding pop and subsequent flash of light dropped the Aureates to their knees. "Keep going," he called to Charlie. Then he jumped past the railing below to ensure they wouldn't be followed.

Charlie exited the stairwell carefully, every single caution he'd learned as a kid rising in him. It was hard to believe this was part of their fun and games growing up, but Charlie didn't feel the least bit sorry for it. It sure had kept him entertained.

The upper floor was empty, and Charlie speculated that all the Aureates had travelled downward to confront him and Jet. Still, he moved with purpose, careful and precise. He reached the door at the end of the corridor, leaned into it, and listened.

Silence.

Charlie moved his ear closer. Maybe they'd gotten the wrong suite after all. There were only two in the whole hotel, and this one had seemed like the more logical option since it was nearer the conference hall.

Abruptly, he heard the drone of speech, but Charlie couldn't make out any words. He'd wait a few more seconds for Jet. A resounding smack and the following groan changed his mind. Jet's racing feet in the background, Charlie pushed the blissfully unlocked door open and walked straight into a shallow kiss. His startled eyes went wide as he shoved the offending figure off him.

"Ah, I thought you were Specter."

Charlie swiped the back of his hand across his lips and smeared the lingering lipstick off. Cardinal Neumann stood behind her near the window, hands bound behind his back. He gave Charlie a hard stare, and Charlie endeavored *not* to read it.

Jet clattered in then, gun raised and ready for action. The woman lifted her own weapon. "It's not much use, Specter. This man, your brother I take it—I estimate he has about eight minutes to live."

Jet took a solemn step back, resting his gun by Charlie's left ear and shrinking down behind him.

"Using your own brother as a human shield? You are quite ruthless, aren't you?"

"Not really," Jet answered. "It's like you said, Belladonna. He's a dead man walking anyways." Jet grabbed a fistful of Charlie's vestment. "You shoot him. I shoot you. I live. You die. And you definitely haven't been in the game long enough to be alright with going out with your mark, even if you *could* shoot me.

Charlie held his composure, not entirely sure what sort of game Jet was playing, but certain he didn't want to resist.

Belladonna smacked her purple lips together in disdain and, with little warning, dove back. The floor beside the brothers exploded, a small thing really that did them no actual harm, but the loud distraction did cause them to stumble, and Belladonna took the moment to break for the window. She shot at it a few times, then curled herself into a ball and hurled herself threw it.

Jet discarded Charlie and raced to the window, but Belladonna was already scrambling across the neighboring rooftop. Jet took aim, found Belladonna in his sights, and...dropped his gun, the Northern Admin's words running rampant through his mind.

Jet turned to find Charlie releasing the cardinal, a worried frown on his face. "You okay?"

Charlie looked at him, confused perplexity still clinging to his features. "I had eight minutes."

"Oh, that," Jet said, taking another glance out the window, "don't worry about it. The capsule you popped earlier counteracts most poisons."

"Most?"

Jet waved him off. "Yeah, most. Hey, if it happens to be one of the few on the entire planet that it doesn't work so well with, well, you're already dead anyways, right?" Charlie glared. "How'd she get you?"

But his older brother merely focused his attention to his task. He could feel Jet's eyes on him, taking in his every feature.

"*Dude*," he drawled, "did she kiss you?"

Charlie said nothing.

Jet broke into a fit of laughter, loud and raucous, like it was truly the funniest thing he'd ever heard. "Next time I see

Belladonna, I'll ask her what she thought. I'm sure *she's* a good kisser."

"Je—"

"I mean, look at her. She's hot."

Cardinal Neumann shot Jet a dry look, completely unamused. "Mister…" He waited for Jet to fill in the blank, to which Jet only grinned. "…Specter, I do not think now is the time for such trivialities."

"Whatever you say, Your Eminence." The cardinal's eyes scoured Jet's visage. Was he being mocked?

"Are you alright, Cardinal?" Charlie asked, studying the growing bruise on the older man's face where Belladonna had struck him.

"Yes," he answered coolly, "I am well. Thank you."

"Germans."

Charlie hissed at him, and his younger brother shot him a glare.

"And the others?" the cardinal asked.

"Everyone's fine, Cardinal. Specter here replaced the toxin with a sleep agent."

Cardinal Neumann eyed Jet with renewed interest. "I'm out of here, Charlie. I've been ordered to evade detection, by the police anyways. Cardinal," he aimed a pointed look at their third-party witness, "good day."

Chapter 26

The Northern Admin's poker face could have won her half a fortune in Vegas. Jet was sure of it.

She'd been staring at him, near unblinkingly, for the past half hour, and Jet was actually starting to consider ceding in their battle of wills, but before her unnerving gaze could break him, the door slammed open, and reflex called his gun out. Detective Hall stilled immediately, long enough for Jet to assess the threat and reclassify it. Impressed by his sensible reaction, Jet's eyes glinted, and he lowered his weapon with unbridled esteem.

"They're here, Admin."

"Good, escort everyone to the conference room."

Jet surveyed the room as soon as he entered. Charlie sat beside Cardinal Neumann, Penny across from him, Detectives Hall and Taylor to one side of her. The Admin gestured for Jet to have a seat, so he claimed the empty one on Penny's left and gave her an amiable smile.

"You will excuse us, Cardinal, I hope, for ushering you away from the scene so quickly. I know you've been questioned by local police and the FBI, but we're a different, separate organization."

"I truly detest secret societies, Miss…" She, too, refused his prompt. "…Miss. They lend themselves to all sorts of vices."

"I'm sure that's true of most, Cardinal, but we aim to keep ourselves in check and desire only to do good."

"Cardinal, if I could just—"

"No, you may not, Father Harper." Charlie bowed his head in submission and trained his eyes on the tabletop.

The reprimand charged the air around Jet, and his hands clenched into fists. But he fought the urge to riposte. Jet knew Charlie wouldn't appreciate it. Besides, everything in his Catholic upbringing was screaming at him to mind his manners, even as everything else in his upbringing was calling him to his brother's defense.

"If you want help, Cardinal, the Dragonfly Club is the most equip to aid you."

"We will see."

"Let's examine our cards then, shall we?" The Admin walked a circle around the room, gazing out of the glass windows at the agents beyond. Jet threw his eyes around, too, realizing with some mild irritation that there were more people in the building than there had been before. He hated being watched. "We know that the Aureate Society, an extremist cult, planned to seize control of the Newberry Hotel and kill all its occupants."

"Their primary targets were the priests," the cardinal informed them, arms folded over his chest, "and Cardinal Weatherford is still missing."

Depression settled over them like a mist. Cardinal Weatherford had been snatched from the hall without any warning, and his abduction was the only red mark on Jet's record, a glitch none of them had anticipated.

No point dwelling on the past. "Belladonna's working for them."

"That assassin who's trying to kill you? What does she have to do with this? Is it common to take more than one contract at a time?"

"Not really."

"So then this somehow involves you, too?" Penny asked. Every eye turned to her, but the attention didn't faze her. Dauntlessly, she awaited an answer, daring them with every contour of her face to deny her that.

"Apparently," Jet told her, smiling affably, "although I'm not sure how."

"Cardinal, aside from speaking at the conference, was there any other reason for your visit to the States?" The Admin asked it evenly, but Jet could hear her suspicion masquerading as respect. Evidently, so could Charlie, because he glared at her while the cardinal wasn't looking.

Cardinal Neumann's square face stayed pinched in displeasure, his lips pressed in a thin line, and Jet struggled against the words forming in own mouth that threatened to get him in real trouble.

"Cardinal, please," Charlie pleaded. "They only want to help."

The cardinal merely stared for a few more seconds before ceding to Charlie's petition. "In the past two years, this Aureate Society has begun to concern us," he explained.

"Cardinal Weatherford and I came to this conference in order to investigate some truly disturbing rumors, subtly of course."

"What rumors have you heard?" the Admin asked.

"They kidnap children and manipulate them into joining their cult or developing a dangerous, extremist view of Christianity." The news clip they'd briefly caught at the rectory just after their arrival immediately sprung to the forefront of Jet's mind. "They intend to use those children to inspire terror in others regarding the faith."

"And so cause hostility between Catholic Christians and everyone else, like 9/11 and Muslims."

Cardinal Neumann nodded. "That is the idea, though they have not tried it yet, as far as we are aware, but the time is coming, and we must be prepared." He paused a moment, then continued, "We have also heard that they kidnap young adults, the future leaders of the Church, and brutally murder them. About six months ago, a group of seven escaped captivity, the first known survivors."

"Wait, wait, hold on," Jet cut in. "Are you talking about the Lucky Seven?"

"That is what the American media has dubbed them."

Jet sat back, and Charlie groaned. "When in trouble…"

"…blame Holly."

"Pardon?"

"Cardinal," the Admin explained, "what the general populace doesn't know is that *eight* victims actually survived, not seven. The eighth was Holly Harper, their—" She signaled at Jet and Charlie. "—younger sister. As a club consultant, we kept word of her out of the media."

"It all makes sense now."

"It does?" asked Penny.

174

Jet sighed, "Yeah, you see, after her escape, Holly was sent in after Renaldo Devenay, who was evidently an Aureate, even if we didn't know it at the time. Do you remember hearing about the Dragonfly Queen?"

"Oh yeah, I saw that on the news. She was awesome."

"That was Holly," Charlie informed her, "chasing Devenay through Birdswick."

"The club was attempting a power play, trying to warn off anyone else from messing with its members."

"Revenge," the cardinal stated, a more pronounced glower on his face.

"No, Cardinal," Charlie explained, "Holly didn't kill him. It was just a publicity stunt, although I'm betting the club didn't know Devenay's friends were so well organized."

"No, we didn't," the Admin answered, "but if scaring them off didn't work, then drawing them out was the next best thing. It makes them an easier target. They're exposed."

"If both of you are Holly's brothers, then why is Belladonna only after you?" the cardinal asked, nodding at Jet.

"Because Charlie wasn't there," Jet answered, a smile creeping onto his face as a few more pieces of the puzzle fell into place. "Charlie was in Jerusalem. I met Holly and Devenay on the rooftop after her op with the Southern Admin and a couple of field agents. Somehow, they must have gotten footage of his capture. My face would have shown up distorted because I had one of Holly's friends inject me with an intradermal signal disrupter. The Aureate Society must've assumed I was one of the higher-ups and hired Belladonna to assassinate me. Actually, considering her appearance at the conference, she's probably on retainer. They hired her to handle their kills."

175

"But if she didn't even know what you looked like, then why is everyone and their mother trying to kill you?" Charlie asked.

"She doesn't know me as Jet Harper. She only knows me as the Ghost, or Specter."

"Real original," Taylor muttered.

"That's the point, *Detective*," Jet drawled. "If there are six or seven Ghosts out there, interested parties would have trouble determining who is who."

"How do you know you're number six then?"

Jet only answered the Admin with a roguish smile. "*Any*ways, someone who knows me as the Ghost from before I was the Ghost had to have given Belladonna a picture of me. I acquired that particular moniker because no one ever saw me in action and I never left any trace I was there behind." Jet tilted his head up in thought and muttered, "I didn't become an assassin until *after* I left the military so that just leaves my family and…" Jet nodded to himself, even if deep down he'd long-since guessed. "I know who Bella's mentor is." The room watched him expectantly. "It's Voight."

"Voight the Void?"

Jet nodded at Charlie. For the benefit of the rest of the room, he added, "Belladonna's mentor is my old mentor, Heinrich Voight, also known as Voight the Void."

Penny issued a surprised gasp.

"Wait," the Admin ordered, "why didn't she go after anyone else in your family then? Surely Charlie would have been an easier target *before* you went on the road together."

"Well, yes, or actually, no—It doesn't matter! The point is, I know Voight. He's leaning over Belladonna's shoulder and making sure she crosses all her i's and dots all her t's.

"Don't you mean crosses all her *t*'s and dots all her *i*'s?" Penny asked.

"No," Jet deadpanned. He spared the remark no more words. "It makes sense when you really think about it. Belladonna accepts the contract for a static image. The Aureates expect her to handle it, so she figures, what the heck! She can build her reputation by figuring out who I am and killing me, but she *can't* figure out who I am, so Voight decides to give his latest protégé a little hint. All he has to do is track down the static image, which he finds hovering around the Harper family. Voight trained me as Jet Harper, before I was the Ghost, so he would've known immediately that that static image was me."

"But Belladonna doesn't know you as Jet Harper. Why wouldn't Voight have just told her that?" Detective Hall asked.

"No, Voight doesn't do that. He calls it mollycoddling. He would have only given Belladonna a nudge in the right direction, a picture and my codename."

"But she knows we're brothers," Charlie pointed out.

"Yeah, she would've figured that out eventually. I mean, who's been riding shotgun with me this whole time? Charlie Harper, big brother of Holly Harper. Eventually, she'd have connected all the dots."

"So then, you arrest this Belladonna woman, and the Aureate Society's assistant assassin is no longer a threat," Cardinal Neumann stated.

"No, Voight would never allow her contract to fall through. It would reflect poorly on him, for those that knew his part in it anyways, so probably the Aureates and a select few others. Considering the likely size of their organization, a tarnished reputation could cost him a lot of contracts in the future. Plus, he would've wasted time training Belladonna for nothing. He'd finish what she started just to get back at us for ending her career early."

"Revenge?"

"Yes," Jet answered smartly, "he's protective that way, although less because he cares and more out of pride."

"Is that why the floor exploded?"

"Yeah, that was Voight keeping an eye on his assets. If you want to separate the Aureate Society from its assassins, you'll need to deal with them both."

The detectives stood, and Cardinal Neumann mimicked theirs movements. "What about the missing children and Cardinal Weatherford?"

"We'll look for the kids as soon as we deal with Belladonna and Void. Hopefully, we'll find Cardinal Weatherford somewhere along the way."

"But Admin," Charlie rushed, "the longer those kids stay with the Aureates, the worse off they'll be in the long run."

"Then you better start looking." She held out a membership card to him, the kind Jet had seen his parents flash every now and again when things had gotten really desperate.

Charlie glanced at it warily. "Jet needs it more."

"Oh, that's right," she said, slipping her hand into her pocket and tossing another one at Jet. He caught it expertly, a flat, three-dimensional piece of gold, three-fourths the size of a credit card. Its front and back were painted black with a three-barred dragonfly on one side and only three words on the other. "Here be dragons…" the Admin read aloud.

"…And so, here am I."

She turned again to Charlie, who was still staring at her hand in indecision. "It'll be easier to track down those children with our resources at your disposal."

Charlie glanced at Jet over her shoulder, who shrugged unhelpfully, then snatched the card from her and tucked it in his pocket. "I serve only one master," he told her sternly.

She nodded at him. "As you say, Father. Come, Mr. Harper, we have work to do."

The detectives filed out of the room behind her, as did Penny. Only Jet lingered in the doorway, first watching Penny exit the room, then peering over at Charlie. "I could help you find them first," he offered.

"No, you'd better go. No point getting on her bad side already. I've got this."

"You sure?"

"Always."

Jet nodded. Then he, too, was gone.

Chapter 27

Charlie could feel the cardinal glaring at his back, his bitter almond eyes digging into the soft spot between Charlie's spine and shoulder blade, so the young priest took a deep breath and twisted around very slowly in a poor attempt to put off the inevitable. Instantly, he wrestled back the grimace that threatened to burst free the second he spotted the scowl on Cardinal Neumann's face.

"Your actions are deplorable."

"Which actions specifically?" If he was going to get scolded, Charlie would know for which part at least.

"I saw the gun in your hands when you entered my suite."

"If you noticed, Cardinal, I never actually fired it." Charlie could very well picture himself, gun in hand, staring dumbly at the assassin who had just kissed him.

"Do you think I'm deaf or merely a fool?"

"Cardinal?"

"I heard the shots."

Charlie thumbed his rosary and sighed. It had taken a lot to convince the detectives to retrieve it from evidence for him. Now it was his only comfort. "My brother and I are both efficient marksman, Cardinal. That means we're good enough to purposefully miss our targets when we want to."

"What good is aiming to miss?"

"It's spatial manipulation. Firing rounds at certain places around our assailants forced them to react in specific, predicable ways, allowing us to control their movements. It's a complex martial arts concept that mixes reaction and anticipation. Of the two, reaction is preferred. Anticipation permits deceit. Together, however, they allow one to see every possible outcome at once, like a chess player controlling the board."

The cardinal studied Charlie carefully. "You think a lot like a militant."

Charlie frowned at the implication. "Both of my parents were field agents for a while, and they didn't want us to grow up TV kids, wasting away in front of a television set, so yeah, we went outside and played all sorts of war games, shooting rubber bands at each other, sparring. It was fun. But our parents never promoted violence. If we used our skills for anything other than self-defense, we'd get in loads of trouble."

The cardinal hummed, unconvinced. "You didn't have to join your brother, the spy, or whatever it is he does, in his quest to find me."

Assassin—you know he's an assassin, Cardinal. Don't be difficult.

"You could have stayed in the hall with the others. Maybe then Cardinal Weatherford would not be missing."

"Is that it then? Are you blaming me for that?"

"I am not. I am merely pointing out that you had a choice, and you chose violence."

"No," Charlie ground back, "I chose action. I think causing someone a small, fleeting physical pain in order save the life of another is justified. Don't you?"

"There is a line—"

"I know there's a line. I've spent the last seven years trying to push myself as far away from it as I possibly could, but all that's ever done is make matters worse. I was in that cohort of seminarians studying in the Holy Land last semester, the cohort of seminarians that was caught in the middle of a violent firefight. I did nothing. I did nothing, Cardinal, and two of my brother seminarians were killed. Two! I'll tread the line carefully. I can promise you that. But God has given me the ability to act, and I damn well will." Charlie wished he could snatch the words back just as soon as he'd said them, but they had already taken shape and slipped into the ears of his superior, who eyed him coolly for them.

"Will you?"

"I'm sorry, Cardinal," Charlie offered. "It's been a very trying week thus far."

The cardinal nodded in curious thought. "I often wonder if Jesus ever slapped Peter upside the head for any of his more careless remarks." Charlie choked down his laughter at the image and merely smiled shyly. "Tread carefully, my young friend, for I see a great, strange potential in you that the Enemy would be a fool not to seek for himself, and in matters of the soul, he is no fool."

Charlie accepted the warning graciously.

"Now, how are we going to find those children?"

Charlie set up a large grid of the United States on a corkboard he had a young agent wheel in from another room.

Penny slipped in with it. "They told me to wait in the lounge, but I'm getting kind of antsy. I'd like to watch if you don't mind," she said. The cardinal, oddly, deferred to Charlie, who, though uncomfortable with the authority, admitted her.

Charlie requisitioned a trolley of supplies—yarn, markers, pins, and a club laptop. He'd need the access. Then he grabbed a pin from a pot-shaped vessel, scrolled down on his computer, and marked a spot on the map: Somerset, Kentucky. "What are you doing?"

"I'm pinning the locations of all the children that went missing and were never found in the last two years. The rate's about twenty percent higher than it should be, which shows a direct correlation to the Aureate Society's kidnapping scheme."

"We have noticed the trend ourselves. It is possible that this is not the first time they have taken to kidnapping."

Charlie concurred, "They likely aren't stupid enough to do it continuously for too long, but it's bad news for us if they've been in business awhile."

"Do you want some help pinning?" Penny asked.

Penny and Cardinal Neumann joined him for the next half hour. There were fifty-two pins, fifty-two children, fifty-two reasons to work harder.

They were brought lunch not too long later, and the cardinal urged Charlie to eat. "Later. I've got to figure this out first."

"Father Harper, do not argue with me. Eating will make you far more productive."

Charlie stared at the map despondently, then conceded. Briefly, he wondered what sort of trouble Jet was getting into, and belatedly, he thought of me, an object of these monsters' ridicule. *Holly!* "Of course," he said to himself, swallowing down the rest of his sandwich and racing back to work.

Penny and the cardinal watched him with several levels of intrigue and concern. "What are you doing?" Penny asked, coming to stand beside him.

Charlie's fingers flew across the keyboard as fast as he could will them. "My sister's the answer. How stupid of me not to realize it until just now." They didn't bother asking again, but he continued regardless, "When my sister was kidnapped, no one bothered to investigate her abductors. You see, the club waited a freakishly long time to start looking for her, and by then, she'd already given them her general location. Since the club didn't know about the Aureate Society then, they went about dismantling the network of men and women involved mainly through their consultants in Birdswick." Charlie shoved the laptop screen out at them. "See!"

"What are we looking at?" Cardinal Neumann whispered to Penny. She shrugged unhelpfully.

"It's the route they traveled when they abducted my sister. See, look," he said again, tracing the northbound line displayed on the screen that formed a misshapen racetrack. "They rented their car from this location, Speedy Track. My sister was abducted here," he said, pointing at the southernmost tip of Texas. "Then they traveled north again past their rental location, here, to a private airstrip, here, owned by one of the guys that took her. From there, they flew her north to Alaska."

"Okay, but what does that have to do with the missing kids?" Penny asked.

"This car rental service was used during each of the eighteen young adult abductions seven months ago. The club never made the connection because they didn't know about the Aureate Society then and they had other means of tracking down those involved. If the Aureates are all part of an intricate network, as I suspect, they probably use what's already available to them. So, all I have to do is search for vehicles rented from Speedy Track in the regions the kids were kidnapped."

"But if it's a popular car service, there could be dozens of them in each location."

"True, except I've never heard of Speedy Track, never seen any commercials, never been pitched a rental for one of their cars at the airport. I've been all over the country, and this is the first I've ever heard of it. It's either a small, little-used car service or just a front for one of the society's many resources."

Charlie's fingers clicked over the keys, pulling up surveillance footage from club consultants in the fifty-two locations children had gone missing and running the Speedy Track logo through a filter. "Look!" Forty of the counties found Speedy Track vehicles in the vicinity around the time the children had gone missing.

"So, twelve of them were probably not kidnapped by the Aureate Society?"

"Actually, several of the children were taken from the same county, so only nine of them are probably not their victims. Now, all we have to do is figure out what locations most of these cars have visited." Charlie frowned at his computer screen.

"What is it?" the cardinal asked.

"Well, the kidnappings took place all over the country. That means there are hundreds of club cameras that likely caught them making the trip."

"Isn't that a good thing?"

"It would be except…that's a lot of footage to look through."

"So, what are we gonna do?"

Charlie thought for a moment, then released an enlightened smirk. "I know a computer algorithm that'll do the work for us. At the very least, we should be able to determine the last place these kids were taken before they went off-grid."

"Where'd you learn how to do that?"

"A BCIS elective."

Penny's brows came together. "All I learned in BCIS was a little coding."

Charlie shrugged. He might have done a little independent study on the side.

It took Charlie a few minutes longer than it should have, out of practice as he was, but eventually, he managed the right string of codes, and moments later, a map was displayed across the screen. Routes were highlighted in blue, and places that overlapped pinged red. "There, Catawba and Peterstown."

"Two?"

"Yeah, an approach from two different directions. The best place to hide a lot of missing kids would be in a sparsely populated area, like a region of the Appalachian Mountains."

"Excellent, let us inform the Admin so that she may send someone to rescue them."

Charlie nodded and swept out.

He found her in the tactical room with several field agents, who sat around observing her discussion with Jet. One looked vaguely familiar, but he couldn't be sure where or when he'd seen him. Charlie gave himself a mental shake. *So not important right now.*

Jet sat on the edge of a table, features drawn low in boredom. He was muttering something about the stupidity of their plan when he caught sight of Charlie standing in the doorway. Jet's tone lightened immediately, and the Admin turned to find the source of his delight.

"We've located the children."

"Really?" she asked in disbelief.

"Yes, they're in the Appalachian Mountains, somewhere between Peterstown and Catawba."

"Somewhere between..." She didn't bother completing her statement. "We don't have time to scour 3,000 square miles, Father Harper. Please, just go."

"It's not 3,000 square miles, and I'm more than capable of—"

"Getting in my way? Clearly. You need to go back to the conference room and wait 'til we're finished here."

Charlie felt his nose twitch. Oh, did he *need* to do anything? Jet shot Charlie a look that tempered him. *Keep calm. Just breathe through it. Count to ten. Yeah, ten. One, two, three...* "Those children can't wait for you to be good and ready, Admin—"

"Then go rescue them yourself."

Charlie looked at Jet.

Jet looked at Charlie. *She told you to do it*, he seemed to be saying, his eyes full of mirth.

Charlie pressed his lips together. *She didn't really mean it.*

Jet smiled. *So?* Then he tilted his head to one side. *What's it going to be, Your Priestliness?*

Charlie stared at Jet a moment longer. "My apologies for disturbing you, Admin. I'll be going then." He shot a nod at Jet and left.

Charlie found the cardinal waiting for him anxiously right where he'd left him. "Where's Penny?"

"She went for a snack," he answered offhandedly. "Well, what did she say?"

Charlie scratched his head. "She told me to go myself."

"What?"

"I don't think she actually meant it, but since she's not going now, I think maybe I might."

"That sounds dangerous."

"Sure, but those kids need me, and I've got the skills to help them, so I will."

"Help who with what?" Penny asked, returning with a granola bar and bottle of apple juice.

"I'm going to rescue those kids myself."

"We," the cardinal quickly amended. "*We* will rescue them." Charlie shot him an incredulous look. "Well, I will not permit you to go alone. Besides, this is *my* investigation, remember? Straight from the Vatican."

"O-kay then."

"I'm going, too."

"No," they both answered.

"But I want to help. I'm an athlete, you know. I can keep up. I've even taken self-defense."

"No, Penny, I need you here," Charlie told her.

"For what?"

He handed her the yarn and markers. "I need you to map the routes on the board, calculate distances, mark times, all of it."

"What for?"

He sighed. "Penny, listen. We need to know everything about their abductions if we're going to help those kids recover from this. Trust me, the more we know, the better. Even the minutest detail could help us help them. Plus, we may need it to catch everyone mixed up in this mess."

"Can't your laptop do all of that?" she grumbled.

"It could if someone actually programmed it to, but I have no idea how to do that, and with those guys twiddling their thumbs in there, as if Jet actually needs their help, they're just wasting time. As soon as we find those kids, the Aureates are gonna scatter like bugs. We need to catch them before they do. Please, Penny. I honestly don't want you to go because it *will* be dangerous and you *could* get hurt, but I also really *do* need you to do this."

"Fine," she said, "if you think it's that important."

"Trust me, it is."

She conceded just as the door swung open to reveal…the vaguely familiar man from Jet's entourage. "Your brother sent me to see if you needed anything for your—" He coughed. "—trip."

The British accent struck a chord in Charlie, and he felt like this man might have something to do with me. "Maybe just a ride."

The slender man reached a hand into the left pocket of his slacks and revealed a set of car keys. He brushed them on his pant leg, pushed his already folded sleeve up farther, and hurled them at the unsuspecting cardinal. Reflexively, Charlie's hand came up to catch them, inches from Cardinal Neumann's startled face. "You *are* a Harper then, so full of surprises."

"You must be Amadeus Twain. Holly's told me all about you."

"I'm honored."

"Are you? I didn't say they were good things."

"It matters little to me." He nodded at the keys in Charlie's hand. "Your brother says he has a spare car stashed nearby and that you are most welcome to it." Twain handed Charlie a slip of paper with an address. "Are you sure you don't need anything else from me? I could get you a weapon, a non-lethal one even if you'd like. Perhaps a bō?"

Oooo, that was tempting. He missed the weight of his own staff laid long and cool in his hands. "No, but thanks for the offer, Mr. Twain."

"As you wish." He departed then.

"Who was that?" Penny asked.

"One of my sister's very weird friends." He turned to Cardinal Neumann. "Shall we?"

The cardinal nodded, and with a wave to Penny, they also left.

Their trip would take nearly seven and a half hours, and Charlie could only hope the car Jet had stored away was comfortable.

Twenty minutes later, they rolled up the door of a storage unit to find a vintage Charger nestled cozily in it. Well, that was rather conspicuous. "Your brother has expensive taste."

Charlie just sighed. *You have no idea.*

Chapter 28

Jet was amused.

No, he was downright tickled. Charlie hadn't pulled something like this in years. The Admin would be sorry. Those five little words she'd uttered would turn a mole hill into a mountain, but as much as he wanted to spend precious seconds picturing what her expression would look like when she realized just what she'd unleashed upon the world, he had to focus on his own problem—getting into Voight's tower without getting dead.

"When?"

"At night."

"What about the nightshift?"

"Voight's tower never shuts down, but the smallest number of employees come in during the nightshift. That means the least number of civilians to worry about."

"And less for you to hide behind."

Jet issued a humorless laugh. This lady was starting to get on his nerves. "Do you always make your final judgment of people when you first meet them? That you even think I'd do something like that is just ridiculous."

"We could try to get them all out beforehand," a nearby agent offered, halting their latest argument before it could start. It definitely wasn't their first dispute, and clearly some of their spectators were getting fed up.

"Good idea," the Admin said. "We'll pull the fire alarm, evacuate the building."

Jet didn't hesitate in shutting her down.

"No?"

"No," Twain agreed, "that won't work. The building compartmentalizes. If we pull the fire alarm on the bottom floor, only the bottom floor will evacuate."

"That has to be against fire code regulation."

Jet and Twain gave *that* agent a hard look, who shrunk back from the force of their collective gazes. "Do you really think Voight gives a damn about fire code regulation? He can change the building's computer commands whenever he wants. It's like flipping a switch."

"What if there's a real emergency?" the Admin asked.

"Compartmentalization *happens* in real emergencies. Voight would rather watch the whole building burn to the ground than risk someone coming up that isn't supposed to, and you're stupider than I already think you are if you don't realize Voight has nifty escape routes on nearly every floor."

She glowered at him. "Then how do we know he won't take off running the moment he sees you?"

"Seasoned assassins don't flee when confronted by other assassins."

"Belladonna did."

"I said *seasoned* assassins, didn't I? Belladonna's a rookie. The second she realized I outmatched her, she ran. I bet she'll stick around when she's got her mentor at her six, or she *thinks* her mentor's at her six. He isn't likely to interfere. She won't learn anything that way, or at least, that's what he always used to tell me. When I beat Belladonna, Voight'll turn up. It's a pride thing. Plus, he thinks he's better than me." *And he's probably looking forward to it*, he silently added.

"Is he?"

Jet shrugged. "Never walk into a fight expecting to win, and never start a fight expecting to lose. You're finished both ways."

"So, how are we getting you in?"

"Air vents?" an agent suggested.

"Incendiary combustion and roasted Jet on the menu."

"Elevator shafts?"

"High-powered lasers. Sliced Jet anyone?"

"Roof entry?"

"Sulfuric acid sprinklers triggered by motion sensors."

"No catchy culinary-related killing for that one?"

Twain scoffed. "Have you ever tried eating something burned by sulfuric acid?"

Even Jet stared at him oddly. "Have you?"

Twain shrugged but didn't answer, so Jet just shook it off. "*We* are going to leave most of the work to *me*."

"And what are *you* going to do exactly?"

Jet smiled. "Why, I'm gonna walk through the front door, of course."

Voight's tower was forty-two stories high. Every floor housed a different organization Voight owned, operated, or sponsored. The ground level, the lobby, had marble floors, reflective paneling, and a silver scheme meant to tip off security about any ill-meaning guests. Jet knew they'd see him coming, but that was rather the point.

The building's first four floors were visible from the lobby, open and welcoming. They were also the only public floors, filled with small shops selling makeup and haircare products. "For appearances," Voight had once told him. "See, Jet, you have to lay careful tracks in the wrong direction for anyone a little too interested in you."

That's why Jet had opted out of a day job. He preferred to go off-grid and simply disappear. Too many variables needed to be accounted for, too many ways to go wrong, exposed and vulnerable in explicit routine. Someone would find you, and someone would kill you. Why set up an extensive and elaborate front for the flies when fading away and existing only in the realm of the dead was easier?

The next sixteen floors were headquarters to more than sixty-three different organizations, and the following ten floors were for manufacturing, testing, and rehabilitation. Voight owned an organization known as Phas-Tech that developed a variety of braces and prosthetic limbs.

Jet rolled his shoulders, uncomfortable with the reminder. Voight was known for his dedication to wounded vets and his philanthropy. Phas-Tech had been created specifically for them. Jet had an intimate knowledge of that. He'd met Voight on one of his routine runs to the lower floors in the rehab clinic.

Jet shook himself.

The next seven floors were for storage. Voight preferred to keep everything together and in one place. It was a calculated risk. Law enforcement only had to gain access to one location to discover all manner of illegality, but Voight was prepared for that. If anyone aside from the man himself stepped foot on any of those floors without explicit permission, they'd be blown sky high. Voight was a fan of explosives. Jet smirked. Smarty would've liked him under different circumstances.

The thirty-eighth floor was home to Voight's personal offices, and the thirty-ninth and fortieth floors were for training, himself and his protégés alike. They were filled with just about every obstacle one could imagine and could be molded into a maze of death under order from the main computer, which he housed in his quarters for safekeeping.

That really only left the top two floors. When Voight was in town, the penthouse was his safest haven—*was* being the operative word. Jet intended to rectify that.

Yes, Jet remembered the building well. It was the place where he'd learned his art, where he'd trained his hands to go farther than they ever had before, where death had become his closest friend and now he returned one last time to say goodbye, at least, to their regular dates.

"Aren't you ready yet?"

Jet glared at the glass doors across the street. "It's not about me being ready. It's about *them* being ready. See that guard glancing at his watch?"

"It's too early for a shift change," the Admin said over the radio.

"You're right. He's getting tired. Tired means sloppy. Sloppy means it's time to go."

Jet stretched once more, letting his joints pop happily. He sighed. Time for the fat lady to sing.

Jet trekked across the street past angry cars. Chicago was so blinding at night, so many lights and lamps and vehicles driving by. Jet was both mesmerized and annoyed. He never could sleep in this part of Chicago, not without the thickest shades known to man blocking out the eternal daylight.

A car behind Jet swerved away from him as if concerned about getting too close. Then Jet pulled open the doors of Voight's tower, and immediately, the eyes of all personnel fell on him. Jet counted four—two security guards, a receptionist, and a lounging custodian.

Jet knew he was quite the sight. Meeting up with the Shoe Crew had brought back a lot of memories, so his chosen wardrobe paid tribute to his days in the desert, figuratively speaking of course.

Jet paused just beyond the threshold and tucked a hand in the pocket of his black cargo pants. Rhythmically, he tapped a steel-toed combat boot on the marble flooring and, after several beats, strolled right up to the front desk, feet away from the startled receptionist. "Hello, Misses—" He annunciated each letter of her name. "—Fleming, would you be so kind as to vacate the premises?" He issued her a smile that could melt the sun.

Her eyes grew wide, and she was suddenly incapable of coherent thought. The security guard nearest to him balked at his audacity. Jet heard him and his partner move, so he drew his sidearm and quickly dispatched them both. "Now, ladies, if you wouldn't mind?"

The woman fled in terror, the confused custodian hot on her heels. He sauntered over to the main elevator, packed himself in it, and aimed for the upper floors.

Naturally, he was stopped on the fourth. Jet groaned. It was going to be a long ride up.

By the time the elevator dinged, Jet had attached himself to the ceiling, and as the doors slid open, an onslaught of bullets sprayed the elevator car beneath him. Jet gripped the grooves of the high walls as tight as he dared. Mentally, he examined the fourth floor.

There were two elevators in the building, one that was wide and made for accessibility and the smaller one that Jet was currently occupying. His elevator rose up by the balcony and spilled onto a long walkway.

Jet fell as soon as the last shot was fired, dropped/rolled out of the elevator, and hurled himself off the balcony so he could swing onto the floor below. He hit the marble hard, broke-fell, and spun up. He estimated it'd take them one minute to descend, so Jet took cover behind a kiosk between both entry points, the elevator and the stairwell, and gripped a gun in each hand. He crossed them over his chest, head bowed and ears alert.

Seconds later, he heard the elevator motor running and footsteps on the stairs. *Three. Two. One.* They never really stood a chance. Jet had been an expert marksman since his youth, and back in the day, he could take on any of his special ops squadmates without any trouble, so as each of his targets dropped, Jet's thoughts strayed to Belladonna. What had her tipping point been, the one that turned her future to harbinger of death? Everyone had a reason.

He rolled back, took a few more shots, then stood at the ready. Twelve down. How many more to go?

Jet hummed a catchy tune as he trailed back to the elevator. The flicker of movement from its inside edge didn't startle him. Jet just raised his left hand at the figure and fired a shot at his neck, then grabbed him with one arm and hauled the man from his ride. Jet hit the button for the thirty-ninth floor. He had a hunch he wouldn't make it any farther.

Jet warmed the corner of the car the way his last mark had, and when the elevator dinged, he took his time easing himself out of it. Jet dove just as the rounds started, leapt up, and began to return fire. These guys were better, more organized, more efficient. That was fine. They could share a cell for a while.

Jet reloaded his guns. Then, dodging around obstacles he was trying very hard to ignore, he went to work. These marks were better covered, so he wove through posts and low-hanging ropes and picked them off carefully. *Take their rearguard.* Jet slipped up behind them. There were five. He snipped off a round and immediately twisted back around for cover, narrowly dodging the spray of bullets that followed. Then he rolled under a large hanging block. *Take their point.* Their backs were to Jet, a response to his prior attack, and firing a round off at their point-turned-rear guard was easy.

Jet frowned to himself. He could read the Marine training all over them. He didn't like picking off ex-military. He was a vet himself after all, but these guys were on the wrong side of his gun, and he sure as hell wasn't backing down, not with all that was on the line.

And wasn't that the story of his life, a rite of passage that kept on coming. Once you were in, there was no getting out.

Jet spun around and shot another. The man dropped immediately as the final shooter took cover. Jet looked for an opening, but every time he peeked out, his opponent let loose a few rounds, inches from his head. Jet sighed, finally acknowledging the structures in the room as more than obstacles…or perhaps *more* as obstacles, an obstacle course to be exact.

Beams were laid across pits that in his early training had been filled with foam. Now, they were empty, like they had been in his later days, where one wrong move could put him back in a chair for the rest of his life. There were swinging ropes, dropping columns, automatic weapons replacing those old-school arrow traps, even blades slicing through the air, or they would've been if the system were on.

Jet kicked a hanging target that looped around to the other side of his cover. Immediately, he rolled out, gun coming up from his low position and taking aim. The soldier had fallen for Jet's feint. Distracted by the movement, he turned too late. Jet was already firing.

Slowly, Jet lowered his weapon. *Fireteam, dealt with.*

But the light tap of boots sprung him up and launched him behind a grounded column. Belladonna was sauntering over, a sharp gleam in her eyes. "Hello, Specter."

Jet sighed in exasperation. "In English, it's Ghost, Bella."

"What you'll be very, very soon."

"Sur—"

The floodlamps came on, pouring out bright, blinding light. Belladonna grunted where she was just as the whirring thrum of a generator tore through the open floor, walls slowly sinking down from the ceiling in a new course, *always* a new course. *Voight's playing with us.*

"Bella—"

"Don't talk!" For a moment, Jet dared hope she'd found a reason to end their feud. "I'm going to kill you now." Or not. "But first, I want to see if the rumors about you are true."

"Which ones?" Jet asked, a little curious in spite of himself.

He heard the click of two mags sliding out and crashing to the floor. "You like playing fair. You have honor, or so they say."

Jet let the mag from one of his own guns slide to the ground, then jumped from cover and aimed. Her eyes were wide with surprise, but he fired with no regret.

A wall dropped out of its slow descent at the last moment, deflecting Jet's shot just as the rest of the walls fell into place. They were in a complex pattern of rooms now. Every room would contain a plethora of obstacles. Some rooms would be small, others large. Some would only contain one or two traps. Some would have several.

Normally, the whole course would've been a breeze, a good workout, if anything, but Belladonna came hurtling through the open doorway connecting her first room to Jet's second. He sighed. He'd have to deal with her the whole time now, too.

She'd left her guns behind, and Jet took a second to wonder about that. Then she was hurtling blow after blow at him, and Jet was waiting for whatever laid behind Door Number 2 to rear its ugly head.

Click. Click. *Click*.

Jet disengaged from Belladonna with a swift kick to the gut just as the flamethrowers roasted the air between them. A shallow hiss sounded in his ear, and Jet dug out his earwig to hang by his throat. He'd need every sense active and unencumbered to survive this.

Belladonna just glared at him from across the room as she waited for the flames to dwindle. Then Jet was somersaulting under a flying row of javelins. Bella jumped to avoid them at the last second as Jet sprung up from his roll, jabbing at her collarbone with his gun before holstering it. *I guess the rumors are true*, Jet thought, acknowledging the change in circumstances.

He swept at her legs and sent her careening down with him just as another row of javelins cut through the air. Then he rolled backwards into a stand, throwing himself through the next door…

…and right off the floor. He dangled over an open pit for a moment, caught a bit off guard. He took a quick glance at what was below. *Mei Hua Zhuang*—it was a room filled with plum blossom piles, high, narrow stumps about as wide as half of Jet's foot.

Belladonna came at him, charging, so Jet kicked at the wall and propelled himself onto a far stump just as she flew into the room and onto one herself. But the piles weren't made of wood. If Jet or Bella tumbled off one of them, they'd splash into a pool of acid. Voight generally changed up the type. Jet couldn't identify which kind it was this time, though it was strong enough to pinch at his temples as he breathed in the noxious fumes.

Belladonna held a javelin in one hand and skipped towards Jet, who immediately hopped backwards towards the exit. He ducked a stab from her javelin and jumped the following swipe. Fighting effectively on *Mei Hua Zhuang* required flexibility Jet's back no longer had. The thought alone was enough to bring up phantom pain, so he caught one of Belladonna's strikes, pulled her forwards, and kicked her back again. Limbs flailing, Belladonna fought for balance. Jet took the opportunity to spin on the ball of his foot and dart towards the door. He made the final leap easily and hauled himself up.

The next room was larger than the others. Jet ran across the system of beams that took up the whole expanse of the floor, Belladonna fast on his heels. This, he could manage.

She caught up to him half way through the maze and the harsh hiss of air being split was their only warning. Jet fell into Belladonna just as the pendulum swung behind him. There were several of them, each swinging on separate rhythms.

Jet and Belladonna locked fists to wrists, and Jet yanked himself back just as another blade sliced the air in front of him, then pushed forward to avoid its returned. He blocked several hits from Belladonna, then skipped over to another beam. She dove after him, catching the dull top of a blade in her ribs. Latching onto it, she let the javelin fall from her hands and rode up to the ceiling.

Jet took the opportunity to escape the room, leaping from beam to beam and across those without any support. He dove through the next door and rolled under a dropping column in a rendering of Bowser's Castle.

He jumped a couple of small open pits and evaded a few more dropping columns. A knife caught him by surprise. He'd turned to locate Belladonna, and only that saved him from a less than stellar end. Her blade cut past his defenses and split his left cheek. Then Belladonna was flying towards him, another knife already in hand.

He vaulted into the next room in time to duck a shot of the Olympic variety. Belladonna followed shortly, flinging her knife at him. He dodged it and narrowly avoided another shot from behind. Just as he reoriented, Belladonna charged, fists raised and ready. He parried her strikes over and over again, dancing around the rocketing projectiles like they were part of her attack. He could hear them, loading up in their chambers to fire, and even with his mind on so many things, Jet was in his element.

Belladonna was a poison specialist. She should have known better than to challenge a frontline combative assault specialist hand to hand. It dawned on Jet then that Bella was likely assuming whatever she'd coated her blade in would be taking effect very soon, but Jet was always prepared, especially for the obvious.

He spun away from her to avoid her fist and an iron ball hurtling through the air, but another fired immediately after. Jet didn't have time to think. He hurled himself sideways and onto the floor.

"Oomph!"

Jet offered her a sympathetic wince. Belladonna was holding her hip, doing everything she could now just to dodge the shots. Jet army-crawled to the doorway and hauled himself up. Belladonna limped after him.

Metal scraped against metal, and even after so many years, Jet recognized the sound at once. He jerked back behind the wall, still in the room where iron projectiles were denting the cement floors and imbedding in the walls. Belladonna followed after him into the open doorway. "Bella, do—"

The guns discharged, and Belladonna was sprayed with a hail of bullets, an assassin no more.

Jet sighed tiredly. *What a waste.*

He scanned the next room from the corner, trying to avoid the projectiles still hurtling through the air. The wall of a hundred guns seemed to be waiting for him, so he surmised it must be motion activated. The door to the final exit was on the opposite end of the room, but not quite aligned with his own.

Jet waited a moment, then lifted one of the shots lying near his foot and rolled it into the next room. The guns fired, and Jet made a break for it, listening intently for the sound of each reloading. He was only half way through when he heard them gear up to fire. But Jet knew Voight. The man wasn't unreasonable. This was a training arena. There had to be a way to win.

So, Jet did what he'd always done when Voight had thrown him a curve ball—he ducked. He ducked and hoped not to get cut off at the knees.

Jet threw himself to the floor on his shins, riding the momentum forward and flattening his back to the floor. The shots fired by row, top to bottom, almost too fast for the human eye or ear to follow. The tsunami of ammunition swished right over Jet's head just as he cleared the door.

He laid on his back for a minute, panting harshly and relishing the rush. *That. Was. Close.* Then he hauled himself to his feet and made for the stairs, popping his earwig back in as he went.

"That was insane—"

"Be quiet!" Jet hissed.

"Sorry."

Jet skipped the next floor, in no mood to deal with another obstacle course from hell. He kicked the door open with his steel-toed boots and dove forward just as the emergency door slid shut behind him. Anyone else would have lost a limb.

Voight's personal quarters were as sparse as the man himself. He'd put up some artwork someone had claimed was the epitome of exquisiteness but had no actual taste for the stuff himself. It was just a front for his real passions, which he'd hidden away in the dark recesses of his soul. His personal effects were nowhere near this building. Jet was absolutely certain of that.

Jet marched forward, gun cradled snuggly in both hands. If he'd lacked a little less finesse, he might have wished for an assault rifle, but Jet had class. He wouldn't waste a single bullet. He pivoted on his heel to scan the front room. Voight had a square couch and a couple of matching armchairs facing a flat screen TV, but Jet knew that the painful-looking lounge chair no one would ever voluntarily choose was really Voight's. Up against the wall, it gave him no view of the TV but impeccable sight of the rest of the room and all its entry points. It was perfectly unassuming, and Voight always claimed it.

A tick from behind him sent him swiveling aggressively. Voight was standing behind the counter of his lavish kitchenette, watching Jet with a tight scowl. His grey eyes were narrower than Jet had ever seen them, and he'd aged ten years in two, his once ebony hair now sprinkled with white and the skin of his high cheekbones less charmingly smooth. "After everything, this is what it comes down to—the Hunter's Game."

Jet's ears twitched. Something wasn't right. "Is that what they're calling it now?"

"Your sister made a startling impression on our dissociated community."

Jet's eyes narrowed. Voight was the only assassin he knew that could make this situation personal, but Jet said nothing about it, sidestepping the trap cautiously and awaiting the next. "Well, aren't you just a ray of sunshine today?"

"Belladonna had potential."

"Your course took her out, not me."

Voight nodded in agreement. "I guess that's true. You always had more anyways."

"Had more?"

"Potential," he drawled, exasperation coating his tongue. "Why did it have to be you?" He shook his head then ever so slightly, eyes never leaving his target. "I have business to conduct and no time for petty disappointments."

Voight raised his gun, previously hidden beneath the counter.

Jet didn't bother poising his own, and Voight fired unhindered.

"Harper!" Jet only blinked, then fired off his own weapon at Voight's figure, which pixelated and vanished. "What just happened?"

"Advanced holographic imaging. Lots of smoke and mirrors," Jet explained.

205

The room silenced, and Jet let the gears in his mind shift further back in time.

"*Disappointments have no place in society. They should all be shot and killed.*"

"*That seems kind of harsh.*"

"*Disappointments are the reasons Man fails and good people die.*"

Sh—!

Jet was running before his brain could finish the expletive. Voight's private elevator dinged, and the resounding boom that followed swept past him in waves. Jet jumped at the first surge, shot the window at the next, and curled up at the last, balling through the semi-shattered glass and toppling out of it just as the trickling blast was reignited by several subsequent detonations. Flame and shrapnel followed him out.

Jet let the empty air rock him, arms still half covering his face, crystal shards glittering past him.

And then he was falling.

Jet shoved a hand under his light Kevlar vest and pulled down. The chute on his back tore open and sent him sailing through the air, bits of building crumbling down behind him. The rest of the structure seemed fairly stable, but the explosion had leveled at least four floors, and already in the distance, Jet could make out the flash of colored light from the racing fire engines below. "You better get your guys in there," Jet advised, "and disable all of Voight's fail-safes. Wouldn't want those innocent firefighters getting caught in his traps."

"Gotcha, Phantom," some agent answered.

"Oh, for the love of—" he cut himself off. "Just pick a translation."

"I thought you said experienced assassins don't run from trouble," the Admin quipped.

"I did," Jet answered grimly. "And he didn't." Jet watched the street below grow. He'd navigated away from the tower. With any luck, everyone would be far too busy staring at the building that was currently on fire, and no one would notice him drifting off down the street. "He was never here to begin with."

Chapter 29

Charlie drove through the night, never so eager to get somewhere as he was then. He glanced at the cardinal, who had reclined in his seat as much as he could, his fingers threaded and resting just below his heart. He wasn't sleeping. Charlie was sure of it. Though his eyes were closed and his breaths were even, they came too shallow and too quick. The man was meditating or praying or both.

Dissonance curled in Charlie's gut, reverberating like the strum of a chord in the belly of a bass, a thrum, thrum, thrum in alternating pitches. Charlie teetered on the line even then, uncertainty tugging at the edge of his focus. Was this the right decision? Or was guilt forcing him into something he shouldn't even be contemplating? The cardinal no longer seemed to care, but Charlie knew the only reason he had so quickly hidden his contempt was because children's lives were on the line and the innocents commanded his entire mind. Charlie envied that benevolent fixation.

Focus!

He pulled into a small town, the name of which he never caught. Cardinal Neumann's eyes came open, and Charlie watched from his peripheral vision as the man took in the time, the digital numbers reading ten past midnight. "I think we should rent a room for the night. Tracking through forestry in the dark is dangerous. We'll get an early start tomorrow."

The cardinal nodded. "I called Bishop Irving. There is a parish not far from here. We will attend their early Mass in the morning."

Early Mass, Charlie thought, nodding distractedly. The rinky-dink motel with a vacancy sign in the window was giving him some creepy vibes, and he wasn't sure he wanted to stop at—

Sunday! Oh Great God of Mercy, it was Sunday! When had that happened? Where had the week gone? What—

But there was nothing to be worried about. He hadn't really missed anything.

Charlie bit his lip, now far more frazzled by his slight oversight than concerned with their sleeping arrangements. He parked the car and entered the lobby. An elderly man with wrinkles on his face and a deep scar over his left eyebrow sat behind the counter. Legs shaking with effort, he stood to greet Charlie. "Hello there."

"Hi, I need a room with double beds, one night only please."

"Of course, Reverend."

The senior rang it up as Charlie opened his wallet, pulling out an array of cards and thumbing through them one at a time. He snagged his Visa after a moment of fumbling and thrust it out, but the man refused it. Charlie offered him a puzzled frown.

"No, that's alright. It's on the house." Charlie was used to getting free stuff. People had the tendency to throw gifts at priests, a mixture of intentions behind them that shifted between honest charity and attempts to buy paradise, but free hotel rooms were not a common offering. "You're something special."

"Sir?" Charlie asked, his card still out as if insisting use.

"A man of God in more ways than one." The elder turned out his collar, and the three-barred dragonfly of the silent club peeked out at him.

The man must've seen the club card in Charlie's wallet. Yeah, that was definitely new. Charlie nodded his thanks, took the proffered room key, and bid the man goodnight. Nothing like startling revelations at one in the morning.

Then, suddenly, he had a much bigger problem. The cardinal had disappeared.

Charlie's eyes flickered over the parking lot and the room fronts of the hotel. A man stood smoking outside one, but the rest were quiet.

So, he swiveled slowly towards the apartment complex across the empty street. The entire first floor of the building was alive with light and music. Someone was grilling outside, and peopled spilled out from every door and window. Charlie squinted, disbelief dropping his jaw. Cardinal Neumann was standing beside the chef with a beer in one hand, chatting amiably.

In a fair amount of amazement, Charlie locked the car and crossed the street. "Um, Cardinal?"

"Charles!" He seemed pleasantly surprised, as if they hadn't just been stuck in a car together for the past seven hours. "Would you like a drink?" he asked, offering Charlie his own.

Still startled and now also mildly concerned, Charlie declined.

"This gentleman is Chuck. Chuck has offered to make us dinner."

At once, Charlie felt guilty. He'd forgotten about food again, only this time, the cardinal had suffered along with him. "Thank you, Chuck."

A blonde woman decked in a pair of Dukes joined them, a cup of water in one hand that she offered to Charlie. He accepted it, dipping his head in thanks.

The cardinal kept to his own cordial conversation, so Charlie took a sip from his cup, if only to fill the silence stretching between him and the newly named Maybelle, the cook's wife. He choked instantly, too polite to spit out the moonshine he'd just swigged but wishing dearly he wasn't so close to tears from the burn of it hitting the back of his throat hard.

Maybelle gave him a toothy grin. "Make it ourselves."

"It's..." Charlie began, searching for a word that wouldn't offend her, "...strong."

"The strongest," she proudly agreed. "Hey honey," she called to a giggling girl, "if you're going to put that on the grill, you gotta skin it first." Maybelle wandered off to assist her, and Charlie took the opportunity to hand off the cup to another passing relative.

Not twenty minutes later, Charlie and the cardinal ambled over to their hotel room, and Cardinal Neumann savored the first bite of his quarter pounder with cheese. "I do not envy the Trappists."

Charlie nearly snickered at that. Then, after a moment, he turned inquiring eyes on his superior.

"Problem?" the man asked between bites of his burger.

Charlie considered him for a moment and shook his head.

"Do not like the way humanity looks on me?"

"It's just…odd to see."

"It is odder seeing it on you." He took another bite. "I think I am rather typical. You have likely seen other priests with the same disposition, but most priests of any kind that I know are not capable of half the things you are. You are a wonder to our kind."

"No," Charlie responded, "just most other priests don't need to do what I can. I've only met one priest that's ever had to physically defend himself, at least, since ordination."

"That could."

Charlie paused, seconds away from taking a bite of his own burger. "Excuse me?"

"How many have you met *that could* defend themselves? Few of us can, not matter the circumstance, and being attacked or injured is more common than you might think. The media just does not wail so loudly about it as it does when one of us has fallen into moral sin. We are Catholics after all. The world is against us."

And because they were Catholics, the world against them, and because Charlie in particular was a Harper, he automatically expected the worst throughout most of Mass the next day.

Cardinal Neumann had taken over the parish for that solemn hour, and Charlie was left to command the troops, a little team of altar servers with wide eyes and worried brows. He tried to focus on them, the Master of Ceremonies he was meant to be, but apprehension for potential pregame trouble didn't allow him to assuage their fears. His anxiousness bled into them.

Finally, once the most harrowing Mass in Charlie's entire life was over, he breathed a deep sigh of discontent and loitered in the nave of the church, subjecting himself to an intentional fast in an effort to keep his mind on the mission. The cardinal had frowned at his declaration, but a reminder of their midnight meal was enough to appease him.

The church was dark. The doors had been locked. Charlie was alone with the Lord and his heart, and in his heart were all his worries, all his failures, all his fears. "Still screwing up, Charlie Harper?"

Red hair.

Red hair and blue eyes.

He was sitting on a pew across the aisle, elbows back over the top of it, feet propped up on the kneeler in front of him. Kenneth Jude looked the same way he had the day he died, except the manic look on his face had been replaced with cool indifference.

"It's only because he refuses to accept what he is, what *we* are?" This said by another Charlie.

Charlie, for his part, just sighed. He knew he wasn't dreaming. This wasn't a vision or a hallucination. It was a manifestation of his innermost thoughts, a common way Villenas coped with severe psychological turmoil, how us latest Harpers solved problems other voices could not fix. It was also one of the major reasons Aunt Hilda wasn't our only relative in Bedlam.

The new Charlie was the same as the old, only calmer and more confident. He stood in the center aisle facing his original and the Kenneth Jude incarnation. "You aren't needed here, Guilt. Leave now."

"Is that what I am? Guilt?" Kenny asked.

"Yes, now beat it. There's no place for you here."

Kenny banished in the blink of an eye, and all Charlie could do was sink lower in his seat. "Is this what I've come to? Dear Aunt Hilda, I'll be seeing you soon."

"Oh, don't be so dramatic. You aren't planning on running off and telling Cardinal Neumann about the conversation you just had with yourself, are you?"

"You know that I'm not."

"Yeah, I know. So, do you want to name me?"

Charlie gave him a glare. "I'm not Holly. We'll just call you Number 2 for now."

The second Charlie rolled his eyes. "I know you've got a creative side. You should use it more often."

Charlie sighed. "What does it matter? I know I'm me and you're you, so are you going to help me out or just whine over irrelevant details?" Number 2 slid into the pew in front of Charlie and leaned back against the top of the one behind him. "You shouldn't give your back to the tabernacle."

"*You* aren't." The reminder that Number 2 wasn't really there remained unspoken.

Charlie muttered unintelligibly.

"Look, you're making this way more complicated than it needs to be."

"Oh yeah, and how's that?"

"Remember when you were a kid, on the road with Uncle Riley and Jet? How many sticky situations did you wind up in?"

Charlie groaned. "Way too many." Letting out a nostalgic sigh, he continued, "It wasn't complicated then."

"What's different now?"

"I'm a priest."

"So, if a bunch of satanic worshipers kidnapped your brother now, you'd do something different?"

"Yeah, I'd call the police," Charlie stated assuredly.

Number 2 gave him an unimpressed frown. "Really? There are two things that you and I both know are wrong with what you just said." Number 2 held his fingers up. "First, if a group of satanic worshipers were able to kidnap Jet now—you know, the ex-special forces, former assassin—somehow I don't think the police would be of much help. Second," he added, taking an exaggerated breath, "you tried calling the police. And do we remember how that turned out?"

Charlie didn't answer, merely leaned forward in his seat and steepled his fingers to rest beneath his chin.

"You and I both know the police can do *their* jobs just fine, but international espionage, psychotic occultists—that's all way above their pay grade, and the FBI, CIA, NSA—they don't get involved until the baddies are standing on their doorsteps playing ding-dong ditch. Sometimes, patience works. Sometimes, it's just disguised procrastination, and nothing good can come of it."

"You don't know that'll happen this time." Charlie jerked suddenly, annoyed realization rising in him. "Are you actually trying to convince me to go?"

"Only because you're trying so hard to convince yourself not to. You don't need any more reasons not to do what you came here to do, but I can give you at least forty-three reasons why you should."

"The kids."

Number 2 nodded intently. "What are your only options?"

"Wait for the club to handle this, call someone to take care of it now, or do it myself."

"And what happens if you wait for the club?"

"Even a single second can scar a child for life. Waiting for the club to act is lessening the potential for any one of those kids to fully recover and putting their lives at risk."

"Right, and if you call someone?" Charlie refused to answer. "What happens if you call the police?"

"They rescue the kids, and we all move on with our lives."

Number 2 snorted. "I don't think so. Come on, master strategist, what happens if you call the police, assuming they even believe you in the first place?"

"They may be incapable of locating the facility. Even if they do, chances are the Aureates will outmatch them, which not only puts their own lives at risk, but also puts the children's lives at *further* risk."

"Well then—"

"But I'm a priest. I can't go in there like Jet, gun blazing and hellfire on my heels."

Here, Number 2 rolled his eyes. "You know all about sins of omission."

"We don't know that this would be one."

"But you don't know that it wouldn't be. What if doing nothing is worse than doing something? More lives are certainly at risk. Damned if you do. Damned if you don't, right? In the end it all really comes down to one thing."

"Oh yeah, and what's that?" Charlie snapped.

"It's not up to you."

"What?"

"The final judgment on your actions—it's not yours. As a priest and a human being, you're permitted to defend yourself if someone intends to inflict harm upon your person—"

"But the martyrs—"

"Charlie, if you died right now, you wouldn't be dying for Christ. You'd be dying for yourself…" Number 2 bowed, catching Charlie's anguished eyes in his own. "…because it's the easy way out." He paused. "God doesn't give us gifts so that we can squander them in death. You can do what you can do because He permits you to do it."

Number 2 took Charlie's hands in his own, the way Bishop had at his ordination. "These hands were anointed to do God's work, and it's not always in the way that we expect, but do it with love, His love—selfless, perfect love—and how can you be wrong? Is there anyone more capable and with a more specific authority to act at this very second? You don't really know if there is, only God does. Trust in Him. He'll silence you should you need not speak, and He will still you should you need not move. For now, those kids need you. Not tomorrow. Not next week. Right. Now."

Charlie bowed his head again, and when he looked up, his second self was gone.

Chapter 30

"Church—you know, that place people go on Sundays for prayer and worship."

"I just—*You're* going to church?"

"Yeah. In case you haven't noticed, I'm kind of Catholic, and we Catholics usually do."

The Northern Admin continued to eye Jet doubtfully, completely unable to wrap her mind around the idea that he might actually want to go. "Okay," she finally agreed, "but at five in the morning?"

"Yes," Jet drawled, "we kind of have work to do. I won't have time later."

She merely scratched her neck nervously. "O-*kay*," she finally answered.

Jet had proceeded to ignore her, driven to Sacred Heart Cathedral, and paid his dues. He sat there, tired, long after the parishioners had filed out. In a small corner of his mind, he wondered how Charlie was fairing in his quest. He got a tickling sensation at the base of his skull that suggested something Harper had already happened.

Heavy bootsteps on the tile tensed him. They thudded all the way up the aisle until they reached the edge of his pew. He looked up, startled out of his seat when she laid a slap across his cheek. "Holly?" The pain had been frighteningly real, but even in my war suit, Jet knew it wasn't really me. "I'm losing it."

"Only as much as Charlie is."

Jet groaned. "Uncle Caleb always *said* it would happen someday." He screwed his face up in thought as he retook his seat. "But I'm not conflicted about anything, so this is completely unnecessary."

"Liar," the apparition accused. "Look, Jet, I'm going to make this real simple—"

"Why's it always you, Holly? Aren't I supposed to be counseling myself?"

"It's always me because you won't listen to anyone else, not even *your*self. You won't really listen to me either, but you worry about me, 'cuz I'm your little sister, the most vulnerable member of the family as far as you're concerned."

"Fine. Whatever. Can we just get this over with?"

"Still miffed about letting Voight get away?"

"I didn't—" he growled. Taking a deep breath, he tried again, "I didn't let him get away. I couldn't have let him get away if he was never really there to begin with."

"And it irks you that he outmaneuvered you. You were so sure he'd be there."

"A slight oversight. That's all."

"Jet," she gently chastised.

"What?" he snapped back.

"Charlie isn't the only one pretending, is he?" Jet frowned. "You guys, always trapped in your own little worlds..." She shook her head. "If you'd just acknowledge what you are, you'd be better off."

"What, that we're Harpers? 'Cuz I accepted that a long time ago."

"No, not what you both are, what *you* are."

"Oh yeah? And what am I?"

She tilted her head to the side, and Jet's gaze landed on a slightly younger version of himself dressed in his crackerjacks, clean-shaven, and adorned with a mischievous smirk.

"Life happens. I'm not that kid anymore."

"I *can* talk, you know."

My counterpart rolled her eyes at both of them. "It's not about being him mentally, doofus."

"Hey!"

"What is he?"

"What?"

"What *is* he?" she repeated.

"A dork."

"Jet!"

"A soldier."

"So what are *you* really?"

Jet sighed. "A soldier."

"Darn right." Jet said nothing, so she continued, "Maybe it's time to stop tapping the glass ceiling of your former career and just bust through it already, because this isn't all you got and you know that, otherwise you wouldn't be here."

He picked at a loose thread on the pew, and when he looked up, she was gone. His second self remained, rose from his seat, and strutted up to Jet, older now and no longer in his navy attire. "She's right, but Holly doesn't know what you don't tell her. It's a nifty defense mechanism to keep your vulnerabilities from acknowledging themselves."

"Voight was a really good friend. He was the only one there when I needed someone." Neither of them mentioned that Jet's lack of support happened to be his own fault—they both already knew that—nor that Voight had trekked the fine line between friend and manipulator so hazardously that even he hadn't really known what side of the line he'd stood on himself.

"It's time to stop being a one-man weapon. That's never how you operated, and Voight can keep up or get left behind because Man was never meant to be alone. He'll learn that the hard way, or he won't learn it at all. You already know that. Accept it, and move on."

He blinked. Of course everything was that simple.

"Now on to problem number two."

Jet sighed. "And what's that?"

"C'mon, even Charlie doesn't reject his sacred gifts the way you do."

"That's because Charlie can control his at will!" Jet hissed. He scrubbed a hand over his face harshly and bowed his head in despair. "Why won't He let me save them? What's the point of this stupid second sight if—if I can't save them?" His voice cracked and his hands jumped to his face as the tears came. "Why couldn't I save them?"

His other laid a hand on his shoulder, bent low, and whispered, "Why don't you ask?"

Jet's eyes found their reflection, then settled on the tabernacle. And he was walking, treading uncertainly up the steps of the sanctuary he'd travelled so many times before. He dropped to his knees before the altar. Silent tears trailed down his cheeks as he cowered before the Lord.

Julius Macintyre.

Mimi Nagasaki.

Oleg Ivanov.

The list was filled with thirty-nine more names, and Jet knew them all, each scored across his temple like a brand. They were the worst sort of people, orchestrators of mass genocide, shameless sadists, the sickest child abusers. And yet, so was he now, wasn't he? Couldn't he be counted among the ranks of those dealers of death? He was a murderer—judge, jury, and executioner. Worse yet, like Charlie's sharp jibe had speared, Jet had always known the error of his ways. He'd robbed each of those persons a chance to change, to twist the S in Saul.

Sorrow and shame warred within him. He shook his head. "Why would He answer me after all I've done? After what I've become?"

"Why wouldn't He?"

"...the heart of Christ bleeds for us. The only question is, can you accept that? Can you accept mercy? Can you accept love?"

"Even me? I've murdered shamelessly, bathed in the blood of my victims like it was the cure for all my pain. I knew it was wrong and did it anyways. How can You want me?"

"How can I not?"

The silent tears turned loud. Crushed beneath the weight of impossibility, Jet doubled over towards the ground, his arms splayed before him, the sobs ripping forth from his agonized soul. He could still see their faces, their blood, their lifeless orbs as he stole away whatever time they had left. "Then why?" he whispered.

"Sir?" He had a gun out and aimed at the poor nun not half a second later, seated back in the pew he'd been in minutes earlier like he'd never left.

Jet gave her a wide-eyed whoops, smiled weakly, and apologized, "Sorry, Sister. You triggered my reflex." He booked it out the door before she could get too good a look at his face.

Okay, he could do this. His mind's rendition of me hadn't been wrong. He was a soldier sure, but he wasn't the same kind of soldier he'd once been, and now there was only one kind of soldier he could afford to be. Oddly, the prospect wasn't all that daunting.

And speaking of soldiers…

Huh, what an interesting idea.

"I'm not sure I agree with this."

"I'm sure you don't," Jet replied, fiddling with his earwig. He was basking in her annoyance. She just knew it. "And for the last time, if you don't keep your eyes out of my ears, we're gonna have a really big problem. Your guys almost got me killed yesterday."

"Fine, but—"

"Oh, and one other thing," he smoothly cut in.

She ground her teeth together, her fists clenching and unclenching at her sides. "*What?*" she bit out.

In a heartbeat, his whole demeanor had shifted. His carefree, youthful, and newly groomed features turned hard and threatening. She took an unwitting step back. "If anything happens to my brother because you're too stupid to split your focus, I *will* destroy you."

Breaths coming a little quicker, she replied, "Are you threatening to kill me?"

"No, death's too easy. You don't think I have pull in the club? Inside and out, honey. You'll lose your title just as quickly as you got it." She moved to speak, but he silenced her with an angry hand. "Don't. If Charlie dies, it'll be 'cuza your incompetence, and that's really all the proof I need to know you don't deserve the title of Club Administrator. I get that you're still settling in, but you do not get to play with people's lives while you figure it out, alright, Sadie Grayson?"

How could he possibly know her name? No one did. It hadn't been published yet. "I—I understand."

"Good." And then the amusing if overly irritating Jet Harper was back, rambling good-naturedly about the alterations to his plan.

Sadie Grayson, aka the Northern Admin, drew in a shaky breath. She had seen a lot, been through a lot. You didn't make Admin by sitting on your butt, but never before had she been so afraid of a single person. An unpleasant thought suddenly crossed her mind and with dawning horror, she spun out the door.

Where *was* Charlie Harper anyways?

Chapter 31

Heinrich Voight had never been a suit and tie kind of guy...
...you know, until he was.
After years of avoiding anything remotely sensible, he'd enlisted, and when that was gone, he found himself standing in front of a mirror in some rent-a-wheel hotel, doing up a shiny blue tie and straightening the lapels on his thrift shop two-piecer. He hadn't known the ins and outs of business then, but he'd learned very quickly that he didn't really need to. All he needed was a quick buck and other people.
Voight had found his quick buck easily, taking on hits for bloodthirsty fools that were too squeamish to get a little dirt on their own hands. He'd graduated to elite soon after with a little guidance and a whole lot of whisky. So, by the time Voight had figured out how to get people to pay him for doing absolutely nothing, he had become a master of shaking hands and making people disappear. Voight knew premeditated

murder better than he'd known his own mother, which may not have been a fair comparison considering his mother had died of lung cancer when he was six.

If Heinrich Voight knew anything else, it was Jet Harper.

He'd met Jet at the rehab clinic on the twenty-sixth floor of his tower. The kid had been remarkably determined to walk again, though his therapists seemed certain it was an impossibility. Even if he could regain *some* function, they had said, it'd never be smooth, unhindered, or pain-free.

Voight had initially felt pity for the boy. "Why bother?" he had asked Jet once. "You'll never do it."

Dr. Stans had hissed at him. Voight rarely interacted with patients and even more rarely did he so assuredly cut them down. "My mind is stronger than my body. I will walk again, even if I have to learn to levitate first."

Voight had been captivated by him from that point forward. He'd come down every day to watch the kid work, first from a distance, then eventually, up close and personal.

"Don't touch me!"

"But Mr. Harper," Dr. Stans whined, a little put out by the sullen attitude that plagued the usually chipper young man, "we need to start your session. You wouldn't want your muscles to atrophy, would you? Missing even one day could make tomorrow that much harder."

Jet had reached down, face filled with faint traces of pain, and wrestled the shoes from his feet. He dropped them on the floor, then tugged at his socks with clenched teeth and added them to the pile. He stared down at his toes and willed them to move.

Voight wondered why the boy had chosen that day of all days to attempt the impossible. How many times had Jet tried it before, had he laid awake at night, putting every ounce of his insurmountable will in trying to get the faintest flicker of movement out of them, had he tried and failed? And why, now, would he try once more, with an audience to pity his defeat?

Jet stared at his toes with the greatest intensity. Naturally, nothing happened. "Mr. Harper—"

But he didn't have eyes for her. For a moment, the anger and frustration and fear melted away, and the light of ill-suited wisdom took its place. Then his toes gave the slightest, most hesitant twitch.

Voight hadn't technically seen it, still up in the rafters overlooking the clinic, but the startled shout of Jet's PT was all he needed to know. The boy had done it. Through sheer will? That didn't seem likely, and yet, what else could it have been?

Only two days later, Jet had been helped to his feet. The exertion from that alone, despite the assistance, saw sweat beading his furrowed brow, an eternal grimace spread across his face, and clear strain in his trembling muscles. A pained yet resolute set of eyes rested strongly and proudly in his finely chiseled skull.

"Okay, Jet," said Dr. Stans, "let's take this nice and slow."

He gripped the parallel bars with the iron in his hands. Physical therapy had already helped him restore some of the muscle he'd lost and allowed him to maintain it, but he hadn't moved his legs in such a long time that fine motor control was simply unattainable. Jet took one step, painstakingly slow, foot only just clearing the ground, a shuffle more than anything. Then, to the wonder of all that watched, he took another.

"That's unbelievable." Voight had come down the moment he'd spotted Jet prepping to launch, and he could barely believe what he was seeing.

"It shouldn't be possible." Dr. Stans and her assistant lowered Jet back to his chair. She continued, Jet too focused on his task to take any notice, "I've never seen someone so motivated. He just won't give up."

Voight had spent weeks watching Jet. Sometimes he'd even stand around and chat with the boy. But something was bothering him about the young man's predicament.

"Where's your family?" he asked one day, not long after Jet had arrived at his session. "They must be eager to help." Jet looked down in shame, so Voight assumed the worst. "Bastards."

"Hey!" Jet snapped back. He had just risen from his chair after several minutes of effort, Dr. Stans at his elbow. He took a hard and angry step forward, ripping his arm from her grasp. "Don't you dare insult my family."

Voight stared back in shock. Jet was trembling in rage, fists clenched at his sides, his face screwed up in a mix of fury and pain. Still stunned, and now also a little scared, Voight watched as Jet took another determined step forward. He grabbed the collar of Voight's shirt and dragged him closer.

"Don't you ever insult my family," Jet repeated, voice low and menacing. "They aren't here because I don't want them to be, and that's all there is to it."

Jet released him, and Dr. Stans, who was also staring wide-eyed at the sailor, took his weight as he latched onto her. She sat him back in his wheelchair as he huffed angrily. "How about we call it a day?"

Voight decided right then and there that Jet would make a marvelous student. He found himself particularly liking the fire in his gut. It helped that the boy was smart, too. He'd be a dream to train, a decent legacy to leave behind.

That's really all Voight wanted. Assassins don't do companionship. There's too much potential for disaster, too much loss to add onto loss, and once his father had passed some twenty years before, Voight hadn't had much else to give. The only people he ever dealt with that didn't wind up dead were other assassins, and generally speaking, befriending them was a bad idea.

But if he apprenticed someone, well, that would be an entirely different story, wouldn't it? There'd be loyalty there to forge friendship. Not that he cared or anything. Why would a man like him care about having someone to talk to, to laugh with, to exist alongside? No, he needed a legacy, something or someone to be remembered by. Now all he had to do was play his cards right, and he'd have it.

So, over the next several weeks, Voight had picked his way through a very delicate game of Operation. "It must be frustrating, not being able to move the way you want," Voight told him when Jet's excitement at another milestone reached had landed him on the floor yet again.

Jet frowned but said nothing, expending most of his energy positioning himself correctly to inch his way back up.

Voight had been the first to ensure he hadn't hurt himself, but knew better than to offer Jet a hand. He'd feel insulted, and Voight had to carefully stir vulnerability and independence inside Jet's troubled, young mind, or Jet wouldn't take the bait. And maybe, some miniscule part of him, wanted the kid to feel strong again…for himself.

Jet took up a pair of crutches less than a month later. They'd wanted him on a walker first, but his pride had outright refused it. "Good day?"

Jet smiled. "Great day! I can do laps on these stupid bars."

Voight smiled back. "I'd say a victory drink is in order. What do you think—Muffaso's or Curnigan's?"

As anticipated, the smile dropped from Jet's face and discomfort took its place. He would have to teach the boy to school his features better. Having emotions was one thing. Showing them was another. "Actually, I think I'm just gonna head home."

"C'mon, Jet, it's on me."

His discomfort remained, a pronounced frown tugging at the corners of his mouth. "No, I'm good."

"Hm," Voight hummed loudly. "That's too bad. So, you aren't a drinker. I had thought when you were finished with this place for good, I might invite you up to my penthouse for some old Highland Malt." Voight felt a little guilty pressuring the boy. Jet was ashamed of his walking aids. The paleness on his once tanned features made that very clear, but Voight needed Jet just uncomfortable enough to buy his next offer, so he feigned obliviousness.

Jet's face colored. "It's not that. I just…" He fiddled with one of his crutches. Voight knew what it was, but Jet needed to admit it, to trust Voight enough to share his unease. "I just don't want to go out…with these," Jet stated, rattling his crutches.

Voight nodded. He could sympathize with that. "Why wait then? I'll spot you a beer now."

"I don't wanna take you away from your work."

Comments like that made Voight question his own resolve. The kid could be unbelievably thoughtful at times. "You wouldn't be. I live on the top floor, well, the top two floors actually. Come on. Come up. Let's have a drink."

Jet hesitated, and Voight wondered at the boy's cautiousness. Where had Jet learned to be so vigilant? Every time Voight looked at him, he saw a young, markless vet, taken out of combat before he'd even seen the worst of it, but every time Voight *spoke* to Jet, he realized the boy was hiding something dark and mature behind those tumultuous brown eyes of his, and Voight was immediately reminded that this particular investment could really pay off.

"You know, when I was a sergeant, we had some real fun with the boots," he told Jet, offering him a beer. Jet was standing by the window, looking out at Chicago like he'd never seen the upper end of it.

"Oh yeah? I had a lot of fun with my XOs, too."

Voight cocked an eyebrow at him. "Didn't that get you in trouble?"

"I fell in when I needed to, so they didn't mind..." His puckish grin made a reappearance. "...too much." Voight got the feeling the kid's XOs had enjoyed themselves immensely. It was rare to be amused by a new recruit, but Jet had the kind of personality that made him difficult to stay angry at.

"So, army?" Jet asked.

Voight twitched. "Marines."

"I thought so." Jet smiled a wry grin.

"What? Then why?"

"Because I knew it'd bug you."

Voight smirked in amusement. *This kid.* "Navy?"

"Got it in one."

"Job?"

"Special forces."

Voight frowned. That wasn't exactly a job. "SEALs, SWCC?"

"The one without a name."

"Funny." Jet smiled knowingly. "You're serious?"

"SEALs had nothing on us."

"I wouldn't say that too loud."

"I wouldn't normally say it at all."

Voight was suitably impressed and a little mystified, too. Just who was Jet Harper? "About your family?" He was digging now, a dangerous job if this kid was as perceptive as he seemed. Sure enough, Jet's smirk partially dissolved. "For someone so eager to defend them, you don't seem very fond of them at all."

"I'm fond of my family," Jet countered, rolling that f-word around on his tongue like it tasted funny. "I just don't think my family's too *fond* of me right now."

"Why?"

"I was discharged from the military nearly six months ago, but I haven't gone home yet…at all."

"Why not?"

Jet stared at the window hard, but Voight knew his gaze was looking far beyond it. "I—I don't want them to see me like this."

"Like what?" Voight wasn't entirely sure why he said what he did next. It certainly wouldn't help his case any, but it didn't seem right that Jet had someone to go back to and, yet, simply wouldn't. "You don't actually have anything to be ashamed of, especially with your family."

"I know, but when I left for the navy, we didn't part on the best of terms, especially my brother and I. I just can't fix that and fix me at the same time, you know?"

Voight nodded. He could understand that, but if Jet was going to have a place beside him, Voight couldn't encourage their happy reunion. The boy needed to grow more estranged. He had to be willing to leave them all behind.

"Why'd you quit the Marines? You're proud enough to be a lifer."

Voight sauntered over to his marble island, and after a few difficult seconds, Jet followed. That had been another offhand line, like Jet was reading his microexpressions with little to no effort. With Jet, Voight just wasn't sure what he could get away with. "I was sick." He personally considered kleptomania an illness. "I tried to hide it—" Or tried not to get caught. "—but eventually, I was found out." His CO had busted him with a busload of illegal contraband. "I was discharged soon after."

For that, they had robbed him of his rank, his freedom, and his dignity. He despised the world of apple-pie lives and political correctness. What did it matter if he had a taste for the illicit? He served his country, would've died for any one of his brothers or sisters-in-arms. He fought with everything he had all day every day, but it wasn't enough. They'd wanted perfection. They'd wanted cookie-cutter culture. And he just couldn't give them that.

Jet had a strange look on his face. Voight had no idea what to make of it. Actually, it kind of mimicked the expression Jet had worn right before he'd wiggled his toes for the first time, a completely out of place comprehension, understanding that had nothing to do with what Voight had actually said. It was disconcerting. Voight forbore the impulse to squirm. Then the look passed, and Jet's features turned curious.

"What?"

Jet only smiled and shook his head. "Nothing."

It wasn't for several more weeks that Jet finally bit the hook. "Voight, can I ask you something?"

They were watching the game, a match Voight had no actual interest in, but it roused something in Jet, so he'd settled himself on the couch against his immediate impulse to take the corner seat with the best view of the room and watched the game beside Jet, whose countenance bespoke a hard day in therapy. "Of course."

"How'd you do it? How'd you take back control of your life after you were discharged?"

Voight blinked and considered Jet for a moment. He knew the importance of how he went about answering this question. "I found something that gave me control back, another place I could hold a gun and fight the good fight."

Jet twitched at that, and Voight bit his lip discreetly. His butchering of that biblical verse may have just given him away. Clearly, Jet had some knowledge of sacred scripture, may have even called himself devout at some point, but luckily, Jet merely shook his head softly and leaned in farther.

"The government says vets like you and me can't do anything now, but maybe we can. What if we could help our comrades from outside the rank-and-file?"

"How?"

Voight smiled victoriously, though he kept the less gleeful side of it from showing on his face. Jet was so easy, so eager to get back to the war, to his comrades, to make up for his perceived mistakes. "There are people out there that are untouchable, protected by *politics*." He spat the word like it was tar. "What if we could circumvent politics?"

"How?" Jet repeated.

"With a knife and a name."

It was an adage of one of Voight's former military mentors. *"Just give me a knife and a name, and I'm good to go."*

Jet had been leery about the whole contract killing thing. He clearly bought all of Voight's pretty words about it, but he'd been raised with a moral mind, and the concept of killing others for money was a little hard to swallow. "You got paid as a soldier," Voight tried to reason.

"For time. For sacrifice. It's not like we got a bonus for every man we cut down," Jet countered.

"Unfortunately, you don't have the luxury of a pseudo-rich government lining your pockets anymore, Jet. You can't do this for free. You need something to sustain you. Don't think of it as blood money. Think of it as compensation for a mission, a mission your old squadmates need you to take, for their sakes. Besides, that's the luxury of being self-employed. You pick the hits you want."

"And what am I supposed to do until I can afford to be that selective?"

Voight could have smiled that Cheshire grin. "I'll handle things for now. I could teach you everything you need to know." Jet's face slid into a frown, and Voight realized he'd just admitted to his vast experience with the game, a slip that no one else on the verge of a life-altering decision would have caught aside from Jet. "I know you wish you could've prevented Stonefield's death and Davis's career-ending injury, but you didn't." Jet's face soured further. He'd been having a really low day when he confided that in Voight. "But you can prevent that sort of thing from happening to anyone else."

"War is messy. People always die."

"Maybe," Voight answered truthfully. It was hard to understand Jet. Sometimes, he seemed incredibly young. Other times, he seemed every bit the soldier he was. "But you can improve their odds, give more of them a chance." He'd already admitted it, so what the heck? "It helps me as much as it helps them, Jet. I feel useful again," he added honestly. "I feel like I'm there, and I'm needed, and it works. Understand?"

Maybe it was his words, or maybe it was the bare look on Voight's face, but Jet finally nodded. "Alright, I'll give it a shot, but I'm not making any promises."

"Fair enough."

Voight wasn't quite sure what actually hooked Jet in the end. He hadn't seemed to like it much the first time or the second or the third, but he kept at it, looking for more jobs, investigating each beforehand even if it cost him the contract. Voight couldn't complain. Jet was exceptional in *everything* he did.

Jet had caught him once, staring at an old photo of his father, the only one he kept on hand. On the anniversary of his death, Voight had stuck to his own family's traditions, and already he was half way through a bottle of bourbon.

"Miss him?"

"He never thought I'd amount to anything." *Of course I miss him, you idiot.*

"I wouldn't worry too much. In the end, fathers usually wind up being proud of all the things you've done right and glossing over all the things you've done wrong."

"Your father's not dead."

Jet turned away with a sheepish grin, but Voight had to wonder if Jet was right. Would his father have been proud of him in the end, despite killing people for a little green and poisoning Jet's mind for his own selfish goals?

Not a month later, Jet had begun straying down his own path, not clearing things with Voight, taking his own hits, and Voight didn't mind. After all, that had been the point. Jet wasn't supposed to stay his apprentice forever, but he hadn't quite expected it to end so suddenly. He'd enjoyed the companionship, and that companionship weakened considerably with Jet's independence. Voight was something of a proud father mixed with an annoyed boss whose best employee had just cut loose.

Voight shook himself out of the memories. Jet Harper had been his greatest work of art, was still his masterpiece. Belladonna hadn't held a candle to him, and Voight hadn't allowed himself to get attached to her, so her death had been a trivial affair, well worth the inconvenience to see Jet playing the game again. If Voight hadn't had other matters to attend to, he'd have been there himself to witness it.

Voight frowned, strolling around the kitchen of his home to pour himself another cup of coffee. This was one of his more reclusive safe houses. It had a great view of the northern Blue Ridge Mountains. The luxurious manor was two stories high, pressed into the side of a mountain. The balcony jutting out of the roof was designed to blend in with the brown and grey rocks around it and hung over the cliff-side invitingly.

Voight hadn't been lying when he'd poked at Jet's weaknesses. His sudden turn away from their lifestyle had been disappointing to say the least. He still couldn't understand why Jet'd had such an extreme change of heart, but he could take a wild guess and say it had something to do with that family of his, forcing the moral hat onto his head like a judgment. If Voight could only break through the wall they'd trapped him behind, the boy would be unstoppable.

But harming Jet's family would've been a mistake. He'd almost warned Belladonna off the elder Harper, though the man was a mystery unto himself. There was a reason he hadn't hesitated when he'd refused the contract, on his own behalf and Belladonna's, for offing Jet's younger sister. Really, Voight was beginning to wonder if the whole family was some sort of jewel of humankind.

He glanced down at the file he had open on the counter. A green-eyed raven barely out of adolescence stared somberly up at him, a petulant gleam in his mien. Belladonna's untimely death had left him with even more work. Now not only did he have to vanish whomever the Aureates wanted, as Bella had been instructed, but he also had to continue investigating other potential hits. Combing through all their members for signs of treachery was a headache and a half, and the boy in front of him was being extra difficult.

Voight's skin prickled, and he looked up suddenly, barely resisting the urge to jump.

Jet was there, stood beside Voight's black sofa in the hall's entry way, partially obscured by darkness, a carefully tempered expression on his face. He had a Gayang strapped to his back, a gun in his left hand, and a pouchful of throwing knives resting just above his tactical blade. The fingertips of his right hand hovered over them at the ready. He wasn't wearing Kevlar this time, but Voight didn't recognize the armor, slimmer than Kevlar but somehow stronger against Jet's slight frame. He wore other pieces aside from his chest plate, though not many, just enough to cover his sensitive joints and, if Voight's high mirror told him anything, Jet's vulnerable spine.

"Jet," Voight said blankly in an attempt to hide his surprise. He hadn't honestly expected the boy—no—man to find him so quickly, at least, not while he still had Bella's job to finish. And Voight had always vetted the information he disclosed to Jet, for an occasion like this, where he was finally pitted against his product. It had never really been his intention to face off with the boy, but some things couldn't be helped.

"Wondering how I found you?"

Voight said nothing. He wasn't afraid, but he *was* cautiously curious.

"You didn't tell me everything. As a matter of fact, you skewed the truth quite a bit, didn't you? I realized you had been dishonorably discharged seconds after you fed me your lies, but I didn't say anything because I didn't think your crimes outweighed the good you did as a Marine." Jet paused, still unmoving in the dark corridor. "And it didn't take me too long to realize that what I was doing was shaming the dead more than honoring them. *My* problem was that I tried to pretend like I didn't know any of it, about you, about the deceit, about my own issues. But *your* problem, Void, was that you underestimated me from the start. I'm resolving my problem. Are you resolving yours?"

"You're wrong, Jet. I knew exactly what I was getting when I took you under my wing." Voight felt confident. He really did, but for the briefest moment, he remembered those eyes, those deep, telling brown eyes that just seemed to know things outside of reason.

"You really think you know me, don't you? Let me guess. I was a wounded soldier with survivor's guilt—plenty of openings there, but I was strong, willful, willing to do whatever it took to regain some semblance of control over my life. I was an easy target."

"Got it in one," Voight mocked, slinging one of Jet's former favorite lines at him, one Voight had only felt made the boy seem younger.

"But let me tell you about everything you didn't see. You didn't see a champion. You didn't see a kid who took out an entire gun smuggling ring with his older brother in place of arts and crafts at summer camp. You didn't see your reckoning."

"Oh, are you here to judge me then?" Voight asked, his amusement clear.

"No, but I'll get you a hell of a lot closer."

"How cryptic."

"Not really."

"Jet, what makes you honestly believe you've surpassed me? You were an elite assassin less than three years. Don't get me wrong. You were prodigy in the craft, but no one excels that fast. Your pride's getting the best of you. I thought I taught you better than that."

"What makes me honestly believe I've surpassed you?" Jet echoed back, chin dipping up in feigned thought. "What makes *you* honestly believe I came here without reassurances stacked as high as the Tower of Babel?"

"Assassins work alone. You don't have time to worry about others."

"Who says backup's my first reassurance?" Jet flicked his wrist at Voight, a throwing knife hurtling through the air at him.

Voight turned his head and let the projectile fly past him. For a brief second, he wondered when the boy had gotten so slow. That had been way too easy to dodge. Then the light flickered on, and he realized Jet's aim had never been truer. The tip of the knife had embedded in the drywall, the blade's small pitching handle angled up 170° to throw the switch. *Damn, that was accurate.*

A tremor between pride and panic trickled through him. Then he saw the wall behind Jet, and the trace-panic turned into rivers of dread. Carved into the wood was a scythe, a straight bar arching down from the center of it to mark the crooked leg its reversed R.

"A scare tactic," Voight chuckled, attempting to shake off the insinuation.

"A warning," Jet countered, "and the only one you'll get."

"No." Voight was shaking his head in denial. "No, he's been around longer than you've been alive."

"And he went off-grid eight years ago, making his first appearance since then only last year. In February, right?" Jet's glee was evident, his smile turning into something truly frightening. Voight marveled at the boy's ability to manipulate others' emotions by his body language alone.

"You've taken up the mantle?"

"Six others came before me, but it's only when you've gone as far as I have that you figure that out—" Jet flicked his wrist again, his knife flying at Voight. Voight turned like he had before but wasn't quite quick enough. The tip of the blade sliced a neat line across his cheek, and blood seeped from it, a match to the newly cleaned scratch Jet had garnered from Belladonna. "—and can take up the mantle yourself."

Voight's composure cracked, his apprehension rising into outright fear. He held the meager ends of his mask together. It wouldn't do to let Jet see him weak. The man was pissed, and that didn't bode well for him. Even as a fledgling, Jet's anger was notorious.

But standing there in the half-light of his hallway, brown eyes ablaze and set with frightening resolution, all Voight could see was impossibility. How exactly had he missed this transformation? What all did it entail? Why was *he* always the one to bear witness to the otherworldliness that was Jet Harper?

It didn't matter, he decided. He'd make do with this meandering course he'd been thrust upon. After all, the man in front of him was *still* Jet Harper. Human. Vulnerable. Regardless of what Jet had said, Voight knew plenty about him, and if Voight managed to kill the younger man, he'd have a new mantle himself, a new legacy. Not quite the one he'd wanted, but it would do.

Voight leveled a heavy glower at Jet. All he had to do was make himself hate the man, take his creation and rend it to pieces. His chest swelled with despair. *No!* He *could* hate Jet Harper. He had to.

The Grim Reaper would die. Voight would make absolutely certain of it.

Chapter 32

Charlie hadn't changed. He knew he really should, but those long, black lengths of fabric were as much of part of him as the scars sliced across his back. Despite all the ways this could go wrong, despite all the ways *he* could go wrong, he would go into it as every aspect of himself, both priest and protector.

Charlie bowed his head and took a moment to simply breathe, in and out, in tune with the rhythmic pulsing of nature. Letting the horrific cries of the lost flood him, he fanned the smoldering fire of his relentless will to summon the part of him that had once earned him the title of Holy Harper, not for his spirituality or his vocation, but because at his absolute ablest, he was nothing less than a holy terror.

He'd done the unthinkable to achieve this state of being. He'd asked the cardinal to drive.

The older man had given Charlie an incredulous look, astonished by his subordinate's request, but Charlie hadn't wavered. He needed to concentrate. So, Cardinal Neumann had ultimately assented, taken the keys in hand, and gotten them both a little closer to God. With a quiet eek behind his teeth, Charlie belatedly recalled that the higher-ups didn't actually drive all that much. That's what seminarians were for after all. *And Jet says* I'm *bad.*

Cardinal Neumann really needed to buff the rust out of his handling. Charlie only wished he'd done it beforehand and while Charlie *wasn't* in the car with him. He signed himself and prayed, *Please, God, get us there in one piece, and I'll never complain about Jet's driving again.* At least his brother was good at it, a speed demon with control.

After effectively, or as effectively as he could, blocking out the rollercoaster ride he'd unwittingly subjected himself to, Charlie dialed a number he'd long ago memorized, even if he'd never before been permitted to use it.

"Hello?"

"I need a number: Peterstown, West Virginia."

The line switched. "Curio's," a man's voice answered.

"Call my card."

"Here be dragons…"

"…And so, here am I."

"Please hold." Charlie tapped his fingers impatiently.

"Dr. Retlan," a woman answered.

"Hi, this is Charlie Harper. I seem to have found myself in a bit of a dangerous situation, and I could use some backup—"

"Sorry, I don't do that sort of thing. I'm a surgeon. If you're not bleeding out or dying, then I'm not the woman for you."

Charlie prayed for patience. "I understand, but we're tracking an organization that's kidnapped a bunch of—" The cardinal swerved around a pothole. "—kids."

"Look—Charlie, was it?—I don't do field work. When you find those kids, I'll be the first one there. I can promise you that. In the meantime, I'm late for work. I'm sorry, but I have to go."

"Could you at least redirect me to someone who can hel—"

He stared at his phone. Had she just hung up on him?

"No luck?"

Charlie shook his head, putting his phone to sleep and stashing it in a pocket.

"I thought club members were supposed to come to each other's aid. Is that not what you said earlier? Whoever was available would join us."

Charlie just moped. "That would've worked in Texas."

Cardinal Neumann parked the car on the side of a secluded road. Charlie hoped nothing happened to it. As blasé as Jet'd seemed about the pile of scrap metal that had once been Charlie's car, he could get a touch irrational when it came to his own.

"So, where do we begin?"

"We'll head north for now."

"Why?"

Charlie bit back a crass reply that might have gotten him slapped and wondered if the cardinal was going to question his every move. "I scanned the map again this morning. There are better routes to enter from if they were south of this location, better routes with better cover, better time, better everything, and some of the mountainous region of the south is bare of trees, not an ideal place to hide a bunch of kidnapped children."

"I see." Charlie wasn't so sure, but he let it slide.

Too many species of trees made up the forest for him to keep up with identifying, though Charlie could pick out many of them, including the oaks and weeping witch hazel, a favorite of Uncle Riley's. Charlie's eyes scanned the ground, inspecting animal tracks along the way, foxes and squirrels and rabbits and anything else he could find.

It was still early in the morning, but already, something sweet hung in the air. Charlie gave it a sniff—bitter apple and cinnamon. They walked another twenty minutes in silence.

Charlie tried to avoid the taller grasses. The thought of deer ticks climbing into his black cassock and thorns tearing at his pant legs made him wary of his surroundings. Just how many articles of clothing had he ruined on this trip already? Two? Three?

"What exactly is our plan, Father?"

"Shhhh!" Charlie hissed. In hindsight, he probably should've given the cardinal a heads up, but in his defense, when he was tracking, the nearer, typical notes eluded him. After all, Jet was a stealth walker, too. Charlie didn't have to remind him to do anything, and Uncle Riley had always just dawdled in the background, if he'd been present at all.

"Excus—"

Bang!

The gunshot rang out loudly, scaring off the local fauna and ditzying up their tracks. "What was that?"

"Moonshiners—the forests are filled with them. We need to go. Now!"

They took off through the trees, weaving around low boughs and stumps and scrambling for a blind of some kind. Charlie caught the sound of the cardinal tripping several times, but the man never actually hit the ground, so Charlie

245

kept running. "I should have worn my Air Max," Cardinal Neumann wheezed.

The jest caught Charlie by surprise. He didn't stop, but he did twist wildly from a dead break, grabbing the cardinal by the back of his own red-piped cassock and yanking him to one side. The man wore even his cape and zucchetto, and Charlie wondered if he'd retain them all by the end of their hike. "Traps," Charlie offered in way of explanation. "They've littered the area with traps. You just narrowly avoided a Burmese Tiger Pit."

Charlie continued his sprint, shoving the cardinal several feet from him so their pursuers had to split their rounds between them. A couple of buck shots sprayed the tree beside Charlie and another wider one he took cover behind. "Uh, Charles?"

The hefty pants gave him away, and Charlie turned just in time to see the cardinal face-plant into an oak. Charlie would've winced if he'd had time for it or laughed if he'd been channeling Jet. Instead, Charlie slid against his momentum on the dirt beneath him, his hand reaching down to push himself up and, yet again, shift directions at breakneck speed. He reached the cardinal just as a couple of hillbillies broke through the foliage.

Charlie yanked Cardinal Neumann to his feet. The man groaned, a biting remark on his tongue, but the shotgun barrels aimed at them shut him up quick and easy.

They were man and wife from what Charlie could see. The way she sat at his hip—it was too suave for siblings, unless something really weird was going on, but Charlie wasn't willing to make that judgment without some real evidence to suggest it was true.

The man stepped forward, but the woman held her gun surer, aimed straight at the cardinal. He, a tall, muscular blond man, inched forward, putting the barrel of his gun into the danger range of Charlie's space. There was no missing at twelve inches.

For a fleeting moment, Charlie considered a hundred and one different options, many of which involved getting the cardinal shot. No, that wouldn't do. He took in the baby blues watching him intently—nope—watching his collar intently. So, the man had some kind of faith, and the white at Charlie's throat made him particularly nervous. "We didn't mean to trespass, nor do we want to cause any trouble. We're just looking for some missing kids."

"We idn' take nobody."

"No, we don't believe you did. Someone else is running through here, and they, well, they'll cause you all sorts of trouble."

"How?" the woman snapped. "Ain't nobody know nothing 'bout our business 'cept you."

"They took kids, innocent children. If the police get involved, they'll sweep everything north of Roanoke. If I spotted your still, so will they." That was a bit of a hard one to sell. Their still had been fairly well hidden, but Charlie's sharp eyes could spot a drop of blood on a matador's cape fifteen feet away.

Their uncertainty was palpable, but then, so was the cardinal's dark bewilderment. Charlie ignored the eyes on his back. He had seen the still. That wasn't a lie.

"Look, we're men of God. We *really* don't want any trouble."

Charlie was rewarded with a flickering eye movement, one he'd dearly hoped to see. *Good, now for one more test.* Charlie flinched wholeheartedly, really put his back into it, so hard it actually hurt. The motion was enough to startle the woman, and the barrel of her gun jumped to Charlie as she took a threatening step forward.

"No, stay back, Leanne." She halted at once.

Well, alright then.

"If hitting a priest can get you excommunicated, I'd hate to think what would happen if you shot one dead." Then with all the grace of a bulldozer, he grabbed the barrel of the man's gun and shoved it away from him. "Good God, man," he yapped in his best McCoy impersonation, "put that thing away before someone gets hurt."

The man dropped his aim to the ground in a loose grip, his finger no longer hovering over the trigger. "*Billy*," Leanne whined.

"Oh, hush, woman. Ain't no point in angering Him, not if these here pastors really are just lookin' for some kids."

"We are. I can assure you of that."

"As can I," the cardinal added.

"Did ya say you were lookin' for someone?" Leanne asked, finally cooling down and lowering her own weapon.

"Yes."

She shared a look with her husband.

Leanne and Billy escorted them to a small, one-man trail, obscured so well Charlie was forced to reassess them. A hidden intelligence lay behind those colored eyes, shielded behind their uncultured accents and overalls. "I on't know 'bout no kids, but this here trail just popped right up outa nowhere. Folla it and it otta take ya somewhere."

"What trail?" the cardinal asked, the dense forestry veiling it from his untrained eye.

The three ignored him.

"Thank you."

"Yes, God will reward you for your help," Cardinal Neumann promised. Even he pretended like he had asked nothing.

They waved goodbye at the couple and trekked carefully along the trail, Charlie taking point and the cardinal losing steam behind him. "Should we be heeding their advice?"

"You just promised them a divine reward for it."

"Yes," the cardinal said, "and they will receive it so long as they were telling us the truth."

"We don't have much choice."

"Why not? I thought you were an exceptional tracker."

"I am, Cardinal. I was backtracking the animals earlier."

"So?"

Charlie tried to hide the sigh in his voice, but the edge of it came out anyways. "I spent an unbelievable amount of time tracking as a kid, so I know what typical wildlife patterns look like. I can see the movement of the animals, the history and the health of the plants, and the presence of humans who have come and gone or stayed. All I have to do is read the *a*-typical patterns. Most of the tracks I was following led away from the northwest, which means the animals around here, even some of the bigger predators, are running from a larger threat." Charlie observed the man's lack of understanding. "Humans," he spelled out.

Cardinal Neumann bobbed his head, but Charlie could see the cardinal's difficulty following his logic and wondered if speaking in German might help. He settled on a simpler English explanation. "The denser the forest, the more abundant the wildlife. Somewhere to the northwest, something's caused a mild disturbance in the middle of the forest. Animals are fleeing away from it in every direction, so I was retracing their tracks to that disturbance."

"Yes, I think I understand now, and you cannot continue doing so because…?"

"The gunshot from behind us frenzied the local fauna back in the direction we were travelling. I could age the tracks to figure out which ones to follow, but that takes time we don't have, and if I rush through it, we'll wind up walking in circles."

The cardinal nodded at Charlie's back. "What exactly is a moonshiner?"

Now Charlie really did sigh. "A person who makes illegal whiskey." He left it at that. Charlie could've prattled on about prohibition and its lingering consequences, but for once, he had no desire to do so.

"And what is a still?"

"An apparatus for distilling alcohol."

"You told them you saw theirs." The accusation was well-concealed. Regardless, Charlie didn't much like it.

"I did," he replied, "right about the time I smelled it."

"Pardon?"

"That bittersweet tang in the air."

"I did not smell anything."

"You wouldn't have."

"I do not understand."

Charlie groaned to himself. "My uncle Riley," he finally offered, "insisted on giving us special training. Jet and I both learned a little martial arts, but Jet was the one that really excelled at that sort of stuff, not me. I did what I had to, then sat around and read. Eventually, my uncle insisted I study something more intensively." Charlie shrugged. "I thought tracking might come in handy."

"And this all has something to do with your heightened sense of smell?"

"Tracking isn't just about what you see. It's about what you hear, what you smell, what you feel, even, sometimes, what you taste, so Uncle Riley helped me sharpen all my senses."

"This uncle of yours must be quite the genius."

"Not really. Just because he taught us how to do it, doesn't me he could do any of it himself." Charlie paused mid step. "We're going the wrong way."

"The trail is wrong?"

"No, the tracks have changed. We're far enough from the gunshot site for that to matter." Time had lapsed. Midday wasn't far now. "The trail isn't necessarily wrong. It's common to increase the length of a path to throw unwanted guests off track. Soon we'll run into other trails that either lead to nowhere or back onto this one. It's a tactic for misleading potential trespassers. Tracking through that is near hopeless. We could be lost for hours."

"So then?"

"We leave the trail. This strategy of theirs means we're getting close. We don't want to stroll up through the front gate anyways."

They marched through a denser patch of trees and brush. Charlie's nose picked up something wet, and after a few more steps, the gentle serenade of running water alerted him to a nearby creek. *Forty meters*, Charlie estimated. They reached it in forty-three. Charlie shook his head. He really was rusty.

Charlie trekked over the creek without much thought, stepping on the raised stones, barely submerged by the flow. The cardinal let out a startled yelp, and Charlie glanced back at him. The man was shaking out his feet, water dripping off them and the bottom few inches of his black vestment.

"How are you still dry?"

Charlie raised the hem of his cassock, revealing the only aspect of his attire he'd altered. His dress shoes had stayed behind in the car. He'd switched them out for Jet's spare pair of leather boots, the kind that cost two pairs of high-end Nikes put together. "I thought they'd better serve me."

"Well, you are not wrong." Cardinal Neumann shook out his shoes once more and squelched along.

They reached a small canyon shortly, and several song sparrows chirped, speaking between each other. Charlie narrowed his eyes, scooped up a bit of dirt, and let the wind carry it away from him. "What is it?"

"Iron—I smell iron in the forest and…" He paused to think. "…decay. We'll need to find a crossing for this canyon. Those scents are on the wind, and they're coming from the other side." Charlie inhaled slowly, picturing the wind carry the dirt. "Two hundred and fifty-one—no!—fifty-four meters that way," Charlie said, pointing east over the opposite edge of the chasm.

"You cannot possibly know that."

"You're right. A 4% margin of error is expected. I'm extremely out of practice."

The cardinal's disbelief was obvious, but before he could say anything, Charlie froze a startled kind of freeze that bespoke a deep consideration for his exceptional senses. "What is the matter now?"

"We need to get out of here."

"Problem?"

"Bear cubs," Charlie explained. "They probably won't attack us, but if their mother feels like they're in danger, she definitely will." He turned slowly away from the canyon. "Let's go."

They found a man-made bridge about eighty meters away, makeshift and a barely stable. Charlie decided it must've been a creation of the Aureates in the region, well used as it was. Boot prints headed from one end to the other, and Charlie hardly felt hikers or hunters would brave it too often. The canyon stretched about twenty feet, and large oaks had been laid across it as though they'd fallen there naturally. Gaps between each log assured trouble for the pair of them, but the wood was chaffed, so Charlie wasn't worried. The Aureates clearly walked it often.

"I'll go first. Follow behind me as soon as I'm clear."

The cardinal nodded, only watching as Charlie slowly made his way across. Though Charlie was careful, he wasn't overly anxious. The logs were still in good health, and his balance was fairly impeccable, even in less shape than he once was. The canyon dropped to lots of rock and a stream that couldn't cushion a feather, but Charlie continued on to the other side worry free.

He signaled for the cardinal who began his own trek. Head ducked, he missed Charlie's gaze sharpen and panic spread across his features. Cardinal Neumann was taking his time, picking his steps very prudently. Charlie bit his tongue until he could hold it no longer. "Cardinal, you may want to hurry it up a bit."

"Slow and steady wins the race, Charles."

"Only when there isn't anything chasing you from behind."

The cardinal turned slowly to face the bear standing on its hindquarters, only a couple of feet from the bridge. "Uh…"

"Don't make any sudden movements."

"Should I play dead?"

"No!" The bear woofed, tilting its head. "No, not for black bears. Back up very slowly," Charlie ordered. "Hey Beary, Beary, Bear, everything's alright."

"What are you doing?"

253

"Letting it know we're human. They don't usually attack humans. It's just curious."

The cardinal reversed with the same caution with which he'd made his previous progress. A whining bawl resounded through the trees, followed shortly by several more. Charlie could have sworn. "Cardinal—" The black bear dropped to its paws, snorted loudly, and charged. "—run!"

Cardinal Neumann stepped back quickly, then twisted half way over the log to dart across. The bear followed, its massive body spreading over several of the oaks and pounding over them easily. The cardinal was off balance. He took a slippery step forward and leapt, his world tilting precariously. With a guttural cry, he careened into the cliff-side, clinging to the rock and grass draped over it.

But the bear was still coming. Charlie shot forward, leaping onto the farthest log to land on a thick stump made from a chopped branch that raised Charlie several feet in the air. He leaned forward, shoulders behind him, arms curved out into tightly clenched fists. Charlie reared back, the bear only a few feet from him now, and roared like a lion. His roar dissolved into a low, dangerous growl, then morphed into a vicious snort, much like a Grizzly. Charlie kept eye contact, adrenaline pushing the brown into thin rings around the black, and expanded his presence more than he ever had before. The bear expelled a puff of air, turned on its hind legs, and fled back to her cubs.

Charlie jumped down, helping the cardinal to his feet where the man had scrambled up the side of the cliff. "What," the older man panted, pallid features throbbing with fright, "was that?"

"I," Charlie croaked. He cleared his throat and tried again, "I imitated the warning sounds of a few large predators, mostly to confuse it." He left out the part about amplifying his presence. The cardinal seemed to have passed the feeling off as residual terror from the bear, and Charlie had no problem allowing him to think as much.

"They sounded very..." The older man searched for an accurate term. "...real."

"I've had lots of practice. Exposure to dangerous wildlife while tracking is expected."

The cardinal said nothing at first, then let loose a low, pathetic whine.

"Cardinal?"

"It is not as easy as you make it seem."

Charlie shrugged. He had worked on them for years. The cardinal wasn't about to figure it out in five minutes. "We better get a move on."

Chapter 33

Hot metal whizzed past Jet's temple as he spun into a leg sweep.

He had freshened up a bit, combed his hair for once, shaved down to the skin, and arranged himself into something resembling a respectable member of society. After that, he'd gone a little nuts arming up with gear, especially with sharp, pointy objects. He'd been tempted to bring his favorite shotgun, too, but alas, Jet knew Daisy wasn't suited for this kind of sport, though she'd served him more than well in the past.

Voight's arm arced down to slice at Jet, but he dodged to one side and blocked a kick. Naturally, Voight had refused to back down and had immediately launched into combat. At some point, the older man'd grabbed his Shamshir off the wall, and Jet had been forced to draw his Gayang to parry it. Their blades clashed marvelously. *Ah*, he sighed to himself, *nothing quite like mixing a gunfight with a sword fight.* Jet had never felt more alive.

But for once, he tempered the feeling. It was the same feeling that had gotten him into this mess and the reason he'd sunk into Voight's cesspool of lies, even as his mind hurled the truth at him relentlessly. If he hadn't taken precautions against Voight, it surely would have driven him mad. So, despite his blindness, Jet had tracked down and investigated every one of Voight's safe houses, hide-a-ways, and storage units. He knew more about the man now than the man knew about himself.

Jet's prescience saved him from a diagonal slice across his spine. He blocked it by dropping his Gayang behind him and pursing it with the strength of his entire arm, shoulder, and upper back. He twisted immediately, ignoring the minor twinge in his vertebral column. He was in the zone.

His foresight came more often now, as if his recent enlightenments had finally allowed him to stop holding it back, and visions flashed before his eyes in constant warning.

Voight hadn't prepared this particular safe house for Jet's onslaught, the result of Voight's overconfidence in his own ability to disappear. It *was* his specialty after all. Voight was an expert at sucking people into the void, himself included, although everyone else was gone a bit more permanently.

The house was set into the side of a small cliff. Its one major balcony overlooked a valley, and most of the walls on the scenic side had a view of the mountainous range and the trees that covered it. Jet knew Charlie would be somewhere nearby in the middle of the Ridge and Valley Province and vaguely wondered how he was faring.

He parried another strike, then swung a knee out at Voight. The man jumped back, and Jet added a bullet to Voight's list of problems to solve. Voight twisted at the last second, barely managing to avoid more than a graze to his throat. He was in far worse shape than Jet, whose breathing had barely sped up, skin coated in only a thin sheen of sweat. Voight had earned a black eye, two new gashes, and more than a couple of bruises. He'd severely underestimated the skill of Jet's weapon-wielding, and he was paying for it now.

Voight panted harshly, swiping a wrist over his forehead to remove the excess sweat. Jet wasn't holding back, and already, Voight's strength was waning. Confident as Jet was that he could cut Voight down at any given second, he wouldn't be reckless, not now. Too many lives were at stake to risk error.

And then they were at it again, gun-slinging, sword-wielding professional ballerinas locked in a beautifully lethal dance.

Voight struck forward with his foot, and Jet stepped back to take heat off the hit, but Voight managed a joint-rending maneuver that locked up Jet's hands, still full of weapons, behind him. Jet stepped back, ready to forcefully release himself, when his arm was yanked back and he lost his gun. Then he was flipped, and only reflex found his feet beneath him. He staggered backwards but kept his balance.

Dark shadows fell into the room from all sides, most behind the walls of glass.

Aureates.

One fired at Jet in his second sight and instinct positioned his blade. The bullet collided and split, its halves shooting into the sheetrock behind him.

All was quiet.

Voight was openly gaping at him, and though surprise didn't quite cover what Jet was feeling, he managed to school it behind a blank mask anyways. No need to let anyone know just what kind of happy accident that had been. Secretly, Jet wanted to samba. After all, it wasn't every day he cut a bullet in half.

"What did I just see?"

Pounding boots from behind him swiveled Jet around. The shadows had come alive and begun an ambush. Voight was already breaking for the stairs behind his human wall of assailants. Yeah, he knew their fight was over.

Jet struck a few of the low level Aureates around him, but their sheer number was absurd. Disengaging, he broke through the ring and dove for the stairs behind Voight. Jet felt the hair on the nape of his neck rise and fought down the instinct to turn and fire as he heard the click of their weapons behind him. Several shot out with a bang before shattering glass silenced them for good.

When Jet hit the roof, Voight was long out of sight. Still, Jet kept running. He could hear the engine roaring, the blades rotating faster and faster 'til they hummed a monotonous melody. Vaguely, an image of Charlie popped into his mind of falling and loss, but Jet's step didn't falter. The time for pain and grief would come later. At the moment, he had a job to do that could not be left unfinished.

Chapter 34

Charlie and the cardinal stood beside a shed beneath a small cove. The grass was yellowing, and several of the trees were sick, evidenced by the mushrooms pluming up from their roots, holes in their trunks, and rot eating through layers of bark.

Charlie squatted, scooped up a handful of soil, and brought it to his nose, letting the fine earth run through his fingers like sand. "It's a graveyard," he said to himself.

"What?" the cardinal whispered in horror.

"Not literally," Charlie answered, his voice just as soft. "Chemical wastes are entering the soil. This is loam. It's nutrient rich. Something else is killing the flora, and it smells like it's in the earth, a mixture of burnt oil and grease."

Cardinal Neumann nodded. "And the children are in here?"

"They're underground. This is the bunker entrance. We'll have to hope they don't have too many guards on hand." He paused for a moment. "We should go now."

"And if they are watching us?"

"They probably are," Charlie admitted. "Time for a little blind faith, Your Eminence."

The door came open easily, exposing the dark interior filled with old lawn care supplies and gardening tools. Nothing moved beyond their human shadows. "Are you certain—"

"With all due respect, Cardinal, now would be a great time to stop asking questions."

The cardinal eyed Charlie for a moment, the tip of his tongue posed to scold, then snapped his jaw shut and nodded.

Charlie looked around. The room was rather dusty, but sunlight leaked in from outside, and Charlie's eye for the smallest elements spotted the disturbed mess on the floor. He shoved a few bags of mulch out of the way and reached for the ring that would open the trap door.

The obstructions were a good sign. Traffic must've been limited lately, so they'd sealed off one of their major exits.

He signaled for the cardinal to get behind him and keep quiet. The man did so without complaint. Then slowly and with deliberate care, Charlie pulled open the trap door. Miraculously, it didn't make a sound. He put his foot down on the upper rung of the ladder and cautiously descended.

The cardinal waited for Charlie's all-clear, then after a brief struggle with his uncooperative cassock, followed sedately. Three rungs from the ground, his foot tangled in the black cotton, and he fell the rest of the way into Charlie's strong arms. With a grimace at the strain of his muscles and a wince at the cardinal's hideous shout, Charlie settled him back on his feet. Thankfully, no one appeared to have heard them.

They couldn't erase their tracks as Charlie would've liked, not without one of them being strong enough to slip through the narrow crack and lower the heavy weight of the mulch behind him, so he hoped instead their obvious breech would signal a noisy entrance from any pursuers.

They treaded through the dank hall in silence. The cardinal's tension rolled off him in waves, but Charlie forced himself to keep calm. *This is just like when you were a kid. Easy.* Of course, when he was a kid, he'd had Jet watching his six, and when he was a kid, Uncle Riley would bail him out if he got into too much trouble, and when he was a kid, he'd been in the middle of martial arts and survival training, but hey—details, details, right?

Charlie was in shape…mostly.

How was he the most qualified person to do this again?

They heard a clatter, followed by a rushed set of startled whispers coming from a door up ahead on their right. Charlie flung himself against the wall, the cardinal at his heels. He twisted the doorknob and yanked the wood open, hands up in defense.

But there was only silence.

Charlie crept in first, examining the room carefully. An emergency light hit the burlap blankets on the top beds of the bunks, but Charlie couldn't make out their occupants in the dim lighting, so he slid on his glasses and triggered night vision.

A child lay on every bunk, seemingly asleep. Their little chests rose and fell, but none of it seemed natural. The cardinal's clumsiness had woken them, and despite their best efforts, they couldn't just drop back into slumber. "Kenzie Donahue?" One of the girls towards the middle of the left row shifted. Her eyes fluttered nervously, but otherwise, she did not move.

"Thomas Schuster?" A young boy lifted his head several inches off his pillow.

"Lindsey McKay?" No one moved. "Has anyone seen Lindsey McKay?"

A boy near the front of the bunks slid out of bed, and after a long few seconds, he took a hesitant step towards them. Charlie noted the bruise under his left eye and the careful suspicion in both. "You're not Mr. J—" He paused. "—and definitely not Mrs. T. I've never seen either of you." Several of the children sat up, curiosity dispelling their caution.

"Have you seen Lindsey McKay?" Charlie asked again, ignoring the accusation.

The boy considered them for a moment. "I think she's with the others."

"What's your name, child?" the cardinal asked.

"Santiago."

Santiago Gonzalez had disappeared on his sixth birthday from the front yard of his childhood home. Charlie had read the report filed nearly two years ago.

"And who are you? 'Cuz you definitely aren't either of the idiots that normally watch us."

He was stupidly brave for an eight-year-old, but Charlie couldn't be sure whether he'd been born with that disposition or if the environment he'd been exposed to for so long had already done a significant amount of damage. A pair of determined brown eyes glared up at him, little flecks of analytical mindfulness splayed in his still large orbs. How long had it taken the Aureates to discover the child genius in their midst and dig into his psyche in slightly more creative ways? Evidently, little Santiago had hung in there.

The light in the room came on, and Charlie went blind. He groped at the glasses on his face, hands already up defensively, reaching out with his senses to counter any incoming attacks. For a moment, he panicked, certain he was so out of practice that he couldn't sense anything at all. Then he belatedly realized that there was nothing *to* sense. Only Cardinal Neumann had changed position, his arm now jutting out at the light switch. Charlie blinked away the blindness and gave the cardinal his most unimpressed glower.

"What?"

Most of the children were staring at Charlie and his raised fists. Santiago gave him a remarkably skeptical look for a boy his age, reminiscent of Jet in his youth.

Charlie inhaled slowly to regulate his temper. "You don't turn on the lights when someone's using night vision unless you're *trying* to blind them, Your *Eminence*," he bit out.

"Ah, sorry, Charles."

Charlie snubbed him in favor of the children. "I'm Father Charlie, and this is Cardinal Neumann."

"We are here to rescue you."

The boy blinked, and Charlie mentally face-palmed when his incredulity only grew. "You? A couple of priests are here to rescue us? They sent *you*?" he reiterated.

"Yes." Santiago had too much attitude in too small a body. "As a matter of fact, they did. If you'd prefer someone else, you're welcome to wait another couple of days until someone's available."

For a moment, the boy's youth shined through, and he actually seemed frightened by Charlie's sarcasm. Then he visibly calmed, took a hard look at the pair of them, and nodded. "Come on, everybody, let's get out of here." The children began to rise.

"Hold on." They halted. "We need to ask you a few more questions before we can go anywhere."

"Why waste time?"

"It's better to be prepared than dead."

Santiago said nothing, eyes grim and guarded.

"Are Mr. J and Mrs. T the only ones who come down here?"

"No, there are others, but only Mr. J and Mrs. T have anything to do with us."

And then a swarm of frightened children besieged Charlie, wrapping him in a cinnamon bun hug and mewling gratitude they weren't old enough to understand.

Charlie patted a few heads, the cardinal taking a few of them in his own comfort, but there was nearly thirty of them, and they only had four arms between them.

Santiago was pushed up against Charlie unwillingly as the crowd surged towards the young priest. He looked up at the man and, standing on his tiptoes, softly warned, "If you get anyone killed, you and I will have a problem." A girl behind Santiago lost her footing and shoved him forward. Off balance, he fell against Charlie, slamming a hand into his kidney while trying to retreat.

A lesser man might have cowered. A prouder man might have sneered. Charlie just sighed tiredly and righted the boy. This was what his life had come to, being threatened by an eight-year-old. "Alright, everyone, listen up please." The children quieted, still huddled around their two saviors. "I know you're all scared and you just want to go home, but the threat is still out there, so we have to be very careful, okay?"

The crowd of them nodded. "Excuse me, Father?"

"Yes?"

"What about my friend Molly? They took her away a few days ago."

"Yeah, Jamie, too."

"We'll find them, but we have to take care of you first."

"I know where they are," Santiago said, arms crossed over his chest.

"You do?"

"Yeah, I could take you to 'em."

Then a shadow behind the cardinal, who was still standing in the doorway, flickered, and suddenly, he was having the life choked out of him. Charlie moved to his aid immediately, but the sea of crying children contained him like quicksand. Nothing short of trampling them would free him from their grasp.

Charlie could barely hear the cardinal gasping over their young wails, and all he could do was pray that it didn't die. Then a loud clang graced his ears, and as the shadow fell and the cardinal collapsed against the doorjamb, Penny Belmonte appeared, the shovel in here hands held like a bat. She'd rung his bell alright, and the shadow man was down for the count.

"Penny? Didn't I tell you to stay behind and work on the profiles?" Charlie hadn't quite meant for that to sound so patronizing.

"I'm not useless because I'm a woman, you know."

"I know," Charlie answered, adjusting his tone. "But you *are* a civilian with no combat experience. I would have left the cardinal behind, too, if he wasn't my superior."

Cardinal Neumann ignored them both, too busy trying to fill his lungs with air to care about Charlie's abrasive remark.

"I finished what you asked anyways—"

Already?

"—so I thought I'd better lend you a hand and took a flight out early this morning. Luckily, someone gave up their seat for me, something about reconnecting with a relative or something. Then this friendly couple dressed in overalls showed me right where to go, although I did wind up lost for a while."

It was a miracle they hadn't shot her first and asked questions later. Maybe they'd learned something from him and the cardinal.

"I saw an adorable family of bears, too, even snapped a picture of them with my phone."

Charlie gawked at her. *Who is this girl?* Dutifully, he reassessed the situation. "Okay, here's the plan: Penny, Cardinal, keep the kids here. Santiago and I will find the others and regroup with you after."

"Why can't we just go now and get a head start?"

"You want to navigate the terrain out there with a bunch of kids?"

"You were about to," she argued, arms cross in displeasure.

"I'm me, and you're you. Maybe you'd make it. Maybe you wouldn't. I, for one, am not about to take that chance."

She frowned at him for a minute, lips pursed disdainfully, but then she shrugged in acceptance and nodded. "You're probably right."

"Good. One of you will need to act as a lookout. Penny, see if you can get a signal on your phone." Charlie whipped out his new pocket watch, something small and unassuming he'd picked up from headquarters, and tossed it to Penny. "If you can, call the number on the inside of that. Tell them we have a dragon, and do whatever you're told."

"What?" she asked in puzzlement.

"Just trust me."

"If you say so."

"Okay, Santiago, lead the way."

Santiago took him to the far end of the hall where the simple path turned into a maze of tunnels. "Most of them go nowhere. You can waste hours trying to get through."

Charlie nodded.

"You know, a normal adult wouldn't have let me come."

"I'm not a normal adult, and you're not a normal kid." Charlie looked around. He noted nothing special about the tunnel the boy had chosen. In fact, it looked a lot like the others. "How do you know the tunnels so well?"

"I've tried to escape dozens of times, but they always catch me. I've got the scars to prove it."

Charlie held back a grimace. "Are there only two groups of kids here?"

"Yeah, after that they join the adults."

"And what did they want from you exactly?"

"To be just like them."

"I heard that some of you are taught to do terrible things in the name of God."

"Yeah, that's true, sort of."

"What do you mean?"

"Some of us are too smart for them. We know better, so they watch us, split us up for lessons, and make sure we don't talk to each other."

Charlie rubbed his temple. "How would they do that?"

"They watch us all the time. Mr. J or Mrs. T sits with us 'til we're all asleep. Then one of them peeks in on us randomly to make sure no one's up. They punish us if we are."

Charlie grimaced. *Poor kids*. Then something occurred to him. "Why were y'all sleeping in the middle of the day?"

Santiago shrugged hardheartedly. "We sleep when they tell us to."

O-kay. "What about Lindsey McKay's group? They're the ones we're looking for now, right?"

Santiago nodded. "I don't know how you're going to convince them to leave. They're proud members of the Aureate Society now."

Charlie froze, eyes turning down at the kid. "Aureate Society?"

"Yeah, didn't you know?"

Charlie ignored his question. "They told you who they were?"

"The half of us who aren't taught to be crazy are taught to be good members of the Aureate Society, although I don't see what the big difference is. You only get moved to that group when you always do what they tell you to." Santiago paused. "I was like that for a while, so they moved me. I thought it'd be better, but then I saw them do something bad, something really bad, and I wouldn't do it, so they sent me back with the others." Santiago stopped again, and his chin dropped to his chest. "They're getting tired of me, and when they get tired of kids, they take them away forever, and I'm old enough to know what that means." He turned his head up.

Those haunted eyes nearly toppled Charlie, but he forced himself to stay on task. "Have you seen another cardinal around here?" Santiago's confusion was evident, so Charlie clarified, "You know the man that was with me?"

Santiago nodded.

"Cardinal Weatherford would be dressed in the same clothes."

He hummed in thought, then shook his head. "I haven't seen anyone like that."

Charlie sighed. "Okay, what happens to the kids who don't join the Aureate Society?"

269

"You mean the ones taught to do terrible things? They get to go home, but only once Mr. J and Mrs. T are sure they're ready."

Put back into society? That was bad news. They'd never track them all down, especially if there were older generations. Who knew how long the Aureate Society had been up to all this?

"Something's got them all thrown out of whack."

"Why do you say that?"

"Mr. J and Mrs. T haven't been checking on us as much as normal the last couple of days. I tried to leave, but the door that goes out by our room is locked or something. I can't open it."

"Is there another exit?"

"Only one, all the way on the other side of the building."

"Do they use them both?"

"That depends."

"On?"

"What's going on out there."

Charlie looked around. The compound halls were primarily made up of bleak cement walls, lights every twenty feet or so, and moisture everywhere. "Do they ever take you outside?"

"I've seen the sun only one time since they took me, and only 'cuz I made it that far before they dragged me back." He sighed tiredly. It didn't suit his youth. "I can't remember what my parents look like anymore. It's only been two years, but I can't remember. Sometimes, they're right there, but I can't reach them, like I dream about them, but then I wake up, and everything's just gone."

"Soon, Santiago. I promise."

"You can't make promises like that. All three of you might die down here."

"Even if we do, we're just the first wave." Charlie stopped again. Dropping to one knee, he stared into the little boy's eyes. "They're coming, Santiago. If we die today, they'll come tomorrow, and when they come, they'll bring a whole army with them. You see? I *can* make that promise. Have a little faith, okay?"

Santiago nodded, a small, strange smile slowly unraveling across his countenance, like his face wasn't quite sure what it was doing. Charlie stood, continuing his trek. "Hey, Father Charlie?"

"Yes?"

"How come you're here now if they're coming later?"

"Because Cardinal Neumann and I didn't want you to have to wait even one more day."

Santiago nodded again. "Hey, Father?"

"Yes?"

"I'm glad you came today. One day's a long time. I've seen lots of bad things happen in a day."

Charlie's step faltered, and finally, he understood.

Nodding, more to himself than at the boy, he waited for Santiago to catch up. "Father, what exactly's going on up there?"

"We've gone to war with the Aureates. Don't worry about it."

The tunnel emptied into a large control room, and Charlie's heart dropped. Chained to the wall was Cardinal Weatherford. His injuries were horrific. Hardly an inch of his flesh was left unmarred, and his white hair was stained by his own blood. Charlie's hands automatically darted to Santiago's face to shield his eyes.

"Was that the man you were looking for?"

"Y—Yes."

"Sorry. They sometimes make the other kids do that to people they catch." Charlie could have wept, his heart seizing painfully. "That's what I couldn't do."

Charlie spun Santiago around, then signed himself with the cross. *God—God, have mercy on their souls.* Charlie wasn't quite sure where that prayer had come from. He sure didn't feel very merciful at the moment.

"Look."

A computer sat on the wall opposite. Charlie fled to it. He clicked on a few of the files and out popped several lists of names, maps, grids, invitations, videos of tortured men and women—a goldmine of Aureate activities that couldn't be accessed by outside servers, brilliant…if Charlie hadn't been sitting right in front of it. He thumbed a pen drive he always had on hand, scholar that he was, and pulled it from his pocket. Then he set his glasses down in front of the screen, plugged in his pen drive, and went to work.

The atmosphere shifted before his senses could decipher the warning. "Father!"

And Charlie draped himself over Santiago just as a shot exploded through the air. He took a minute to ensure there would be no more, then raised himself off the boy.

Blood.

"Huh, looks like the kiddies are getting a new toy to play with." Charlie rose from his knees, steel eyes locking on the figure in front of him. "And my, you don't look too happy." In arrogance, he advanced on Charlie.

What. A. Fool.

Hands up in seeming surrender, Charlie wasted less than three seconds disarming the man. Then he leveled a spinning roundhouse kick at his skull that connected fiercely and knocked him unconscious.

"Wow!" Charlie spun around. The little figure seated on the floor was looking up at him in awe. "That was pretty impressive. I didn't see that coming at all."

"Santiago! You're okay?"

"Well, my arm really hurts, like *really* hurts, but yeah, I'm okay."

Charlie took a closer look. Sure enough, the kid had a bullet lodged in his small bicep, but he was otherwise unharmed. "Oh, thank you, God."

Clearly, the child was extremely desensitized to pain. That didn't bode well for his psychological health, but Charlie ignored that for the time being. Santiago's physical health was of greater importance at the moment.

Charlie reached through the slits in his cassock to grab at his belt. He yanked it off and out, then wrapped it around the boy's tiny arm. "I'm not going to pull it too tight, just enough to slow down the bleeding. I don't want to completely cut off your circulation."

"Okay," the kid chirped, keeping the perplexity off his face. "You're really good. You're almost as good as me."

Another figure entered the corridor. Charlie attacked her immediately. Block. Block. Right palm strike heart. Left palm strike cheek. Right uppercut. She was down. Two more men appeared in her place. Dodge left. Duck. Sweep punch. Charlie kicked at the inside of one's knee as another man joined them. He swept his legs out from beneath him, elbowed the other in the nose, and push-kicked the first back. The man with a now broken nose launched himself at Charlie, who let the man's momentum roll off him and flipped him onto one of his buddies. He roundhouse-kicked the last one in the temple and sent him to the ground.

Left fist raised in front of him, right hand by his ear, palm facing out and elbow bent, Charlie embraced his favorite martial arts style, the one crafted specially for him by a master of the trade.

"I take that back. Maybe you're just a *smidge* better than me."

"Come on, Santiago. Time to go."

But before he could move, a group of children entered. Many of them were in their teens. "Santiago, what are you doing here?"

"This is Father Charlie. He's come to rescue us." One or two of the kids looked hopeful. Most looked confused. A few looked angry.

"Who needs rescuing?"

They charged at Charlie.

"I told you they wouldn't want to leave."

The duo made a run for it.

Charlie could've easily handled a bunch of kids, but he wasn't eager to hurt them, so he searched his thoughts for a new course of action. "Santiago, can you get me to the other exit?"

"Yeah, this way." Charlie could run, and with his long legs, the teens couldn't keep up. Unfortunately, neither could Santiago, and soon, heavier footsteps pulled up behind them. Charlie considered lessening his presence. He hadn't used that particular gift in a while, but... He glanced down. It wouldn't help Santiago. "Just go straight until you hit a crossing, then enter the first hall on your right."

"What? I'm not leaving you."

"I'll hold them off for a bit, then hide. They won't kill me. You can get me out later when your friends come."

Charlie didn't hesitate. He booked it down the hall, then dove into a lightless tunnel. A large iron door slid shut behind him, and Charlie was nearly positive this wasn't the way out.

He was in a narrow tunnel, long and straight, an eerie reminder of a freezing winter and lots of blood. Charlie could almost smell it, the thick iron tang of someone's life splattered all over the walls. He could see nothing in the pitch blackness, certainly not without his glasses, and though he could see nothing, Charlie could sense everything.

The whirl of his own mind dropped him into Illinois, gentle mutterings drifting from somewhere up ahead in a slightly wider tunnel, whispering of trivial matters like school and chores. A decision approached Charlie, the adjacent tunnel calling to him, darkness crawling up his legs as he trekked, devouring him inch by inch, eager to swallow him up like Jonah and the whale. He couldn't stop. He couldn't turn around. He couldn't—

And then he was back in the emptiness, and Charlie remembered his fate, his fear, and his redemption.

There wasn't a particle of light in the tunnel, so Charlie couldn't make out a thing, but he could feel the walls several inches from his arms. He reached his hands up, flinching when his fingertips met a sticky wetness. Three feet—the tunnel was three feet wide. Charlie lowered his center of gravity, bringing his wet fingers up to his nose. He flinched harder at the abrasive smell of blood.

Okay, so he hadn't been imagining it. There really was blood in the air. A heavy clank behind him pushed him forward, and as the sound of something spinning approached, Charlie sprinted towards the other end of the tunnel, the revving device behind him chomping at his heels. He forced his step harder and leaned forward, a significant gap forming between him and mechanical beast behind him.

Charlie sensed the wall coming just in time to put his hands up and cushion the impact. His wrists ached, but he didn't dwell on it. Whatever was behind him was coming up fast.

He reached out with his sense of touch. Air flowed through the tunnel, pushed forward by the rotor behind him, and as it struck the wall, the air channeled up, sucked into its only means of escape. With no other choice, Charlie squatted, then leapt vertically, open hands finding a narrow ledge. He grasped onto it, then hauled himself up, pulling his feet clear of the rotating device just as it hit the wall, chopping at it with a hack, hack, hack!

Charlie stayed low on the ledge, resting on the balls of his feet braced against the shaft's narrow edges. The vertical tunnel was three feet around, he decided, but still, he saw nothing. He sniffed the air, noticing instantly the metallic scent had vanished, replaced by mossy must.

Charlie groped around for something, and eventually, his efforts were rewarded when his hand smacked against a metal pipe. Charlie stood, and the panel beneath him slid shut. Instantly, water poured into the shaft. He reached for the pipe and hoisted himself onto it, finding himself in a maze of bars crossing all around like a backwards version of KerPlunk.

Charlie slipped through a pair of them that he only just fit between, then used more to pull himself up. Clearly the path had been built for someone a bit smaller, and Charlie squeezed through a couple of narrow crevices with a sucked in gut and some tight maneuvering. *Boy am I going to feel this tomorrow.*

The water was slower than he'd thought it'd be, and for a moment, Charlie was pleased with himself. He'd make it to the top with plenty of time to spare, but just as he reached the end of the shaft, his hand struck another pipe and another and another. Crossing over each other, two in a V and one making an A out of it, Charlie's adult body could not dream of fitting through them.

The water was rising, and this time, Charlie was less than thrilled with its pace. His fingers found the spot where pipe met wall. It was cemented in. The pipes were aluminum, and the cement itself was intact, so really, he was stuck.

The water was only feet from him now, and he worked his brain over for something, anything that could help.

He flicked the metal pipe with his index finger, his ear pressed up against it, listening intently. The vibrations ended early.

"God, forgive me," Charlie begged, yanking off his wrought-iron crucifix. His old crucifix had been made of sterling silver and plastic, but Charlie had learned fast that it couldn't hold up against his black cloud and had it re-casted accordingly.

He jabbed the long end of the crossbar at the place where aluminum met cement, striking it repeatedly. He just needed the cement to crack a little. And it did, a thin sort of break that didn't give Charlie too much hope. He slammed his crucifix down on it a few more times, then hung back on a lower bar and kicked at the juncture. It gave a little, but hung in there stubbornly. He struck it again, putting all his weight into his heavy heel, and this time, the cement fractured, the metal bar scraping across the wall to rest on its final breath. Charlie yanked on it as the water lapped at his dipping back and soaked into his dangling fascia. And the pipe came free. Charlie hoisted himself up, then once more out of the shaft and back onto solid ground.

Charlie panted lightly. That had been close. And then a panel was sliding shut again, and Charlie was at the ready, immediately assessing the black tunnel reminiscent of the first. Charlie slapped a hand against the wall. He still couldn't see, but his fine-tuned senses had created a different sort of sight that sent Charlie running again before he'd had a chance to catch his breath.

Something was coming at him from the front, low enough to sweep his legs. He jumped, took two more steps, then slid under a swinging something on his folded knees. He pushed off the ground with his forelegs, flexed his abs, and snapped his lower body off the ground and to his feet. Yeah, his muscles would not be thanking him for that later.

Charlie took several more steps before the sound of his feet echoed strangely in his ears. He jumped suddenly, aware of the pit-to-who-knew-where beneath him. His hands and feet hit the walls, and he spider-climbed the rest of the way until he kicked the door and dropped to solid ground.

He walked through the next doorway, and when the panel slid shut behind him, a blinding white light burst on, flooding the room with spots across Charlie's vision. It took him more than a few moments, but the spots faded somewhat and he found himself staring at a short corridor with a barred iron door at the end of it.

It opened unceremoniously.

A woman stood on the other side, a sweet smile on her face and a 9mm nestled in her grip. She gestured for him to exit, so he did. "Mrs. T, I take it?"

Her smile widened, and she adjusted her spectacles, flicking at the loose strands of her messy bun. "You've heard of me. I'm flattered."

And then he was chained to the wall beside the departed Cardinal Weatherford, freed of his cassock but glad she hadn't forced him out of shirt like she had his superior. His hands were up above him, but his feet rested comfortably on the ground, and for that, he was grateful.

"I hope you weren't expecting too much from your little helper," she said, gesturing to the child behind her. Santiago stepped forward, eyes downcast. Charlie watched him carefully. "He didn't make a mistake, you know. He knows the tunnels very well." She frowned. "You don't look very surprised to see him."

Charlie's eyes flickered over to her. What had she come from? Where had she been to wind up in a place like this, tormenting adults and children alike? He saw suffering in her eyes, shielded by power and pseudo control. "I'm not." She gave him a curious look, but Santiago's shock was clearer, and the boy almost opened his mouth. "He's a survivor," Charlie said simply. Santiago held his gaze a moment, then dropped his eyes remorsefully.

"That he is." Mrs. T approached him. "Won't you make such a lovely plaything for the children?"

Charlie said nothing.

"Come, Santiago." The child shuffled forward. His eyes rose, but he kept them averted. She held a knife in front him. "Why don't you show this young man of God what's in store for him?"

Santiago startled, taking the knife on reflex but treating it like the source of all evil. He turned his large, scared eyes to Charlie. Charlie held his gaze, strong and reassuring. The child's mouth fell agape.

"I'm waiting," Mrs. T snapped. "Don't act like you haven't done worse."

Santiago flinched, and Charlie was moved with pity.

No, Charlie wasn't afraid. Pain was nothing foreign to him, and he just couldn't bring himself to fear the gleaming blade. He was more concerned about the boy in front of him. *God, spare this child further torment.*

The knife dropped to Charlie's midsection, but Santiago's eyes remained on Charlie's, enchanted by his gaze, even as the tip of the knife drug across his unresisting body. Despite his lack of fear, Charlie bit back a hiss. Yup, pain was still a thing. His calming eyes faltered a second, breaking the trance on Santiago. The boy awoke startled, stumbling backwards, the knife clattering to the ground. Angry, Mrs. T approached him, scooping the knife up as she went. Now Charlie pulled at his bindings. No. *No!* "Stop!"

Fear was taking over, and Santiago's eyes welled with tears. The child should've run, but the terror chaining him to the floor was just as real as Charlie's metal cuffs, and then a pinkette pulled the boy behind her and kicked at the startled woman's knife hand, effectively disarming her.

With renewed courage, Santiago rushed forward, delivering a hard kick to the woman's shin. The dancer followed his hit with a strike to her head using the blunt side of the knife she'd retrieved. They watched as she crumbled to the ground unconscious.

"Penny?"

She gave him a pretty smile, marred by the quick frown that replaced it once she'd caught sight of the blood seeping through his shirt. "Are you alright?"

"Huh?" Charlie looked down. He always had been a bleeder. "Yeah, I'm fine. It's just a scratch really."

Penny moved forward, pointedly keeping her eyes off the corpse still strung against the wall. "Was that…?" she trailed off, tilting her head in the cardinal's direction.

"Yes." He paused to look at Mrs. T. "I think she has the keys on her."

"I'm not going anywhere near that monster." Penny reached into her hair and drew out a couple of hairpins, and Charlie glanced at his restraints. They were a fairly simple model. Bobby pins would work. "My dad liked being on the wrong side of the law. We used to spend Saturday mornings going through locks and all the ways to pick them."

Charlie blanched. He suddenly understood the strange looks Jet had been giving her in the conference room of headquarters, though he'd been too distracted at the time to give it much thought. Jet was smitten. Charlie just wondered if his little brother knew that. He could be denser than Charlie when lives were on the line.

The cuffs clicked, and Charlie's arms dropped. After reassuring himself that his cut was, in fact, only a small thing, he flung his cassock on once more. "Thanks for your help, Penny."

"No problem—"

"I'm sorry!" Santiago was trembling head to toe. "It was—"

"Don't worry about it," Charlie cut in. He didn't have time for this right now. "Penny, take Santiago and get back to the group. Were you able to reach the club?"

"Yes, they told us to stay put for now."

Charlie nodded. "Do that."

"What about you?"

"I'll make sure you aren't followed."

"Okay." She paused for a moment. "Don't you want to know wh—"

"No." And then he was ushering the pair of them out the door.

Charlie snatched his glasses off the table and slipped them on while plucking his pen drive from the PC. He sped through the hallways, away from the innocents, dealing with any strays without hesitation. He hit an intersection. Echoes of young voices down one hall scrapped that option. Charlie glanced at the other two and chose the less humid one, a new pair of adult feet following up behind him.

And then he reached a set of stairs, took them two at a time, and shot through the door he threw open with a bang. The clatter alerted some nearby men to his presence, but Charlie disposed of them quickly before continuing on his way.

Something told him he didn't want to face the approaching figure, so Charlie kept running, anything to avoid dealing with the bombshell sneaking up behind him. His heart was racing, and he couldn't help but wonder if it was from exertion or anxiety. Charlie came up to a cliff's edge and slid to a stop. He shifted immediately, but the click of the gun and a sharp, "Don't," made him halt. "Turn around."

Charlie did. In the next second, the blood drained from his face, and he suddenly felt very queasy. "Kenny?"

The stranger's eye quirked.

"No, Simon," he self-corrected, feeling a little faint. So this was point of all his recent reveries.

Surprise adorned Simon's face for half a second, then seriousness overshadowed it. "Do I know you?"

"Simon—" Breathing was oddly difficult. "—it's me, Charlie, Charlie Harper."

"Oh yeah, Charlie. Well, what a surprise! I wanted to be just like you, and here I am."

"What?"

"Yeah, clandestine adventure at its best. The society offered me that, and I took it."

"Simon, this is nothing like what Jet and I used to do. You're on the wrong side."

"Is there a right side?"

"Yes," he answered immediately.

Simon's eyes flicked around a bit, his gun still trained on Charlie. "Ah, well, what're ya gonna do?" His gun hand firmed up, and his finger dropped to the trigger. "Now give me that flash drive, and I won't kill you where you stand."

"Because death by torture is so much more appealing."

"Ah, I guess you found Cardinal Weatherford. Poor sap. His heart gave out long before we got to the good stuff."

Charlie couldn't help but watch his old friend in venomous shock. "What did they do to make you such a heartless..." The pejorative died on his tongue. "Simon, this isn't right."

The man yawned. "Are you done?"

Charlie gave himself an emotional shake. No point in appealing to the child Simon. Years of brainwashing couldn't be undone with a couple of sweet words.

"So, a quick death or a long, torturous one? Your choice."

It seemed they were at an impasse. The information Charlie carried was vital to the dissolution of the Aureate Society and the end to all its heinous crimes against humanity, but it didn't seem Simon intended to slip up. He was too far from Charlie for Charlie to do anything more than gaze at him somberly, and he was too far gone mentally to be captured by Charlie's empathetic influence.

Charlie cast his eyes to the trees. Adjusting his glasses, he feigned consideration. The lenses scoped his sight, and he almost sighed in relief. Apparently, the club had caught up with them early. He didn't want to see Simon die, but—

And then a cluster of teenagers surrounded the redhead. "He's got shooters in the trees, Mr. J, but they won't shoot at you with us in the way."

Charlie knew that probably wasn't true. Sure, it was no one's desire to kill a child, but most of the Dragonflies on site would be prepared to do what they had to, and Charlie was the victim here in their eyes. They'd protect him at the children's expense. The thought made him cringe, and he readjusted his lenses, this time tapping into the short range radio chatter buzzing around the busy air.

"The target's been surrounded by a group of four kids."

"Hostages?"

"No, sir, doesn't seem like it. They put themselves in the line of fire."

"Orders, sir?"

"Shooters, find your targets. If they further threaten Father Harper, take them all out."

Charlie frowned. No, that would not do. He'd come here to rescue these kids, not get them killed. Slightly anxious at the turn of events, Charlie shuffled back a step, conscious of the cliff's edge behind him. Somewhere, far but not too far, Charlie could hear the sound of running water. Below him—it was definitely coming from below him.

Charlie glanced over his shoulder. A rock-infested ravine twisted through the cliffs. Charlie sighed. Down meant certain death, and where else was there to go?

"I was listening, you know, when you claimed to be completely unsurprised by little Santiago's betrayal. I find that hard to believe."

"Like I told your friend, he's a survivor."

"It still must have stung, discovering your brave little soldier had slipped one past you."

Charlie said nothing, staring intently into Simon's eyes, watching them narrow in suspicion.

"Unless…unless you *knew* he was sending you the wrong way."

"Santiago, he isn't like the other kids. He's intelligent and cunning." Charlie paused. "He's also eight and, like I said before, a survivor. If I were him and a couple of priests had shown up to save me, I'd have been pretty skeptical, too, and if I was a survivor like Santiago, I would have ensured my position was secure either way. Santiago helped me until he was certain we'd fail, which was the moment we were forced to retreat. And he volunteered to what? Stay behind and confront his captors? I don't think so. He's been severely traumatized. He sent me into a trap and hung around to get his pat on the back, an assurance of his survival."

"Then why did you go?"

"Because Penny had only called in our friends a few minutes before that. Haven't you figured it out yet, Simon?" Charlie wasn't one to boast, but he let the pride bleed into his words for the sake of effect.

Simon clenched his jaw and tensed. "You were just a distraction."

Charlie smiled pompously. "All we needed was to find the kids, to verify that they were, in fact, here. That's it." Charlie stood back on his heels, arms crossed pretentiously, a smug grin on his face. "Then all I had to do was make sure we didn't get cornered and killed before backup could arrive, so I let Santiago take me on that wild goose chase. I'll admit I had trouble placing his allegiance at first, but he dropped enough accidental hints for me to figure it out long before he actually 'betrayed' me. That course of yours was a bit of a challenge. I'm out of shape, but it did eat up quite a bit of time, didn't it?"

"You let yourself get captured." The smirk remained on Charlie's face. His tactical skills were second to none. "You could've been killed."

But he wasn't prideful, not really. "I knew by then that Santiago was supposed to be keeping watch over the other children. He kept running away, and your normal tactics for brainwashing weren't working very well, so you gave him a position of power, like in the Stanford Prison Project, and watched him fall into his role. I knew the other children would rat him out just as soon as the cardinal and Penny made them comfortable. Penny would come looking for me. She's blessed, so I knew she'd stumble around to the right path, and if she hadn't made it in time, well, c'est la vie."

A silence fell between them, and Charlie shifted temperaments as quickly as he dared.

"Kenny's dead."

Simon froze for half a second, then resumed his manic shifting, as if Charlie'd said nothing. "Eh, it's probably for the best. He always was a nuisance. No more pattering after me like a lost puppy."

No.

No.

Charlie thought of Jet when they were nine and six respectively. Jet's favorite pastimes had included poking Charlie, hitting Charlie, breaking Charlie's stuff, pulling Charlie's hair, sticking his nose in Charlie's business, and ratting Charlie out to Mom and Dad.

No.

Absolutely not.

He couldn't imagine a world without his little brother around to annoy him. He just didn't work without Jet, not then and not now. Charlie had barely managed to cope during the few short years they'd had nothing to do with each other, when there hadn't been anyone to balance his strict and prudently efficacious strategies. Memories could only sustain someone for so long. And Jet's reckless yet effective adaptability had salvaged more than one plan blown out of the water by the insanity of people. Charlie could read people better than he could read books, but they weren't always fighting people, and Jet could read the future almost as well as he could see it.

Charlie raised the flash drive. The intel was still saved on the computer down in the bunker. The club had arrived. It didn't matter anymore. They'd already won, with or without Charlie's life hanging in the balance.

An explosion from the ground level door forced Charlie back a step in pure reflex. Simon and his brood didn't budge. "We tied up the loose ends, Mr. J. That drive is now the only means to our exposure." Lindsey McKay smiled, and though the tilt of her lips was all amiable application, her eyes spoke the truth. Eyes always speak the truth.

Charlie tried not to think of the ones he'd left behind. He could only hope the club had gotten everyone out in time. Instead, his string of endless thoughts flew to something else. He was now the only one with the information that might bring them closer to the end of this madness.

Was that really necessary? Charlie asked, eyes raised to heaven.

The drive was in his left hand, held up with its twin in surrender. A quick death for Charlie now seemed like Simon's only option. Charlie only had a second.

So, he pulled the spectacles from his face, used his chest and nimble fingers to fold the frames, then slipped them in his sleeve.

"Don't want to see death coming? Not a very brave priest, are you, Charlie?" Simon tutted. "What would my younger self have thought of your cowardice?"

287

Charlie shut his eyes, dropped his shoulders back, and stiffened like a board, his arms coming up in something less like surrender and something more like acceptance, crucifixion against the wide, open sky.

Charlie leaned back.

"Hey, what—"

Back.

The collective sound of cacophonous shouts assaulted Charlie's sensitive ears, equal parts angry, surprised, and disturbed.

Back.

And Charlie fell.

Chapter 35

But that was just one of the things about him. When he was motivated, he could fly.

Off the rail-less terrace, Jet soared. With only rock below, even a chute couldn't save him if his hands didn't meet their mark. He was way too close to the ground for that. Weightless, wingless, he missed the landing skid completely and dove beneath it. From his tactical pouch, he pulled a hook no bigger than his hand and flung it at the skid, a trail of thick, black rope tailing it. The sleek grappling hook twisted around the skid several times before catching on itself. Jet waited for the sudden tension and swung into the jerk to avoid injury.

"Structure is clear, Grim Reaper. Should we catch up to you?"

Jet swung a hand up to the radio on his neck. "Negative, hold your positions. Eyes on me."

"Roger that, Grim Reaper."

Jet freed his hand to the line and began to climb. The gunmen occupying the copter had seen his pseudo fall and assumed the best…for them anyways. Another minute and Jet had grabbed the skid, hoisting himself up easily.

A startled invective echoed inside his mind that wasn't his own, and with a flinch, he realized his team was projecting through his second sight. His mind must have been working overtime to hear them hundreds of meters in the air, thirty seconds from the past. Jet shook his head. He could ignore that…hopefully.

Jet stood, the ground below a sea of green. They'd gained quite some height very quickly.

A tall man riding the edge of the craft kicked out at Jet, so Jet slid to the edge of the skid in evasion. With nothing to impede his momentum, the man flew out into the open air, and even Jet's second sight wasn't quick enough to grab him. He stared wide-eyed for a second at the free-falling figure, then noticed a round, black dot flagging open in the distance. *They have chutes?* Jet's lips formed a wicked grin, and he tapped his radio again. "Did y'all just see that?"

"Affirmative."

"How 'bout we play a jumbo-sized game of catch?"

Jet could hear the grin in the other man's voice when he answered, "Roger that, Grim Reaper."

And then Jet was in the bird, dodging limbs and ducking shots. Naturally, one of them clipped the pilot. "Really? Are you a complete idiot? Did you see me firing off rounds like a lunatic? The least you could do is not shoot your own freakin' guys!"

The helicopter lurched right, and Jet flung a few of the off-balance men from the craft. A vision of brief, intense pain and lots of blood called his Gayang into his hand once more and across his head. He turned it to its flat side just as Voight let out a round, and the bullet ricocheted harmlessly into the air. Jet knocked a few of the others out.

Then it was just Jet and Voight. Still lacking a gun, Jet held his blade in front of him. "A Filipino Gayang—you always were a fan of the foreign."

"I'm a fan of the efficient," Jet replied.

They moved towards each other, and just as Voight's gun aligned with Jet, the copter twisted. Jet moved under his splayed, flapping limbs and cut across Voight's back. Voight growled, his own chute now ruined. He raised his gun again, but the instability of the craft threw his aim, and Jet danced around the shots with ease.

"One other thing you never knew about me, Voight," Jet stated, finding his feet and internally groaning when he realized their ride was leaking fuel. *That's alright. I can still land it.* "I have this uncanny ability to know things are going to happen before they do."

Jet can admit his prescience, even now, isn't perfect, so when the bird gave a sudden twist and chucked Voight at the door, only instinct pushed Jet forward. He caught Voight by the ankle as his own hooked around the door handle. His shoulder strained, as did his back, but he held on, re-sheathing his Gayang briskly.

"Why?" Voight shouted.

"No one's beyond redemption."

Voight's eyed narrowed. "You're wrong." He snagged a small blade of his own and flung it at Jet's grip with all his might. Jet released him to avoid losing a finger and watched Voight flutter through the air.

Jet groaned. Why did Voight always have to be so difficult? Jet swiped his spare pair of motorcycle shades and shoved them on his face. Then he unhooked his boot and slid into the sky after Voight. Saving Voight with only one chute between them would be such a pain.

And then he was falling yet again, and really, how was that fair?

Just inside his range of hearing, Jet picked up a gun firing, so he spun midair, torrents of wind washing over him. One of the drifting Aureates was shooting at him from his spot in the clouds. Jet scanned the sky. Spying a man gliding ten feet from him, about fifteen feet down, Jet angled himself just right, then slammed his arms to his body and his legs together and shot towards his target. He struck the man from behind, kneed him in the head once when he immediately attacked Jet, and relieved him of his gun. He kicked off the man and back into the open air, taking aim at the hands of anyone who so much as looked in his direction.

Once the threats were neutralized, Jet sought out Voight. The man had darted some distance from him, and Jet had to do quite a bit of repositioning before he could soar towards Voight with any accuracy. Voight raised his own gun to Jet and fired, but Jet saw it coming and dove beneath him, twisting midair and throwing his arms out to slow his decent. He slammed into Voight from below and grappled with him.

"You're losing altitude way too quickly, Grim Reaper. Disengage."

But Jet refused. He wrestled the gun out of Voight's grasp, whose hands then hooked onto Jet's chest armor just as Jet locked his knees around the assassin's torso, Voight's back to the fast approaching ground and Jet essentially kneeling above him. Jet laid the barrel of his gun to the center of Voight's head.

"Deploy your chute, Grim Reaper."

"Have you grown that soft?" Voight asked him. "Can't you kill me? You're an assassin."

"No, I'm not. I'm a soldier, damn it, and so are you, Sergeant."

Flecks of uncertainty filtered into Voight's eyes. Charlie had always been better at reading them, but Jet could see it just as easily as he could see the sun. Staring at it made his own eyes sting. He'd known Voight's weakness almost as long as he'd known the man. Voight had never left the war, and he just hadn't had any way to cope without it.

"Damn it, Harper. Deploy your chute!"

Jet let his gun slide, then chucked it carelessly aside. "Let me show you an alternative. Let me show you where people like you and me still fit in." Jet extended his hand, offering hope in seasoned friendship they had never really left behind, regardless of what Voight thought. The man really wasn't as manipulative as he seemed to think he was.

The uncertainty remained as Voight's eyes skipped between the sincerity in Jet's own and the younger man's olive branch. He raised a hand from Jet's vest.

And then there was blood and gore and *What just happened?* followed quickly by a sudden jerk as Voight's lifeless left hand yanked out Jet's drogue, and Jet was hauled back by the strength of the wind to hover above the macabre sight while Voight's disfigured corpse continued its decent.

Jet's second sight saw the next shot too late and the strength of the hit blasted him backwards in compressed pain.

Chapter 36

Marcus Ren swore loudly. "Grim Reaper's taken a hit," he announced over his radio, scoping the area the shot had come from and doing the math as quickly as he could.

"There," Coffer hissed beside him on the roof, pointing needlessly, "on the rocks."

Ren adjusted his rifle, listening intently as Coffer offered his read of the elements. "Target in sight."

"Don't kill him!"

Coffer let out a notable sigh of relief and dropped his head to the cement roofing, but as much as Ren would have loved to express the same sentiment, the majority of his focus was on the man who had just nearly killed his friend. "I won't."

Ren pulled the trigger, watching as his round shattered the other man's rifle.

"Somebody, get that guy," Jet ordered.

"Davis, here. En route, Grim Reaper."

"Roger that, Davis." Pain laced Jet's voice, but no one questioned it. They'd have time for that later. "Wick, give me a sitrep."

"We've apprehended seven of the twelve targets. As expected, Ms. Talks-A-Lot has ordered her guys onto the field. They're scouting the last five of them."

"Who's got Davis's six?"

"Bird, if he can keep up," Wick quipped.

"That's a negative," Ren cut in. "Davis is on site. Bird's still 100 meters out." Ren loaded another round and prepped as backup.

"Where's Smarty?"

"Dunlap Duty." The Shoe Crew's nickname for babysitting, short, of course, for dung in the lap.

"Roger that."

Ren ignored them, eyes on Davis as he danced around the target. Davis took a few good hits, but he was tough all over, and after a minute of fumbling for a decent foothold, he swung his steel leg out and caught the guy in the side of his head. "Target is down, and Bird's on site."

"Roger that," Jet stated. "Secure the prisoner, and rendezvous at what's left of Voight's shack. That goes for you too, Smarty. Ditch the load and buddy-up with Wick."

"Roger that," he answered.

It only took them twenty minutes to regroup in the ruins of Voight's manor. The prisoner was tossed down between Davis and Bird, his rock-camo cowl ripped from his head roughly. Jet tore the radio from his ear to kill the buzz of the Northern Admin, who demanded to know what he thought he was doing.

Ren inspected the kid but didn't see any signs of severe trauma.

"How did you survive?" their prisoner asked. Ren studied the rival sniper. The kid, because really he was one too, was a decent shot if nothing else. He was baby-faced, just a little older than Jet, with a full head of black hair. "That shot should have taken your heart right out of your chest." An Italian, Ren noted with intrigue, maybe Tuscan. He couldn't be sure. Bird was the linguist among them.

"Yeah, and who are you, hotshot?" That was Wick, not at all pleased by the bullet this kid had aimed at their kid, highly trained assassin or not.

"You're Belladonna's brother."

They all turned to Jet, who had leant up against the nearest wall nonchalantly.

"That is what you called her, and yes, you killed my sister."

Jet kicked off the wall and waltzed over. Ren couldn't tell if he was adding swag to his step to look cool or was just channeling his pain into a smooth limp. "First of all, I didn't kill your sister. Voight and his funhouse of doom did. Second of all, your sister was an assassin. What did you expect? Mourn in solitude and leave me the hell alone." It was definitely pain. Jet could be vicious when he was hurting.

"I know how she died. That is why I killed Voight first, but if she had slipped up at all, you would have killed her, too."

"Probably," Jet threw out, "she *was* trying to assassinate me, but for the record, you moron, my guns were loaded with nonlethal rounds."

That was news to everyone. A shot from Ren's gun was definitely of more consequence. "What?"

"I'm leaving the game, done, through. Voight was my last target, and I meant to bring him back alive. Belladonna, too.

If she didn't make it, that's on her. Sorry. Too bad. Move on. Was it really worth the trouble you're in now?"

"She was my twin sister, so yes, it was."

Jet stared at the kid awhile longer, then waved his hand at Bird and Davis, and staggered on his way.

"Jet? Jet!" Ren called. The kid stopped, giving Ren a moment to catch up. "Are you alright? You shouldn't have survived that."

Jet tapped his vest. "This isn't Kevlar," he explained. "It spreads out the force of impact and is pretty much impenetrable."

"Yeah, well, I still think you should have your chest looked over."

Jet waved uncaringly.

"*Jet.*"

"Oh my gosh! You're starting to sound like Charlie, Ren. I'll have someone look at it later, alright? Just chill."

"Charlie must get a kick out of dealing with you," Davis quipped, a bounce in his step. Wick and Smarty followed with the prisoner, dragging him, uncooperatively, along by his bonds.

"How's your leg?" Ren asked.

"What, this one?" Davis asked, repeating his earlier joke. Jet rolled his eyes. "It's fine, Ren. Actually, it's better than fine. Whatever this thing is made of, it feels great. They should put it on the market."

"You wouldn't want to buy it if it was," Jet told him.

"Why not?"

"It'd cost you your other leg, both your arms, and probably most of your internal organs."

"What?!"

"Just be glad someone in the club likes doing me favors."

Jet turned off from the path they were trekking and took a trail through the trees. "Uh, Jet, where you going?" Wick asked. "Mobile command's this way."

"Yeah, but the Admin's *this* way, and I need to find out what happened with Charlie."

He had an odd expression on his face, his eyes shadowed and his face grim. It was somewhat familiar... Ren flinched at the reminder. It was the same expression Jet had worn at Stonefield's funeral. That couldn't bode well for him. "You need a hand?"

"Nah, I got it. See you." He waved at them and walked into the trees.

Deep down, someplace Ren had stored the memories of the shattered kid who'd lost his friend and his legs at the same time, Ren knew Jet couldn't survive another major loss, not so soon after the last, so he hoped with all that was in him that the kid wouldn't have to.

Chapter 37

Jet ached all over. He hadn't exactly lied to Ren. That shot had hurt like hell but hadn't done any real damage. His knees, on the other hand, hadn't been fond of his low altitude drop, especially so soon after base-jumping, and his back wasn't thanking him for it either, even with his new metal spine to cushion the fall. He'd tried to curb most of the impact on landing, had cut his chords and dropped/rolled the hell out of it, but damn, that had still hurt.

His mind, despite the pain in his body, was much further away. Charlie had taken a steep dive into a rocky ravine. Other than that, Jet didn't know much. He begged for another vision, something of him and Charlie chatting around a dining table, cracking jokes and ribbing each other. He got only silence and his first sight.

Jet rubbed a tired hand over his forehead. He'd only experienced visions while awake a few times in his life.

Mostly, his prescience acted in his sleep or in his subconscious, where it rarely disturbed his train of thought. But while his mind was active, the future, the past, whatever he was called to witness, lapped over his eyes without, somehow, obscuring his first sight, like a watermark with startling clarity. And never before had the visions come so quickly.

Jet hissed, scrubbing a hand across his face and over his chest where the sniper's round had struck him. As promised, the armor hadn't even dented, and Jet was sure that once the newly laid fabric surrounding it was removed, there'd be no trace of action at all.

Charlie had better still be alive.

Jet shivered. He'd lived apart from his brother for years, but he'd never forgotten their bond. They were great brothers for each other, especially when they weren't trapped inside their own lies.

They worked well together even when they weren't as well working together. Not even his old squadmates could quite match him the way Charlie could. It might have had something to do with being a Harper or spending all that time together with Uncle Riley, but it wasn't something he'd ever willingly forfeit. Jet was the one always seeking danger. Jet was the one with a notorious track record for attracting it. The thought that Charlie had actually died before him—

Jet shook himself. He could see the Admin off in an open clearing, yapping at a poised, grey-haired woman who accepted her words with only half an ear. Several guys were running to and from a grounded military-grade helicopter. Jet strolled up to the troublesome woman without any trace of pain, bypassing the other entirely. "Where's Charlie? What happened?"

She shifted away from him immediately, her face dark. "There was an incident. Father Harper—Hey!" Her hand was on her Bluetooth. "I want every last one of those kids assessed before they go anywhere."

"Admin?"

She waved him off, and he almost lunged for her.

Dread held him back. *Charlie.* He scrubbed his hands over his face again. *I'm getting on the next flight outa here.* He didn't want to know yet, didn't want to have to think about the fall he'd seen or the rocks so far below it.

Jet lugged himself into the quiet bird. "Charlie?"

He was seated against the wall on an uncomfortable slab of metal the defense industry called a bench. "Hey, Jet."

"Why are you all wet?"

Charlie was soaked through completely. Sagged in his seat next to a very uncomfortable-looking Cardinal Neumann, he answered, "Went cliff diving. Why do you look like you were caught in a windstorm?"

"Went skydiving."

They were both quiet for a second.

"Reminds me of the summer of '06."

"I was just thinking the same thing," Jet replied.

"I feel like your uncle really should have been reported for child endangerment."

"Actually," Charlie answered, "that was vacation with our mom and dad."

The expression on the cardinal's face was priceless, and Jet couldn't help the effervescent laughter that bubbled its way up his throat. He unhooked his radio completely and yanked off his chest plate, dropping down next to Charlie contently.

"What is *with* your family? Has God commanded, 'Look, but never touch'?"

"Huh?"

"Cain," Charlie explained.

Jet could dig that. It did always seem like when something bad happened to them, their transgressors would get it back seven times worse, mostly courtesy of the Harpers, but hey, God used just about anyone when He felt like it. No one could say for sure it wasn't simply God's vengeance raining down on them—divine justice and all that.

...Right?

Charlie wasn't quite sure what Jet's immense look of relief was for, but he liked that his miserable frown had disappeared only seconds after spotting him. Charlie could bet it had something to do with Jet's prescience, but this wasn't the place to discuss it.

The Northern Admin, an elegant, older woman, and a couple of club members had bunched in with them only minutes after Jet's arrival. The Admin had ordered the pilot to take off, and they were now on their way back to headquarters.

A woman identified as Dr. Retlan appeared on a screen that Charlie hadn't noticed. *I must be more tired than I thought.* "We've just wrapped up the last of the physicals, Admin."

"Good, how's it looking?"

Dr. Reltan frowned. "About as well as could be expected. Most of them are fine, physically. Bumps, bruises, lots of scars on some, but anything dire was treated well, so none of them are in any danger, except the little one with the gunshot wound, but we've given him some blood and taken care of it."

Charlie sighed in relief. "So, Santiago's alright?" Jet gave him a curious look but didn't ask.

"Physically, he'll be fine. He's a tough nugget, too. Didn't even flinch when I was inspecting his wound." The doctor smiled coolly. "I told you I'd be the first one here when you found those kids, Father."

Charlie only nodded.

"They'll all need psychological evaluations, Admin. We can't release them until then. It seems like night terrors will be the worst of it for some of them, but some of the older ones...well, brainwashing's no simple thing to undo."

The Admin nodded. "Do what you need to, but keep us updated."

"Of course." The doctor signed out just as they landed.

Cardinal Neumann fled from them immediately, requesting a way back to his own comfort zone. The Admin gestured for a lingering agent to handle it, but the unnamed elder woman flocked to him first and escorted him inside herself.

Charlie just wanted a shower and a long nap. "Explain this to me in your own words, Father Harper, because I've heard six different versions of the same story several times over. What happened?"

Charlie groaned. "The cardinal and I found the bunker and some of the kidnapped kids. Then Penny showed up to lend a hand—" Charlie ignored Jet's vocal delight. "—and Santiago informed us that there were other kids somewhere else in the bunker, so I had him take me to find them. Meanwhile, Penny made contact with the local club and the agents you so helpfully sent our way, and they rescued the first group of kids. Santiago and I found Cardinal

Weatherford's body and information on the Aureate Society—"

"Yes, yes, yes," she interrupted, "get to the interesting part."

"Someone needs to teach you patience. Pity the man who has to do it."

The woman scoffed, her cheeks turning the same shade of red as her hair.

"Santiago volunteered to fend off the brainwashed children, since I wouldn't defend us against them, and stayed behind." Charlie flagged a hand up. "Before you start laying into me for that, I already knew he was playing both sides. The Aureates—not so much. So, I *let* him play me, both for his protection and to give the club enough time to arrive."

"I understand that you initially intended to escort the kids out yourself."

"Not really."

"Miss Belmonte said—"

"Yeah, I made have misled her a bit, not so much to keep her in the dark, but because I figured we were likely being watched."

"Then what was your original plan?"

"There was no original plan."

"Wha…?"

"That's not how Charlie operates," Jet explained, "at least, not since we were kids."

"I don't understand."

"I've been hearing that a lot today."

"Yeah, don't you miss it?"

The Admin's eyes narrowed, realizing, somewhat belatedly, that they were sharing a joke at her expense.

After several seconds, Jet took pity on her and elaborated, "Charlie plans by the moment." She stared at him, a clear sign she was still lost without actually having to state it. "Ever had the awesomest plan ever that goes straight to pieces before you've gotten more than a few seconds into it? Typically, you have Plan B, C, D, etc. Well, instead of worrying about having the right plan for every potential scenario, Charlie sets a few general goals for himself, like find the kids and ensure they all make it out alive. The rest of the plan comes later. It's formed based on the decisions of the other players."

"So, you make it up as go?"

"Essentially," Jet answered on his behalf.

"That sounds obscenely dangerous. What if you get stuck?"

"It *is* dangerous, and not everyone can do it, but Charlie's a master strategist, which involves split-second problem-solving, so kids," Jet said, eying the remaining agents, "don't try this at home."

Charlie shook his head. Honestly, sometimes Jet gave him way too much credit. "Anyways, after Santiago and I split up, I just killed a lot of time 'til I was chased outside by Simon Jude."

"*What?*" Jet sputtered.

"Turns out the Aureate Society kidnapped him all those years ago, and he may be one of their older victims of brainwashing." Charlie quieted for a moment. The vague image of a twelve-year-old Jet speaking to a strange man at the park hovered near the outskirts of his memory. Just how close had Jet gotten to becoming a statistic?

Putting the thought aside for the time being, Charlie continued, "The other brainwashed kids used themselves as human shields against the club snipers. I was cornered at the cliff edge, and they blew up the computer that had all the intel on it. Simon was going to kill me for the flash drive, which I knew would mean the deaths of all five of them."

"How'd you figure?" the Admin questioned.

"Logic," he stated simply, "and I was tuned into the club's radio frequency. I could hear 'em talking. So, I figured, it was them or me, and I...tried something new."

"Cliff diving," Jet guessed.

"A trust fall with God."

"It's a miracle you're not dead—that you missed every single rock at the bottom." The Admin shook her head in wonder.

Charlie shrugged. "He caught me."

"He could've spared the intel, too, but Simon crushed it before our guys could stop him."

"What? The flash drive?"

She nodded despairingly, turning toward the stairs that would take them down from the helipad.

"That wasn't the intel." The Admin looked stunned. Jet smirked at her despite not having a clue what was going on himself. Charlie was a master of his art after all. This little op didn't scratch the surface of what he could do.

Charlie slipped a hand into his sleeve and retrieved his glasses. "That flash drive had less than a gig of memory on it. I only used it to transfer files occasionally—my penance for relying a little too much on technology as of late. I couldn't have dumped half a computer on it. A nice decoy though, wasn't it? I connected my glasses to the computer wirelessly and transferred all the intel into them." He handed them to her.

"Your...glasses?" She took them hesitantly.

Another hand snatched them up. "Yes, his glasses, as in the ones I made for him as a favor to his sister." The Brit was far too smug for his own good.

"I've been figuring them out since I got them, and they can do all sorts of things, like store 64 gigs of data."

Twain frowned. "They need an update."

"The water didn't ruin them?" the Admin asked.

"They're waterproof and impact resistant." Twain dropped them on the floor and slammed his heel into them.

Charlie was a little put out by that. "We didn't need a demonstration."

Amadeus Twain just shrugged. "I'll download the intel and give them back to you, with an update, of course."

"What's next? Laser vision?" Jet asked.

Twain smiled maniacally, and the brothers shivered. Something was very not right about that man. Twain fled the roof, and with much less enthusiasm, they turned to follow.

"Hey, Charlie?"

"Yeah, Jet?"

"What'd cha do with my car?"

Chapter 38

His Charger was intact…as far as anyone knew. Charlie had abandoned it on the side of the road somewhere like an unwanted animal, exposed and vulnerable, but the Admin had sent someone to get it, so there was that at least.

Jet took a breath. As long as Charlie hadn't scratched the paint, it was no big deal, so Charlie had better pray he hadn't scratched the paint. Although if Jet knew Charlie, the only thing his big brother cared about at this point was having a shower and napping. Jet's car was the last thing on his mind.

But unlike Charlie, Jet didn't have the luxury of even a brief rest. He still had one last job to do.

The Shoe Crew, down only their man lost years ago, was assembled in one of the vast training rooms of northern headquarters. Belladonna's tepid sibling sat on the ground in the middle of them, bound and gagged. Jet stalked towards him puckishly. "How's your day been?" he asked. "Because mine's been just all sorts of exciting, especially when I took a shot to the chest from a high-powered sniper rifle."

The man only watched him, not that he could have answered if he'd wanted to, but his eyes held no response.

"Marco Amico." That got a startled jerk out of him. "Former member of Italian special forces, the 9th Paratroopers Assault Regiment, Col Moschin, right?" Amico's eyes narrowed. "Note the 'former,' Sergeant." Jet paused for the fun of it. "The Italian military has disavowed you. As far as anyone's concerned, the Marco Amico in front of me isn't even a citizen of Italy. I'll ask again. Was it worth it?"

This time, Amico lowered his eyes.

"Hmm, I'm in a glorious mood all of a sudden. That was a damn good shot you took to kill Voight, thrilled as I am about that," Jet peevishly added. "I'd pass it off as luck, but you took nearly the same shot at me only a few seconds later. Now, at the very least, you'll be going to prison for murder and attempted murder. At the most—and let's face it, you pissed off the club, so you'll probably get the most—at the most, you'll be incarcerated as a terrorist. After all, you are a foreigner no one seems to know anything about, who tried to kill a United States veteran for seemingly no reason at all."

Amico's eyes narrowed, but he kept them aimed at the wall.

"Lucky for you, Nightshade, I'm a firm believer in rehabilitation over retribution, for some things anyways. I am a reformed assassin myself after all. So, you can go to prison for the rest of your life, or you can join my team."

At once, there was an uproar.

"Whoa, whoa, whoa, hold on a second. What?"

"This guy just shot you, and you wanna put a gun in his hands and have him stand at your six."

"What are you, insane?!"

"Ah, I'm over it. That was so three hours ago, guys. I think Nightshade will agree that he no longer finds me at fault for his sister's death. Camilla, right?"

The newly dubbed Nightshade nodded, his demeanor bemused.

"Hey, Bird, ungag him, would ya?" The man did so. "What do you say, Nightshade?"

"I do not think your friends agree with your decision."

Jet quirked an eyebrow at him. "So, you're so scared of my friends, you'd rather spend the rest of your life in Gitmo?"

The man blinked. "I accept your offer."

Jet smiled. "I thought you might. Don't worry, Nightshade. We'll teach you better ways to handle your problems than by putting a bullet in them."

"Why do you keep calling me that? Is it my new codename or call sign?"

"Psh, I'm the only one cool enough for a call sign around here, and we don't do codenames."

Nightshade gave him an unimpressed frown, shifting a bit to get more comfortable. No one had moved to untie him yet. "Bird and…Smarty, was it? Those are not their real names."

"Actually, there are people with the surname Bird, ya know. Like someone in Italy being called *friend*," Coffer stated, giving Nightshade a pointed look. "But you got lucky this time. He's actually Brian Song. We call him Bird 'cuz birds sing and 'cuz when he talks in any of the twelve languages he knows, it's all bird to us—that is, bird like Pidgin. He's our linguist, anyways, and our intelligence officer."

Nightshade blinked at him some more, but Coffer kept going, "Smarty's name just comes from his actual name. He's

Sergio Martinez, so S Mart, Smart, or Smarty. It helps that he's got a mouth on him at times."

"I think my mouth's always around, Randy."

Coffer rolled his eyes. "He's our explosives expert. That," he said pointing, "is Marcus Ren, our sniper and field medic. I'm his spotter, Randy Coffer. That's Devon Davis, our munitions specialist, and that's Wick."

"What's his other name?"

"Hell if I know. Hell if anyone knows. He's our on-and-off again squad leader."

"What?"

"Lieutenant Stonefield used to be our number one, but he died in the line of duty three years ago." The room silenced for a moment of respect. "Wick was our second, but he doesn't much like being in charge, so Harper's our acting squad leader now, which is kinda weird 'cuz back in the day, he was the rookie."

Amico nodded. "And I'm Nightshade because?"

"*Atropa belladonna* is also known as the deadly nightshade. Seeing as how you're twins, and I don't ever think you should forget how much you gave up for her, I think Nightshade suits you," Jet explained.

"What exactly does your team do? Neutralize threats?"

"Actually, we take orders from the club in hostile, no-go zones. The seven of us used to be Navy Special Forces, but thanks to some pull from the club, all these guys, minus Davis and me, have been put on reserve."

"Why do I feel like this is going to get crazy?" Ren asked, scratching at the back of his head anxiously.

"We gonna have lots of fun now, boys." It was the door behind him that contained Jet's maniacal grin. Someone had entered the room. "Penny?"

"Oh, hey, hi, I—I was just looking for the bathroom, I swear."

"Walk back ten feet and take a right. It's at the end of the hall."

"Right. Thanks." She lingered in the doorway, eying the men around her, especially Nightshade, who was still seated on the floor, bound at hands and feet.

"We were just talking. Penny, this is my team, well, not *my* team. Well, I guess now it *is* my team." Jet could feel the eyes on him and chuckled nervously. With the threat of death no longer hanging over his head, Penny was somehow much more endearing, not that she hadn't been before. When had he missed that? "I was a member of this squad when I was in the navy. I never told you I was in the navy, did I?"

She shook her head shyly.

"Right, well, I heard you gave Charlie a hand. Thanks for that."

"No problem. I couldn't just let them handle it alone, although I did underestimate your brother."

"Everyone does. It's the collar. Anyway, he said you did pretty well and that you have some nice moves."

"Really? A priest said that?"

"Well, not in so many words, but it was implied."

"Right," she said, nodding a little, a light blush on her pretty cheeks. "Maybe you could show me how to make them better—my moves, I mean."

"Yeah, definitely."

She nodded more intently. "Right, great, I should—" run right into the doorframe. "Ow!—go." Then she was half way down the hall.

For a hopeful moment, all was quiet.

Then, "What the hell was that?!"

Thanks, Devon.

"Dude, you like her, like *like* her like her."

"What are you, ten, Randy?"

"No, this is perfect," said Smarty.

"And about time," Ren threw in.

"It's supposed to be this way, Jet," explained Smarty. "Guy meets girl. Guy falls in love with girl. Guy and girl get married and live happily ever after."

"Yeah, that's not how my life works. You forgot guy gets girl kidnapped, and girl helps save kids from cult, not to mention, guy gets constantly shot at, and girl gets stuck in the middle of it."

"Ah, c'mon, Jet," Bird chuckled.

Wick just shook his head like he thought they were all acting juvenile.

"C'mon, what? You realize she's only involved in any of this because she talked to me for two minutes."

"'Twas fate!" sung Coffer.

"Oh, shut up," Jet snapped. "You guys are worse than Charlie." He made for the door, his team following.

"Hey?"

"That's because he has boundaries," Ren pointed out, "you know, being a priest and all."

"Hello?"

"And you don't, Mother?" Ren rolled his eyes.

"Hey!"

And then they were all gone, and Marco Amico tugged weakly at his wrists and wondered just what the hell he'd signed himself up for.

Chapter 39

"Father Charlie, your brother's here to see—" Margarita Luna shrieked in terror.

Charlie's letter opener had pierced the wall beside her right ear, the fly's wings still twitching. "Thank you, Miss Luna." She nodded her head quickly, squirmed, and fled.

"Is that what passes for knife-throwing these days?" Jet asked, yanking the surprisingly buried letter opener from the wall and tapping the tip of it on the trashcan until the bisected insect fell from it.

"Like you could do any better."

"What? Of course I could do better."

"You're the martial artist."

"And you're the tracker."

"I'm the better knife-thrower," they said in unison.

Then they were in the rectory.

Charlie had erected an old dart board at one end of the dining room. They were standing on the opposite side of the house in the living area, tossing up steak knives in order to test their weight. They faced each other, chatting amiably. Jet flung his knife first without so much as glancing at the target, and the tip imbedded in the center of the bullseye.

"That all you got?" asked Charlie. He mirrored the movement, flicked his wrist out, and left-handed, forced the tip of the knife to slide in right beside his brother's.

"You call that a precision hit." Jet raised his next knife, but Charlie put a hand on it.

"No handle shots."

"Aw, c'mon, Charlie."

"No, they're not my knives. They're Father Johann's."

"Fine," Jet conceded. "But that means we get to play dirty."

"You're on."

Jet spun the knife on his finger, snatched it suddenly, and—

"So, you and Penny, huh?"

The knife flew wide, very wide, right into the wooden frame of the door Father Johann had just opened. The man stared stunned at the knife still vibrating mere inches from his face. Jet looked nearly as stunned. He was frozen in pitcher's position, his wrist dangling midair, and pink on his cheeks. "Heh, sorry."

Charlie held back the laughter building in him, only for Father Johann's sake. The man edged around the knife, giving it a wide berth, as if it could somehow still do him harm. Cardinal Neumann entered behind him, and the mirth in Charlie died. Jet, too, stiffened.

"Father Johann, Cardinal." The cardinal's face was blank, and Charlie took a protective step forward so he was level with Jet. "To what do we owe the pleasure of this visit, Your Eminence?"

"I need a word with you, Father Harper, on official business."

Father Johann offered him a nervous head jerk. "Of course, Cardinal, whatever you'd like."

"I'm gonna head out then," Jet announced, laying the rest of the knives in his hand down on the nearest end table.

"You never actually told me why you were here, Jet."

"We'll catch up later."

The three clergymen trotted back to the main building, where Father Johann offered up his office and left the two of them to talk. Cardinal Neumann had Charlie take his pastor's seat, while the man himself paced around the room, looking at Father Johann's books and baubles. "Do you know why Cardinal Weatherford and I were tasked with investigating the abductions?"

"No, Cardinal."

"We work...worked with a particular office in the Vatican that conducts external investigations related to the Church. Unfortunately, incidents like this business with the Aureate Society are beyond our capabilities. Cardinal Weatherford and I volunteered to investigate, but what really was there for us to do, even if we had come to all the correct conclusions?"

Charlie watched him wearily. Initially, he'd believed word of his more...active response to the Aureates might've graced the pope's ears and that he was now in quite a bit of trouble for it, as he had been when Bishop had found out, but now, he wasn't so sure.

"We have been given—I have been given," the cardinal amended, a pained expression on his face, "permission to create a special task force to conduct investigations such as this and deal with them accordingly."

Oh no. Charlie could already see where this was going. "Cardinal, honored as I am to be considered for a position on this team, I'm a simple, diocesan priest."

"I do not wish to recruit you to the team."

"You don't?"

"I want you to run it."

"Oh, that's so much worse."

"Charlie—" And that level of casualty was never good. "—you already have the necessary skills."

"But Cardinal, I'm trying to tame my reflexive impulses, to temper them, not develop them."

"I thought you had resolved to do what you must."

"Which is why I've begun a training regimen meant to keep me in shape and prepared for the inevitable trouble my family attracts. It's not something I'm going to actively seek."

"You would not be the first response," the cardinal argued. *Just how desperate is he?* "The team will be made up of a handful of men from the Swiss Guard."

Charlie took a deliberate breath. "Cardinal, if there's one thing I've always known, it's that I belong among the people. I'm a parish priest. This is where my calling lies, not off chasing trouble."

"How many of your brother priests run a parish and an office? You are an intelligent man of…sturdy character, Father Charlie. It is only a matter of time before you are made the next exorcist, the next liturgist, even the next chancellor—"

"But Swiss Guards mean the Vatican."

Cardinal Neumann's face soured, and he glared at the desktop. "Not necessarily."

"Cardinal?"

"They do not have to stay in Vatican City." Really desperate, it seemed.

"I'm sure some of them have families," Charlie snapped. He could appreciate the importance of the team's existence, but the cardinal was really taking this too far.

"Yes, but in America, families are permitted to live on base. If they are based here, I see no reason why their families could not be moved with them."

"But they're not American military."

"I was only making a comparison. We will provide housing for them, or if your bishop is feeling generous, perhaps he will."

"They have no jurisdiction here."

"They will not be doing anything that the law does not already permit them to do."

"And they'll be alright with this? All of it?"

"If they are not, I will drop the matter entirely."

Charlie glanced around the office. The skies above him never calmed long. He should've been used to it, but Charlie was still settling into his old persona and just starting to stir it in gently with his new. He hadn't expected to be thrown a curve ball so soon, but he supposed if he had been, then he was more than capable of handling it.

Charlie began to sigh, then cut himself off. He decided then and there he'd endeavor to so less—sigh, that is.

He peered out the window at a woman who was peering in at him. She reminded him, marginally, of Aunt Hilda. Then, uninvited, she approached. Charlie stood, prepared for whatever oddity was coming his way.

And wasn't being home just fabulous?

Chapter 40

"It's simple really. You lied. We used the information you gave us, and we nearly died."

"I don't know how it could've been wrong."

"I do. You lied." My image was morbidly curious, crouched beside the kneeling man I'd once known as Jonathan Hicks, blood trickling down his face from an excess of injuries that would make him less recognizable to anyone else. "Why would you do that knowing what it meant?"

"Please, Holl—" The butt of the gun collided with his head, and he dropped from his knees to his side from the impact.

"You really shouldn't make her mad. She's dead serious." The young man beside me was new, although something familiar was found in his features—deep black hair over an elvish face that sported a pair of green emeralds for eyes.

I was dressed in my Queen of the Dragonflies gear, but someone had carefully spray-painted a standard Aureate brooch on the upper right side of my chest plate. "Jonathan, you saved my life once. I thought I could return the favor, but you just wouldn't let me."

Hicks was twitching in the sand, one hand trapped beneath him and the other trembling at his side. I gestured at the young man with us, who immediately hoisted Hicks back to his knees. Laying the long side of the gun's barrel to my forehead, I let my finger hover over the trigger.

Then I leveled the muzzle at Hicks and fired.

Jet came awake with the hateful bang, more panic-stricken than he'd been in a long time. A clang of something in the kitchen roused him fully, and he slipped out of bed, a gun already in hand. He'd just started renting this new place. He wasn't keen on losing it so soon. Mrs. Butterfly hadn't taken news of the gunfire well, and he doubted his knew landlord would feel any better about it.

He slid the bolts out on his bedroom door carefully, then pushed it open, and crept into the hallway. "Good morning," I greeted.

"Holly?" He unwound slowly.

"Belgium waffle?"

"Hey, Jet." Charlie was behind me, lounging at one of the dining room chairs, scrolling through something on his phone, a cup of hot tea in his free hand.

"Nice bruise," I told him. The brown and yellow splotch wrapped around his torso, already in the final stages of healing. "Makes you look rugged."

"Thanks." He seemed wary, and after the dream he'd just had, it was clear why he would be. "What are you guys doing here?" Then after a moment of thought, he added, "And how did you get in without me noticing?"

"Well, we *are* related."

"You said we'd catch up later. Holly was coming by, so I thought it'd just be easier to meet here."

"Right, okay, yeah. Waffles sound good." Jet seated himself in a chair, trying to unwind from that heavy nightmare that had felt too much like a vision for comfort. "How are your summer ops coming, Holl?"

"Classified."

It would be. Everything would be. We would be one of the few families where international secrets were the topic of Saturday morning breakfast.

"Although I guess no one would care anymore now that you're official members."

Jet shrugged. "Well, you're not dead, so it must not be going too badly."

Charlie rolled his eyes at Jet's crass reply. "Are you almost done tying up Devenay's loose ends?"

I sighed. "Not nearly. We'd have to catch most of the Aureate Society for that." I stabbed a piece of waffle. "To be fair, your intel has helped a lot, but not all of it's my prerogative. I imagine some of it will be headed your way, Jet."

"Bring it on. My guys are ready for anything."

"Looks like I might be working with Jonathan Hicks again."

Jet froze, some of the color draining from his face. He schooled his features, sat back in his chair, and swallowed down the bit of waffle he'd already bitten into. "At least you know you've got each other's backs, right?"

The whole room tensed, and even Charlie looked up, eyes swinging between Jet and me.

My hands balled into fists, and I smiled connivingly at him, a wicked gleam in my eyes. "Oh Jet, don't you know me at all?"

Made in the USA
Middletown, DE
24 August 2018